ABDUCTION

Gillian Jackson

SAPERE BOOKS

ABDUCTION

Published by Sapere Books.

20 Windermere Drive, Leeds, England, LS17 7UZ,
United Kingdom

saperebooks.com

ISBN: 978-1-913028-61-9

For my husband, Derek and our children, David, Stephen, Ruth and Paul.
Thanks also to neighbour and friend, Sean Jackson for sharing his knowledge and advice regarding police procedure.

Prologue

Elise McDonald, April 2014

I always believed that I would recognise her when I saw her again. To me, it was a certainty, simply a matter of time, and today was the day. Grace was not ten yards away from me. The family likeness was unmistakable: high cheekbones, a rather too long aquiline nose, wide-set blue eyes, and full lips — features that left absolutely no doubt in my mind that this was my sister. Her proximity caused my heart to beat faster, and my palms were clammy in spite of the air conditioning in the department store.

Grace was oblivious to my scrutiny, idly examining a rack of overpriced jeans that seemed to have caught her attention. Moving to a better vantage point beside a full-length mirror, I could continue to stare at her reflection without being seen. She had the same hairstyle I had favoured at that age — long honey-blonde hair, poker straight, with a thick fringe almost touching her eyes. It was quite uncanny really.

Suddenly, Grace began to move, setting off with a purpose that brought panic to my already nervous mind. I could not let her disappear again, yet I had no plan, no idea of how, or even if, I should approach her. Following in a pathetic zigzag pattern, I touched the racks of clothes as I passed, feigning an interest.

Grace left the clothing department, heading for the escalator, which forced me to quicken my step to keep her within sight. She was leaving the store; if I let her get out into the busy mall I might lose track of her altogether, but I was still undecided about whether to make an approach or not. My legs were trembling and my breathing erratic as I almost ran to catch up to her before she reached the door. Still without a clue what to say, I intercepted her as she paused to examine a new brand of perfume, spraying the fragrance liberally on her wrist.

'Hi.' I forced myself to smile, trying to sound casual. 'It's Grace, isn't it?'

'No, sorry, you've got the wrong person.' The girl returned my smile. Her youthful, innocent face almost undid my resolve. It was like looking at a pleasing blend of my mother and me, but Grace obviously could not see it. I wanted to blurt out that she was my long lost sister, even if she didn't know it. I had not seen her since she was three … but I knew it was Grace!

'Excuse me.' She smiled again, a gentle expression, patiently waiting for me to move. Still blocking the exit, I searched frantically for some way to delay this young woman, to find out more about her, but I could think of nothing that didn't smack of desperation. Mercifully, fate decided to solve the dilemma and the baby within me suddenly kicked, causing a sharp pain beneath my ribs. An audible gasp escaped me as my hand went to my swollen belly.

'Are you all right? Can I do anything?' The polite smile was replaced by genuine concern and I seized the opportunity.

'Perhaps if I could sit down for a while?'

'Of course, there's a bench just outside the door — can I help you there?'

Allowing Grace to take my bag, light though it was, we left the store together. When we were seated on the bench, she anxiously asked if I was any better.

'Yes, much better, thank you. It's a boy and I'm sure he's wearing football boots already.'

Laughter lit up Grace's whole face, and it was all I could do to stop myself from flinging my arms around her in a futile attempt to make up for those lost years. Politely she asked how much longer it was until the baby was due, and I replied that it was only six weeks.

'Well, if there's nothing more I can do I'd better go.'

An icy panic gripped me. I'd hoped for more time, time to quiz this girl about her life, her memories. But why should she want to spend time with a stranger?

'Oh, but you've been so kind. Can I give you a lift home perhaps?'

'Thanks, but I live out of town in Carlton Wells.' Grace stood to leave.

'I'll happily take you — it's not far.' *Please don't let me sound too desperate.*

'Actually I'm going to meet my dad first. He's a doctor at the Central Health Centre, but thanks for the offer.'

My brain was working overtime, and trying to sound casual I asked, 'It's not Doctor Carter, is it?' I had no idea which doctors worked there and had plucked the name from thin air.

'No, it's Doctor Solomon, and I'm Jane by the way.'

'I'm Elise. It's been lovely to meet you, Jane, and thank you so much for your help.' With a name and a vague location, I could relax and let Jane Solomon leave before her suspicions were aroused. I watched her slender, lithe body moving fluidly at a fast pace, bag flung casually over her left shoulder. Resisting the urge to call her back, I blinked back the tears from my eyes. She was alive! I'd never given up hope, even when the rest of my family had. And now there was no doubt in my mind that this beautiful teenager was my lost sister, Grace!

2000

Chapter 1

Margaret Bryson

If I had to pinpoint just one feature that sold Lilac House in River View to us, it would be the garden. Not that I didn't love the house itself, I did, but there was so much work to do on it. Almost an acre of garden was divided into sections, sloping gently to the south where a high brick wall offered privacy from the river behind and the overgrown path running along its banks. An orchard of fruit trees bordered the property's west side, providing an abundance of apples, pears and plums, where I envisaged children laughing with delight as they harvested our very own crop. The only formal part of the garden was directly behind the house where a generous sized patio was laid out, with a lawn immediately behind and well-stocked flower beds.

Two tall lilac trees at the far corners of the lawn gave the house its name and provided fragrant shade through the early summer. Beyond this, the garden began to slope and mature shrubs grew wild, creating a haven for birds and small mammals, most of which I tried not to think about. Ancient red brick paths weaved in and out of the shrubs which, although overgrown, were magnificently natural in appearance, creating an exciting space for children to play.

We wanted three children, maybe even four, and when we moved into Lilac House I was pregnant with our first child, Elise. Stephen and I knew how blessed we were. No couple could have been happier and when Elise was six, our second daughter, Grace, made an appearance into the world.

Grace turned three years old today — the eighth of August — a perfect month for an outdoor birthday party. I had thoroughly enjoyed preparing for the party to which eight of Grace's friends had been invited. The centrepiece, of course, was the cake, a large teddy bear-shaped sponge, covered with chocolate icing and the legs covered with 'Smartie' trousers 'held up' by liquorice braces. Grace adored teddy bears and had a considerable collection in her bedroom.

Elise had taken to the role of big sister with enthusiasm and now at the grand old age of nine was proving to be an invaluable help. The guests were mostly around Grace's age, six giggly little girls and two boys, but rather than feel left out Elise managed to occupy the children and keep them all happy and in order, like a little mother hen. The younger children adored Elise, and her boundless energy was invaluable to me; I was almost certain that our third child was on the way and Stephen and I were ecstatic.

Bea and Peter came to help with the party, for which I was grateful. My sister had prepared much of the food, too. She was a rock on such occasions, and although I knew that they would dearly have loved children of their own, Bea never complained and generously invested all her love into our daughters. I considered telling my sister about the baby that afternoon, but somehow it never seemed appropriate. This was a day that seemed to underscore the fact that I had so many good things in life while she did not.

Our neighbour, Christine Robinson, was also on hand to help. She and her husband Harry had become good friends over the nine years we'd lived in Lilac House. We had much in common, and although they didn't have children of their own, they were hoping to start a family soon. Christine was always keen to help out with our girls if I ever needed it. Practice, she would say — a dress rehearsal for her own family.

The party was magical: perfect weather, contented children and a happy relaxed atmosphere as we played games after tea. Our garden was a superb place to play hide and seek, and squeals of laughter rose into the air as the children took their turn to be 'it' while the others hid.

Elise was helping Bea to clear the tea things back into the house while Christine and I supervised the games. James, the younger of the two little boy guests, was leaning on the lilac tree, eyes squeezed tightly shut and counting slowly to twenty, or as near as he could get. The other children had scurried swiftly away through the maze of shrubs, their giggles turning to whispers and then to silence as they crouched into tiny spaces, or hid behind trees in the orchard.

I took James's hand to help search for his friends; it was a daunting task for one little boy on his own in such a large unfamiliar garden. Following the sound of muffled laughter, we found the first two girls hidden behind tree trunks, and as they followed on we made our way through the labyrinth of shrubs that grew untamed at the bottom of the garden.

Soon I had a line of children behind me, following on gaily like baby ducklings. We found all the children except Grace. Unsurprising really, as she was the one who knew the very best hiding places.

I began calling for her as the others were getting restless, ready to move on to a new game, but my daughter remained hidden from sight. Elise had returned to the garden and I asked her to keep looking for Grace, hoping she too would know those perfect, secret hiding places.

Ten minutes can seem such a long time to children, and they were bored with hide and seek so I led them back to the lawn while Elise continued to search for her sister. Another five minutes passed and my girls had not appeared. A small knot of anxiety began to wring my stomach, but logic told me she had to be somewhere in the garden — there was no way she could have got out without being seen.

Bea appeared from the kitchen, and I asked if she and Christine would watch the children while I went to help Elise, who was walking round and round the paths calling for her sister.

'Grace isn't answering, Mummy. Do you think she's gone to sleep somewhere?'

'I don't know, darling, but we'll soon find her now we are both looking.'

I was feeling concerned now, edgy. We went right to the boundary wall at the bottom of the garden. It was quiet here; the noise of the children playing on the lawn was just a whisper on the light summer breeze. Surely Grace would hear our calls. I began lifting the overgrown shrubs in the hope that Elise had been right and her sister had fallen asleep somewhere, but by then I was fearful. To my relief, Stephen appeared to help.

'Bea said you couldn't find Grace? She must be here somewhere.' My husband's reassuring smile didn't quite reach his eyes.

'I know, but we've searched everywhere; perhaps she's fallen asleep and not heard us.' I glanced at my watch — it was twenty minutes since we'd begun the game, not a long time but enough to stir panic inside of me.

'Are you sure you've looked everywhere?' Stephen asked.

'Yes, but she could have moved around, trying to stay hidden.' I looked hopefully at Stephen.

'Grace!' he called, more sternly this time. 'The game is finished now, and your friends are waiting for you. Come out where we can see you — it's time to blow your candles out!'

Elise moved closer to me, wrapping her thin arms around my waist.

'She's not here, is she, Mummy?'

Huge tears were running down her face. I wanted to comfort her yet I felt like crying myself.

Stephen told us to go back to the house to get Peter, and together they would search while I saw to the other children. It was an effort to move. My mind was spinning with such terrible thoughts but I needed to hold it all together. Grace had to be somewhere in the garden. I was just being silly and passing my edginess on to Elise. I took her hand and purposefully walked back to the others. We were both sniffing and trying to act unconcerned.

Bea flashed me a questioning look as we approached.

'Where's Peter?' I asked.

'He went in for a beer and to catch the football results — shall I get him?'

My nod sent Bea scurrying inside to find her husband. They appeared in a couple of minutes and I pointed to the bottom of the garden.

'Could you go and help Stephen?' I could say no more than that. To actually speak the words that we could not find Grace would have broken me, and there were eight little children in my care.

Bea and Christine stoically organised a game of pass the parcel, asking Elise to operate the CD player in an effort to keep her mind off Grace. I felt totally useless. My logical self was attempting the 'pull yourself together, they will find her soon' speech, but my heart was breaking as all kinds of scenarios flashed before my eyes — alarming, horrid images, which stubbornly refused to shift from my mind.

It was another fifteen minutes before Stephen appeared, hurrying towards us, followed by Peter but no Grace. His expression told me all I needed to know as he took my hand to lead me into the house. Bea and Peter needed no instruction to look after the children. They were wonderful and carried on with the games, even though I knew they must share our concerns and fears for Grace.

'I think we need to call the police.' Stephen's face was ashen. I nodded and he went to the telephone in the hall.

I'd never had occasion to dial 999 before and neither had my husband. I listened to his side of the conversation, the recital of our address and a description of Grace. It was those words which were my undoing. I heard a low feral moan followed by a loud sobbing and realised those awful noises were coming from me.

Stephen replaced the receiver and took hold of me, drawing me close and stroking my hair.

'She can't have gone far, Margaret. They'll soon find her … or she'll come wandering in, laughing as always.'

He didn't believe that any more than I did. My husband's arms around me offered only a small measure of comfort as we sat holding each other until the police arrived. I had been hoping that somehow Grace would be with them — you know, like that moment in the film *Mary Poppins* when the Banks children are brought home by a friendly constable. But of course she was not — this was stark reality, not some charming, happy-ever-after film.

Two uniformed officers came inside to ask their questions, and the sound of others told us that our garden was again being searched. An inspector very quickly joined the two in our home, introducing himself as Detective Inspector Jim Duncan — a small man with an air of efficiency who appeared to be in charge of the investigation.

Very soon after the police had arrived, parents began coming to collect their children. Christine saw the visitors out after a woman officer took the details of each child and their family before allowing them to leave.

It was surreal, a nightmare, it couldn't be happening. *But it was.* I quickly lost track of time. Bea and Peter were watching Elise in the conservatory, trying to keep her from seeing the police swarming all over the house and garden. I wanted her close to me, but it was better that she did not witness our distress and the barrage of probing questions from the police. Every inch of the garden was combed by several uniformed officers with no sign of Grace whatsoever.

I sat gripping Stephen's hands in the lounge of our home: the hub of our perfect life, now cruelly shattered into a million fragments. At some point, another police officer arrived and was introduced as Detective Sergeant Jack Priestly. We were told that he was to be our Family Liaison Officer, or FLO. Something in my mind connected with that title and I couldn't bear it anymore; the sobs began again, more violent than before.

'They think she's dead,' I moaned, completely at a loss.

Jack Priestly folded his six foot frame, squatted down in front of me and took hold of my hand, wide brown eyes meeting my own, his round face open and honest.

'Listen to me, Margaret. We're not thinking that at all. My role is to keep you informed with what we are doing and any progress we make — that's why I am here. Grace has only been missing for two hours, and the chances of finding her are good. There are officers searching the area and knocking on doors right now. We are doing everything possible to find your little girl.'

Those kindly eyes were filled with compassion; there was something about the man that inspired trust and I nodded my thanks, grateful to have someone so understanding with us. I asked him why there were so many people in our house — noises were coming from almost every room, banging and scraping sounds that echoed through my aching head.

'It's something we have to do — procedure. Each room needs to be searched, I'm afraid, but they will be gone soon.'

I turned to Stephen, horrified again. 'They think we've killed her! Our own daughter — and they think we've killed her and hidden her somewhere!' Could this possibly get any worse?

'Darling, it's exactly what Jack said, procedure, that's all.' He looked so tired, no longer a man in his prime. The skin around his eyes was red and swollen, and he had aged at least ten years in the past couple of hours.

I felt helpless to do anything. I knew I should offer some kind of comfort to Stephen but could barely hold myself together.

At some point, Bea and Peter brought Elise in to see us. They were taking her home with them; it was the sensible thing to do. I hugged my daughter, attempting a reassuring smile. Bea and Peter kissed me in turn then hugged Stephen, telling us to call if there was anything at all they could do.

As they left, Christine and Harry appeared, anxious to see if they could help. Harry engaged Jack in discussion. I couldn't hear the conversation, but Christine told me he was offering to join them in the search. I could hardly respond to their kindness, but Christine seemed to understand and hugged me for the second time before leaving.

My mind was racing and suddenly became focussed on the word 'kidnap', which to me was synonymous with ransom.

'If she's been taken for money, do you think someone might call?' I asked Jack.

His face was solemn as he replied, 'Kidnapping for ransom is not as common as people think, and as you're not particularly rich, or famous, that scenario is unlikely. We do have someone coming to put a device on your telephone though, just in case.'

His words brought no comfort; if Grace hadn't been kidnapped for money, then why was she taken? I attempted to discipline my mind not to go there.

I needed the bathroom and stood to go upstairs. Our home was still swarming with uniformed police officers — one or two acknowledging me with a solemn nod as I passed by. The door to the bathroom was open, and a policeman was on his knees lifting off the side panel of the bath. He didn't hear my approach — there was still so much noise. I watched in horror as he shone a torch under and around the sides of the bath. I gasped and he turned to look at me, a weak apology in his eyes. But I knew then that the possibility of Grace being found alive was slim. The police were looking for a body, not a child.

It was Jack Priestly who called our GP. He had been with us for hours — a calm, unflappable presence making endless cups of coffee, and he had the gift of being able to melt away into the very fabric of the house to give us some degree of privacy, while being on hand to help and answer questions.

I cannot describe my feelings at that darkest of times: numb, distraught, frantic ... such a fusion of emotions. Each time the phone rang or a police officer came into the room, I jumped to my feet, anticipating and yet simultaneously dreading any news.

Dr Morrison was kind and gentle; he had been our family GP since we were married. He wanted to give us both

19

something to make us sleep, but I could not think of sleep until we knew … one way or another. A bottle of sleeping pills was placed on the mantel shelf in case we changed our minds, and the doctor left after a gentle lecture about looking after ourselves for Elise and for each other.

By midnight we were exhausted, and Stephen almost bullied me into taking a pill and going to sleep. I was too tired to argue and obediently crawled, fully clothed, into our bed, muffling my last exhausted sobs with the pillow. Stephen stayed downstairs with Jack Priestly. I think they cat-napped throughout the night, neither man wanting to be far from the telephone.

I forced myself to squeeze my eyes shut, not wanting to see how dark it was out there or think about how frightened Grace must be. It's impossible though, isn't it? To control your thoughts. The more you try not to think about something, the more you do think about it.

Eventually the pill took effect and I drifted off into a fitful sleep. If I had dreams I do not remember. The next thing I was aware of was waking when it was almost daylight and feeling dampness on the sheets beneath me. Throwing back the covers revealed a pool of blood.

I screamed for Stephen who was beside me in a minute. We both knew what had happened and cried together for the loss of our baby and the absence of Grace.

Stephen wanted to come to hospital with me but I refused, knowing that I would probably be admitted and discharged within a matter of hours and wanting someone at home for when Grace came back. I was also afraid he might connect the dots and realise that this could have been my fault. Doctor Morrison should have been told that I was pregnant before prescribing medication, yet I had not thought to tell him.

Guilt washed over me, guilt about the baby and about Grace. She was in my care when she disappeared — how could I have let it happen? How could I have let my children down so badly?

The hours in the hospital were a blur. I cannot remember ever feeling so low as at that point in time. Guilt was eating away at me, coupled with self-loathing. I was berating myself for every detail of the events that had occurred in the last twenty-four hours, and there was still no news of Grace.

Stephen came to pick me up that same afternoon, and as we left the hospital I caught a glimpse of my reflection in the plate glass door. It could have been an old lady walking beside my husband — there was no life or youth left in me as I shuffled along to the waiting car.

As we arrived home the church bells were chiming, calling parishioners to Evensong. They sounded hollow and distant. Nothing had changed when I gazed at our home, and everything had.

Jack Priestly opened the door wearing fresh clothing. Stephen told me that he'd been home to grab a few hours' sleep. He shook his head before we even asked if there was news. It was over twenty-four hours now, and I knew that with each passing minute, hope was diminishing.

While I had been in hospital, the police asked Stephen to appear on national television and appeal for information from the public — a hastily arranged interview that the police wanted to do immediately while there was more chance of someone remembering something. He told me about it in the car on the way home, and I could tell that the emotional experience had taken its toll.

We watched it together on the early evening news. Television cameras had filmed police frogmen searching the river behind our home. I was horrified to think that Grace could have been drowned, that she could have been so close and needing me — it was one scenario that had not so far occurred to me.

A brief report then preceded Stephen's appeal, brief because there was nothing to say, brief because nothing had happened. My husband's grief was plain to see; he begged for help of any kind. I had an overwhelming feeling of having let him down by not being at his side and that awful, weighty feeling of guilt was compounded even more.

Jack explained why they'd wanted to do the appeal so soon and why they couldn't wait for me. I understood and appreciated all they were trying to do. He reminded me that police officers were still out there searching and that Harry Robinson had enlisted the help of neighbours and friends to assist the police in the search. Most of the words went over my head, but I remember thinking how kind it was of Harry and how we never know our true friends until a time of need.

Jack left us alone and went into the kitchen: more coffee, I assumed, but he reappeared fifteen minutes later to tell us that a meal was ready. I hadn't thought about food in the last twenty-four hours, surviving on biscuits unenthusiastically nibbled with the stream of tea and coffee, but suddenly I was hungry.

Stephen helped me into the kitchen where our little breakfast table was set for three and a huge casserole dish stood in the centre, a plate of fresh vegetables beside it. I looked from my husband to Jack.

'Where did this come from?' More guilt washed over me with the realisation that I should have been the one to provide for these men.

'I'd love to say that I made it, but my wife sent it for you. She sort of expected that food would be the last thing on your minds at the moment, so … voilà!'

'That is so kind — please thank her for me, it's really thoughtful.'

We sat and ate in silence. The food was good, and I managed more than I expected to. Jack insisted on clearing up, steering me to the lounge with a mug of tea and I gratefully sank into the sofa, exhausted physically and emotionally. I asked for one of the sleeping pills, wanting to sink into oblivion and escape from reality, to sleep and find respite from this nightmare we were living.

Stephen put me to bed and sleep did come, but so too did the morning and the nightmare continued.

Chapter 2

Jack Priestly

I had volunteered to train for the role of Family Liaison Officer three years ago, encouraged by my superintendent and my wife, Sarah. Both could see qualities in me that I was unsure about, but after twelve years on the Force it was time for a change and the work of a FLO interested me.

I'd been involved in countless serious crimes, including a handful of homicides, and looked upon this change as a way to offer more direct help than simply being part of the investigating team. The role of a FLO certainly did bring me closer to the victims of crime and offered things I had never quite expected. I became expert at finding my way around other people's kitchens — I was tea maker, ever ready shoulder to cry on, tissue provider, punch-bag (metaphorically and physically), fount of information, bearer of news — both good and bad, listener, accumulator of information and watcher of family dynamics — or as some would say, a spy.

Generally, I managed to give of myself one hundred percent but had the gift of being able to 'box' my feelings when off duty. This case, however, was the first assignment involving child abduction in my two years as a FLO and hopefully I would still manage to do so. Inevitably anything to do with a child, especially one so young, affects the officers working the crime and I was no exception.

When the call came to attend the incident, it was with mixed emotions that I headed to the Bryson family home. An average suburban house from the front, it appeared large enough for a family to live comfortably, but what made this house stand out was the garden area surrounding it. Built on a corner plot, it must have covered at least an acre of land.

Before going inside to meet the family, I skirted round the house to the garden to seek out the officer in charge of the search. He walked me through the area, explaining about the game the children had been playing and I could see the problems it presented. Where the garden began to slope, it became a paradise for children. I had two boys of my own, the youngest a similar age to the Bryson's missing daughter, and I knew they would absolutely adore this place. The shrubs and trees offered shade and excitement for adventurous youngsters. A tyre swing swayed gently in the breeze. If only it could talk, our job would be so much easier.

There was evidence of a tree house under construction, and for a brief moment I wondered if the family would ever enjoy this magnificent garden again. A huge, rampant buddleia marked the beginning of the wilder area of the garden, bright purple spikes attracting fluttering butterflies, which appeared to be playing their own game of hide and seek.

Most of the officers were obscured from sight by the thick undergrowth and there were some big, burly men amongst them; it would be easy to miss spotting a child here, which made me question whether she had still been in the garden when her parents were searching or had already been taken away — each minute putting unwelcome distance between Grace and her family.

Thanking my colleague for his time, I approached the house again, noting the exits to and from the garden. There were two gates at the front — a single pedestrian one from where I had come, and a detached double gate for vehicle access, opening onto a gravelled drive and car parking area beside a double garage, which housed the family's people carrier.

An adjacent sliver of grass ran down the west side of the house leading to the back of the property. From there, looking south towards the river, the fruit orchard was on the right, beginning from the side of the garage and continuing to the far end of the garden which, because of the camber of the land, could not be seen from where I stood. To the left was the lawn and patio area; a gazebo with pink balloons tied to each corner saddened my heart as they bounced merrily on the breeze — the sorry remnants of the party.

About ninety yards from the house the shrubbery began: wild and overgrown from the spell of good weather of late. Again, the furthest point was unseen from the lawn, but I'd already visited the boundary wall and the arched wooden door, bolted from the inside. I knew that the river flowed on the other side of the wall and frogmen were already assembling to search it.

Before I went to the house, I peered through the tiny glass pane in the garage door and discovered another egress from the property in the form of a single door on the far wall. Having committed the outside layout of the house to memory, I rang the bell and steeled myself to meet the Brysons.

Margaret and Stephen Bryson were about my own age, Stephen possibly a little older, a tall man with a shock of sandy hair cut short to his head. Margaret was shorter than her husband by a good six inches, an attractive woman with light honey brown hair falling in natural waves around her face and neck. Cornflower blue eyes, wide with anxiety, met my own, tears threatening to spill over at any moment.

Margaret's mind was working fast, connecting the dots and wondering why a FLO was needed, so I attempted to explain my role and reassure them both that my presence was not because we were assuming their daughter was dead. I hoped they believed me — it was important to gain their trust in order to be as effective as possible.

My first impression of the couple was that they were genuinely distressed, and my heart ached for them. The fact that they had called us in so soon was in their favour. I began to explain our procedures — things like searching the house, which was a mandatory part of our methodology — but Mr and Mrs Bryson were an intelligent couple and picked up on the fact that we had to consider the possibility that they were somehow involved in their daughter's disappearance.

When Margaret found a policeman removing the bath panel, she became almost hysterical. It was then that I suggested to Stephen that we should ring for a doctor, something he readily agreed with, and while he comforted his wife I made the call and then began to familiarise myself with their kitchen. Providing tea and coffee was routine and very often the only practical thing I could do. Until we found Grace, her parents would have no peace and yet I could offer no guarantees as to when, or even if, we would find her.

The GP arrived swiftly and was sensitive and kindly, encouraging them to stay strong for each other and for their older child, Elise. Margaret initially refused medication to help her sleep, but the doctor left some anyway. I think he understood that we were preparing for the long haul with this investigation and when he left, generously offered to come back at any time should they need him, day or night.

Evening melted into night and one by one my colleagues left, their solemn expressions an indication of the frustration and sadness each one felt. The search of the river and the immediate neighbourhood had yielded nothing but would resume with a wider perimeter at first light. Neither of the Brysons would eat but drank endless cups of coffee in an attempt to stay awake. I encouraged them to at least eat the odd biscuit to maintain some degree of strength.

By midnight Margaret was persuaded to take the medication and go to bed. Barely able to rise from the chair, Stephen helped his wife upstairs before returning to sit with me. I could have left for a few hours' sleep myself by then but was happy to stay for as long as Stephen wanted me to. My wife knew that I may be out all night and so would not worry.

We dozed in our respective armchairs until a shout from upstairs jolted us back to reality. Stephen ran upstairs as I waited in the lounge. It struck me as incredibly cruel when I found out the reason for Margaret's distress. How people survive such blows is beyond me. An ambulance took Margaret away and, as it was still very early, I persuaded Stephen to try to get a few more hours of sleep and went home to do the same myself. It was the early hours of Sunday morning, and we had no way of predicting what the new day would bring.

Sarah woke as I opened the bedroom door, in spite of my attempt to be quiet. She had probably been expecting me most of the night.

'Any news?' In the soft light of the bedroom her concern was still evident. Perhaps only a mother can fully understand the feelings of another in such awful circumstances.

I shook my head. 'No, love, try to get some more sleep — it's still early.'

I quickly peeled off my clothes and climbed into bed beside her, pulling her soft warm body into mine for comfort as exhaustion finally claimed me.

Three hours later, the noise of my sons' laughter woke me and I was filled with an urge to see them both, to hug them close and assure myself that they were safe and well. Sarah watched as I did just that, and the boys giggled as if we were playing some kind of impromptu game. I savoured every minute with my family, but I was also anxious to be back at my post. Sarah understood completely.

As I arrived at River View at seven thirty a.m., the inevitable cogs of the investigation had begun to turn once more and had taken hold of the Bryson home. A smaller team than yesterday were already walking the river banks — their colleagues would be assigned to door knocking and gathering any possible CCTV footage that may be available from businesses or private homes in the area.

Inspector Jim Duncan was the Senior Investigating Officer for this case and arrived shortly after me; he wanted to know my initial impressions of the family, even though it had not yet been a full twenty-four hours. Although I was primarily there to support and inform the Brysons, I was still a police officer and one situated in an ideal position to observe the family's interactions. It's such a distressing fact that many abducted children are harmed by a family member, which is why we begin at the very core of the family and move the investigation methodically outwards from that point.

Jim was a slightly built man for a police officer but wiry and with a tenacity that was almost tangible. His face was lined from weather as much as age, and his intelligent brown eyes missed nothing as they scanned the room.

If I was in the Brysons' shoes, I would have welcomed a man like Jim Duncan being in charge. He motioned me with a nod to follow him to the kitchen, and I smiled at Stephen who was looking haggard and tired after a restless night. He was about to call the hospital for an update on Margaret, so I took the opportunity to follow Jim and find out if the situation had altered overnight. Sadly it had not, which was to be expected really.

I knew Jim wanted a concise, verbal update as to my views on the parents, so I reported that there had been nothing incongruent in their words or actions, nothing to warrant concern or make me doubt that everything they had told us was true. I told him about Margaret's miscarriage, and he shook his head sadly — Jim was a father, too, and fully motivated to offer his very best in the search for Grace.

A press conference had been hastily arranged, and Jim wanted me to ask Stephen if he would be willing to make a general appeal for information. Normally we would ask both parents to do this, but in the circumstances the father would suffice. I was to take Stephen to the station around midday, coaching him beforehand as to what to expect and what questions to avoid answering, although both DI Duncan and I would be there to see that the appeal was handled correctly and would yield the best possible outcome.

The rest of the day's investigations would be focussed on the wider family, Margaret's sister and her husband, the parents of the other children who were at the party and the neighbours, Christine and Harry Robinson. Specially trained officers would talk to the children themselves and particularly to Elise Bryson, Grace's older sister.

Chapter 3

Bea Cartwright

Sleep did not come easily on that hot August night — no surprise really, but I would have welcomed the respite of oblivion from the awful reality of events. Poor Elise had been so confused and upset — wanting her mother, yet being old enough to understand the situation — and having witnessed her parents' distress, she accepted being with Peter and me.

The happiest of occasions had turned into a nightmare that I could hardly believe was true. Who would want to take Grace and why? Actually, I didn't really want to know the answer to the 'why' question; it was unthinkable, appalling! My poor sister — how ever would Margaret be feeling?

I desperately wanted to go back to her last night, when Elise had finally fallen asleep, but Peter was the voice of reason. If the police were not still with them, they would most probably be trying to rest, although I doubted that was possible.

I settled for a telephone call. Stephen answered, but there was no good news to impart. Margaret was in a state and refusing to sleep, and a police officer was still with them and would probably stay all night, he said. The conversation was short, neither of us knowing what to say nor having any words of comfort to offer each other. This wasn't a situation that could be eased by banal comments or platitudes. Grace was missing, and with each passing minute the horror of what might become of her was evolving into a grotesque reality in my mind; most surely it would be the same for Stephen and

Margaret. And now, with the hours of darkness over, I dreaded what the new day would bring.

We had always been close, even with nearly ten years between us. Margaret was our parents' afterthought, a child who would keep them young, which she most certainly did. I doted on my little sister, and I like to think she looked up to me, too.

Our shared childhood was idyllic with much love and happiness, which only served to make the loss of our parents in a motor accident so hard to bear. I'd been married to Peter for ten years at the time, and Margaret had recently become engaged to Stephen. In an attempt to be pragmatic, we determinedly counted our blessings and remained thankful for the years we did have with our parents, and the fact that they had lived long enough to see our futures mapped out and decided.

With only six months between the funeral and Margaret's wedding, we determinedly focussed on the latter and kept ourselves busy with the preparations. I was thrilled when Margaret asked Peter to step in and give her away, a role he happily accepted. Planning for the wedding eased our grief enormously, and afterwards we picked up the threads of our respective lives as married women.

Margaret became pregnant with Elise after their first year of marriage, while Peter and I remained childless. After over ten years of trying we had given up hope of ever conceiving a child, but rather than feeling any jealousy towards my sister, I was delighted at her news and readily on hand to babysit. Margaret was so generous in letting me share in Elise's life and we spent most weekends together, the four of us and Elise, mainly at Lilac House, the home they were restoring.

I loved the place almost as much as they did; not that I wasn't happy with my own little cottage. I was, but Peter found it difficult to find work and there were often periods when we had little or no income except for my meagre wage at a newsagents. But I'd become a dab hand at restoring furniture and making do, and although I often dreamed of owning a little shop where we could sell restored items, a vintage, shabby chic emporium, I knew that raising the capital for such a venture was an unattainable dream.

When Grace was born, my love for her equalled my feelings for Elise, but I wasn't their mother and I knew that Margaret's pain would cut even deeper than my own at this dreadful time. As parents, I knew they must both be going through absolute hell.

By seven o'clock that morning I was restless and wanted to ring to see if there was news, but I didn't wish to disturb any sleep they might have managed to snatch. Elise was still in bed, having eventually cried herself to sleep at about eleven, exhausted and distressed. She had always been mature for her years and after Grace came along was such a help to Margaret. I may be biased, but I don't think I've ever known a closer, more loving family than my sisters'.

As I dithered over what time would be best to ring, Peter appeared in the kitchen holding Elise's hand.

'Look who I found wide awake and hungry.' His tone was purposefully light and he smiled down at Elise. 'At least I hope she's hungry, because I am!' He grinned.

Elise's face was pale with red circles around her eyes.

'I'm not very hungry, Uncle Peter.' She then turned to me. 'Have they found Grace yet, Auntie Bea?'

How I would have loved to say yes, to put a smile on that sad little face, but it wasn't within my power.

'No, darling, but it's light now and the police will be out searching again.' What cold comfort to a child whose world had just collapsed around her.

I poured orange juice for the three of us and switched on the kettle before rummaging through the cereal cupboard, looking for something to tempt Elise. Cornflakes would have to suffice.

When we were settled around the kitchen table, I searched my mind for something to say to cheer us all up but failed miserably. We ate in silence until Jasper appeared in the kitchen doorway.

'Look, Elise, Jasper's come home for his breakfast. Would you feed him for me love?'

Elise wriggled down off her chair and scooped Jasper up into her arms. The cat did not protest, seeming to know that his own special brand of comfort was required more than ever at that particular moment. Elise kissed his face over and over again — I didn't like to think where he'd been through the night, but it was not a time to worry about hygiene. Eventually, she put him down and went to find some food, Jasper following, almost tripping her up as he weaved in and out between her stick thin legs. She put the dried food in his bowl, filled the water bowl with fresh water and then lay full length on the floor beside him while he ate.

Jasper could soothe Elise without even trying; they seemed to have a special bond. When we first bought him as a kitten less than a year ago, she had spent hours playing with him, ignoring the scratches from his sharp little claws and the nips from his exploring teeth. In truth, he was really more her cat than ours. Elise made the time to play with him, and hopefully now Jasper would bring some comfort to her troubled little soul.

I whispered to Peter that I was going to phone Margaret, and he got the message to keep Elise occupied.

'Stephen, it's Bea, how are you?'

'Oh, Bea, I'm sorry, I should have phoned you earlier. Margaret was taken into hospital in the early hours this morning. She's had a miscarriage … the stress, I should imagine.' I gasped, shocked, as he continued, 'I've spoken to someone on the ward this morning, and they're hoping to discharge her later today. There's still no news on Grace.'

I was stunned into silence. A miscarriage — she must have been in the very early stages, or I'm sure Margaret would have told me she was pregnant! I'd guessed that there would be no news about Grace; if there was, I would surely have heard immediately. I didn't know what to say.

'Are they still looking?' What a stupid question — of course they were!

'Yes. Harry's even enlisted some of the neighbours to help, and I'm doing some sort of appeal for the news over lunchtime. I hate that sort of thing, but if it helps, and the police said it often does… How's Elise?'

'All things considered, not so bad. She did eventually sleep and seems to be bearing up today. Let me know if you want me to bring her over. I'll ring later to find out about Margaret, okay?'

'Yes, and I'm sorry, Bea, for not letting you know; I honestly don't know where I am at the moment — forgive me?'

'There's nothing to forgive. We'll keep Elise as long as necessary. God bless you both, Stephen.'

I replaced the receiver, feeling deflated and totally useless — a miscarriage on top of everything else, how utterly awful. Returning to the kitchen, I was greeted by the inquisitive faces of my husband and niece.

'I spoke to your daddy and he sends his love. The police are still looking for Grace, so we'll have to wait and see.'

I wished for positive, encouraging words to offer, but there were none. Peter glanced at me and frowned — we both knew that the longer Grace was missing, the less chance there would be of finding her safe and well.

The phone rang before I had a chance to sit down again. It was a detective, Jim Duncan, who wanted to speak to both Peter and me. I gave him our address, reminding him that we still had Elise with us. DI Duncan said he would come immediately to talk to us individually while the other one looked after Elise. Another officer, specifically trained in such circumstances, would be in touch about talking to Elise later that day.

Peter sighed and nodded when I told them. The poor girl was being drawn into something no child should ever have to face.

Jim Duncan was with us in less than half an hour. I was glad of his speed and the fact that they were making an early start even after such a late finish the night before. A young detective constable was with him, who was introduced to us as DC Dave Bennet. DC Bennet was a nervous looking man, but DI Duncan was obviously efficient and within a minute of them entering our home, Peter had taken Elise into the garden with Jasper while I was interviewed first.

'What we are trying to do now is to build up a picture of exactly what happened around the time that Grace disappeared. Nothing is too trivial to mention, Mrs Cartwright — what seems irrelevant to you may have meaning when added to other information from other sources. So, if you could run through everything you remember about yesterday afternoon, it would be a great help.'

DI Duncan's grey eyes stared directly into my own as if he was trying to read my thoughts. It was relatively easy to tell them exactly what I remembered; I had thought of nothing else since, so I began from after lunch when Peter and I arrived at Lilac House.

DC Bennet took notes and occasionally DI Duncan stopped me to clarify a point, or to ask exactly where I was in the house or garden at each particular time. They were certainly thorough, and when I'd covered everything the constable read it back to me to double check. It was then Peter's turn, so I went out into the garden to take over with Elise. I expected that Peter was asked pretty much the same questions.

'Have they found her yet, Auntie Bea?' Elise's voice trembled, and once again there were tears in her eyes.

'Not yet, darling.' I was afraid to say more for fear of losing control of my own emotions, so I knelt down on the grass and hugged my niece as she sobbed gently on my shoulder.

It had been less than twenty-four hours, the longest day of my life. I had never been the religious sort, but I held Elise close and whispered a prayer for Grace.

Chapter 4

Jack Priestly

When there was still no news by early evening on Sunday, the atmosphere in the Brysons' home was tense and at times I could feel their resentment of my presence. Understandable really — who wants a stranger witnessing the most harrowing time of their lives?

On the other hand, they were beginning to use me, asking questions about procedure as well as specifics relating to Grace's case. I couldn't offer them the news they desperately wanted to hear, but I was able to update them on the investigation — at least the positive aspects of it. The response from the television appeal earlier that day had been good, and it would be repeated on later news bulletins when we expected even more feedback. The public in general were keen to help if they could, and a few suspicious incidents from the same afternoon had been reported.

I explained to Stephen and Margaret that a team were working solely on the information gathered as a direct result of the appeal. They would interview every person who had come forward, which would take time, but anything deemed to be in the slightest way significant would be followed up immediately.

I did not, however, mention the crackpot calls that always come in with the genuine ones. We didn't dismiss them out of hand but could usually recognise those people whose motives were far from altruistic. It was the same with the hate calls and mail. One of the things I asked to be allowed to do when I was with the Brysons was to screen their telephone calls and check their mail as far as possible without breaching their privacy. Although they agreed without question, I think they knew why I wished to do this and as the hours ticked by, they had become almost relieved to have me monitoring their calls, particularly when the media started to ring, offering money for exclusive interviews.

Margaret was weak from the loss of the baby as well as the stress of her youngest daughter's disappearance. She did, however, revive slightly when Elise was brought to see her at about six p.m. There were hugs and tears all round, and it was good for the parents to be with their daughter again. The girl would remind them of why they needed to stay strong and would provide an alternative focus other than the main agenda of finding Grace.

A female officer had interviewed Elise earlier that afternoon at the Cartwrights' home with Bea Cartwright present as an appropriate adult. The main characters had now all been questioned, and back at the incident room a picture was being put together of each person's movements on the previous afternoon. We were trying to account for minutes rather than hours; it only takes a few seconds to snatch a child.

Stephen Bryson had supplied us with photographs of Grace: a pretty child with fair hair and blue eyes, a sprinkling of freckles over her nose but no distinguishing marks — a description that could fit several thousand children throughout the country. By now, copies of the photographs had been widely circulated and appeared on the television at the lunchtime appeal. All the national and local newspapers would run with them tomorrow, and with any luck someone somewhere would recognise her.

The appeal was shown again later that evening, prompting a fresh surge of telephone calls to the incident room, and officers would work well into the night following up any new leads. There would be no complaints at having to work overtime; the unity of officers in such cases was incredible.

Elise returned to her aunt's house, bravely saying goodnight to her parents and blinking back the tears.

'Jasper will be missing you,' Mrs Cartwright coaxed, and the child nodded solemnly and turned away from her parents.

Margaret was persuaded to eat a little pasta; it was packet stuff, as I had been in charge of food again that day. I know that at home Sarah was spending her Sunday baking and cooking for the Brysons — everyone wanted to help in whatever way they could.

I left at around eight p.m. to go home and rest. Stephen had my phone number as well as that of the incident room, which would be manned round the clock, and had been persuaded to call me if there was anything at all I could do. By nine-thirty I was climbing the stairs to bed, exhausted and wanting to be fresh for the following day. Hopefully Monday morning would bring the breakthrough we so desperately wanted.

There were signs of activity on the phones as I stopped by the incident room on my way to Lilac House the next morning. Nearly all the national newspapers carried photographs of Grace Bryson on their front pages, and even though it was only seven-thirty in the morning, the phones were ringing.

A chat with Jim Duncan gave me nothing of importance to take to the Brysons. There had been the expected time-wasters, one or two sightings of Grace before she was actually taken and a woman claiming that Grace had come to her in a vision and told her that she had been killed by her mother. These callers were anything but helpful, yet had to be logged —

activity that ate into manpower hours, time that could be better spent on more solid leads.

Today we were going to interview the parents and aunt and uncle again, and widen the door-to-door inquiries. The neighbour who was helping at the party, Christine Robinson, would also be seen again together with her husband Harry, who had been out of town for a conference and was driving home at the time of the party.

'What do you make of the father, Stephen?' Jim asked, never one to beat about the bush.

'He's shocked, numb almost. I think he's genuine.'

'Don't you think he's rather cold? Most fathers would be insisting on joining the search, wanting to see exactly what we are doing.'

I could see where Jim was coming from, but I had read Stephen differently.

'Being quiet and withdrawn could be his way of coping, and there's a miscarriage in the mix now to compound the situation. Surely the logistics of it all rule him out, don't they?'

'Not necessarily; it only takes a minute or two to grab a child, and he's in a good position to have planned every detail.'

'But what would be the motive? And wouldn't he have needed an accomplice? He didn't have time to get her any distance from the house. When parents are involved it's usually a spontaneous episode, discipline gone too far, temper lost, that kind of thing. I don't see any of the family involved, but it is still early yet.'

'There's the aunt and uncle, too — what's your take on them, Jack?'

'Again, it's very early and I haven't seen much of them. They brought the elder girl round to see her parents yesterday but took her back to stay with them. Poor little mite, she'll not know what's hit her. I would wonder at the motive if it was either of the Cartwrights, and they seem pretty genuine — almost as upset as the parents.'

'We'll widen the search and repeat the door-to-door to try and find out the neighbours' views of the family. That goes for the Cartwrights, too. Surely we'll find some nosey neighbour who's dying to share all the gossip. Anyway, before you go, come and have a look at this diagram of the house and gardens. I presume you've had a good look round?'

A detailed plan of the Brysons' home was pinned onto a freestanding board, a picture of Grace above it, smiling, carefree and happy, as is the right of any child. It was a pretty good plan of the property.

'I took the opportunity to nose around on Saturday before going into the house. What are your theories so far?'

Jim began pointing out the exits, and they were as I remembered them: an old but solid gate on the southern boundary wall, a door from the rear of the garage leading onto the west side of the property and the front double gate for vehicle access with a single gate for pedestrians a few yards away, both leading to River View, a quiet leafy street in the suburbs of Leeds.

'They were both locked from the inside.' Jim tapped the south gate and the door at the rear of the garage with his finger. 'So either it was someone inside the house who locked up again after getting her out, or she was taken by persons unknown through one of the gates at the front of the property.'

I nodded, taking in his meaning but not fully understanding why a family member would do this. 'If it had been one of the family, and I assume we're thinking primarily the parents or the aunt and uncle, why would they lock the exits afterwards?

Surely they would have left them open to make it appear that someone had sneaked into the garden, taken Grace and left through the south gate or the garage. Locking them would throw suspicion in their direction, don't you think?'

Jim stroked his chin thoughtfully. 'So, if it was an outsider, they would certainly have had to use one of the gates at the front. That gives us a good chance that someone saw something. I don't consider scaling the southern wall a viable possibility. How would the abductor know he wouldn't be seen and that the girl would be there anyway?' Jim's fingers moved to the area of lawn at the back of the house. 'This is where they were playing and where Grace was last seen. The children ran into the shrubs to hide, but Grace could quite easily have gone into the orchard. Was someone already there perhaps, watching the party and waiting for his chance? I don't somehow see it myself. Anyway, an open mind is the way to go. She can't have vanished into thin air, and hopefully today will be the day we'll get that vital lead. There's also the neighbour to meet, Harry Robinson; his house is next door and the properties share a boundary wall, but it's too high to scale, unless it was meticulously planned. We'll need to check his alibi, too.'

We walked back through the incident room, which was now even busier, with almost every phone in use. As we passed, a DC leaned back to catch Jim's eye, his hand over the receiver of the telephone.

'Sir! I think you might want to talk to this lady.' He then thanked his caller and asked if she would repeat her story to the SIO. Jim took the phone, glancing at the DC's notes, which gave the caller's name.

'Hello, Mrs Graham, I'm DI Duncan. I believe you have some information which might be helpful?'

I waited, listening to one side of the conversation, which was nothing more informative than a few positive sounding noises. Jim's eyes had widened, and he swung the notepad round and began to scribble. He thanked the caller profusely, taking her address and number to contact her later then replaced the receiver.

'This one sounds interesting; we'll make this a priority.' He glanced at the notes. 'Mrs Graham, who lives in the next road to River View, has been worried about a man she's seen several times in the local park. She's pretty certain he's just moved into the area, the big house at the end of Burton Road which is now flats, you know? She's seen him going in there, but the interesting thing is that he's been regularly watching the local children playing in the park at Smithfield Lane. Mrs Graham walks her dog there at least twice a day and had thought it strange that he should be there so often and alone. The park is less than a hundred yards from River View.

'Jack, off you go to the Brysons, and without giving too much away find out if Mrs Bryson takes the children there. I'm going to visit these flats and find our park watcher. Good work, Sam.'

DI Duncan patted the young DC's shoulder before purposefully heading out, barking instructions to officers as he went. Two constables were ordered to the park to talk to parents, joggers, dog walkers, anyone who frequented the park, and DC Bennet was tasked with accompanying DI Duncan. The wheels were in motion once again, and I headed to Lilac House to be of whatever help I could and to find out more about the family in general.

An almost tangible sadness lingered over Lilac House as I arrived that morning. Although it was only eight-thirty, both Stephen and Margaret looked as if they had been awake for a considerable time, if indeed they had slept at all.

It seems almost incongruous to enter someone's home with a smile when you have no good news to impart, so I tried to appear expressionless as I followed Stephen into the kitchen. His enquiring look had asked the question, and my slight shake of the head answered it. Margaret also held that hopeful look in her eyes but assumed the worst when all I could say was, 'Good morning.'

The kettle was still warm and Stephen automatically began to make coffee for me, adding one spoonful of sugar without the need to ask. I suspected we were going to learn several minor details about each other; being thrown together by such a tragic event was not the ideal way to form relationships.

'There have been several calls.' I tried to sound optimistic. 'Even throughout the night, and a team is taking note of every one. They will all be carefully looked into.'

'But did anyone see Grace or someone taking her?' Margaret asked.

'Nothing as direct as that, I'm afraid, but one or two names have cropped up which are of interest, and DI Duncan is hoping to see one of them this morning.'

Perhaps I had said too much, but I wanted to give them something to grasp at, to let them know that we were doing everything possible to find their daughter.

'Who is it — someone we know?' Stephen was anxious.

'I don't think so, and I can't give you a name but we are following every lead.'

'Is he a known paedophile?' His voice was low, but Margaret heard and let out a groan before dropping her head into her hands and sobbing once again.

'Just someone of interest, we'll have to leave it at that.'

Stephen held his wife, and I moved into the lounge to afford them some privacy. After a few minutes, Stephen came to find me.

'Why can't you say?' He appeared more hurt than angry.

'Look, I'm sorry; it's just the way things work. We can't go around naming people in an investigation without a solid reason to do so — I only told you so you would know that leads are being followed up. As soon as we have anything significant, I'll tell you.'

He nodded, grudgingly understanding.

'Perhaps if I could build up a picture of Margaret and the children's day-to-day activities it might help. Is she up to that?'

'Yes, doing something positive is better than simply waiting. I'll fetch her.'

In less than a minute they returned, Margaret red-eyed but eager to help.

'I know Elise is usually at school, and Grace attends pre-school for how many days?' I began.

'Three — Monday, Wednesday and Friday. I take Elise to school at Burton Road then on to pre-school at Marlow Terrace.'

'And which way do you go?'

'If it's fine we like to walk, so it's straight down the road to school, just a couple of blocks over. Then Grace and I cut through the park to get to pre-school.'

My heart leapt; could this be the link we were looking for?

'What about the holidays, Margaret — they broke up for summer a couple of weeks ago, didn't they?'

'Yes. We haven't been away so far; we were waiting until after Grace's birthday … then we intended to go to Devon for a couple of weeks.' She stopped to blow her nose and dab at her eyes.

'So what have you been doing? Going to the park, into town?'

'The park a few times, yes, but not usually to town. Elise enjoys shopping, but Grace gets bored; she's more the outdoors type. We often take a picnic and then feed the ducks in the river, and there's a good playground with swings and climbing frames. Grace would spend all day there if she could.'

I felt a rush of excitement and needed to ring Jim Duncan without the Brysons hearing me. 'Will you excuse me for a moment? I need to make a quick call.' I went out through the kitchen into the garden and dialled the number of the SIO. 'Jim, I think the park could be relevant. Mrs Bryson walks Grace through there to get to pre-school and during the holidays they are regular visitors.'

'Great! I've just seen Mrs Graham and we're heading on over to Burton Road now.' He sounded positive, upbeat.

'Burton Road is where Elise Bryson goes to school!' I almost shouted.

'Interesting.' Jim was as calm as ever. 'We're not sure which flat this chap lives in, but we have a description and if he's a new tenant someone should know. I'll ring to update you when we've seen him, Jack. Bye for now.'

I felt a sudden rush of adrenaline and the need to do something physical, but I had to temper my enthusiasm and go back inside. I didn't want to build Stephen and Margaret's hopes up until there was something more concrete to tell them.

Inside again, I continued asking about their everyday routines, plucking questions out of thin air in an effort to keep

Margaret occupied, and who was to know whether some vital piece of information would be unearthed? If I'd done this little exercise sooner, perhaps the park might have appeared significant. I knew that by now uniformed officers would be in the park talking to anyone who so much as walked past with any degree of regularity. This was the most positive breakthrough so far, and I waited anxiously for word from the DI.

The wait was an hour and a half. When my phone did ring, I excused myself to go outside again — the caller ID showed it was Jim Duncan.

'Yes, I'm alone.' I was longing for good news.

'The man we're looking at is Will Hogarth, thirty-six years old, moved into Leeds a couple of months ago. We're running his details through the system now.' Jim spoke quickly as if on the move.

'Are you taking him in?'

'Not enough to do that, but he has agreed to come in voluntarily so at least we'll keep tabs on him until we see if he's known to us. Took umbrage, though, when I asked if we could have a look round the flat, so I'm applying for a warrant. I think there are sufficient grounds for concern.'

'Can I tell the parents?'

There was a pause.

'Tell them we have someone whom we're questioning. It'll be all over the media soon, especially with the activity in the park, so it's best if they hear it from us, but don't build their hopes up too much.'

'What's your instinct, Jim?'

'He fits the profile. Loner, out of work, spends time in the park to watch the world go round. It's possible, but I'll reserve judgement until we see if he's got a record. Dave's running his name through the system now.'

'Right, I'll tell them the bones of it. I think any news will be welcomed today — it's been a long hard weekend.'

I had actually already told them most of this, but at least now I could let them know he was at the station, co-operating, even if I could not divulge a name.

Again, two pairs of anxious eyes met mine with their silent enquiry.

'That was DI Duncan. There is a man at the station about to be interviewed. At present, he's only a person of interest and is there voluntarily to help with the inquiry. There's not much more to tell you for the moment, but the DI will keep us informed.'

'Do they think he took Grace?' Margaret looked so pale and fragile, almost near to collapse.

'We don't know; that's what they will be asking about now.'

I could tell there were other questions whirling around in their minds, unspoken so as not to make them real. What we were all really wondering was whether or not Grace was still alive.

Chapter 5

Margaret Bryson

It was no surprise that sleep did not come naturally, and once again I relied on a sleeping tablet out of sheer desperation. It was a temptation to take another one when I woke after six hours of fitful sleep. The oblivion would be so welcome, respite from the agony of not knowing where my baby was or what horrors she might be going through. But I couldn't give in to such actions; there was still Elise and Stephen to think about, and I needed to be brave for them. So, at five a.m., I began to scrub the kitchen floor.

Stephen heard my movement in the silence of the empty house and appeared in the doorway.

'What are you doing, Margaret? It's only five o'clock.'

'Sorry if I disturbed you. I can't sleep and needed to do something practical.'

'The floor doesn't need cleaning, especially on your hands and knees. You've just come out of hospital for goodness' sake.'

He was right but I was so desperate, what could I do to escape the agony? I would happily walk the streets day and night if I thought I might find Grace, but common sense told me she was hidden away somewhere, or dead. Tears began to well up inside; I would have thought there would be no more tears having shed so many. Stephen was at my side, lifting me from my knees.

'Come back to bed, Margaret.'

Following meekly, I climbed into bed beside my husband, his arms circling my trembling body as I clung to him for comfort and he kissed my hair, my cheek and my lips. We made love … gently at first, then with an urgent, silent passion, our bodies entwined as one. The comfort of his nearness brought a brief surge of strength throughout my being, while at the same time I was consumed with guilt at the very act of desire I'd needed so badly.

Afterwards we cried silently, Stephen's hot tears on my face mingling with my own. Exhausted, we both slept for a brief time before reality and the brutal truth of what was happening in our lives once again swamped us, and the intrusive harsh sunlight revealed the stark fact that Grace was still missing.

Jack Priestly arrived early, his face blank, reflecting the fact that there was no good news. We knew the police were doing all they could and for that we were grateful, but I longed for even the slightest snippet of news to cling on to, any indication that my daughter was well.

Jack mentioned that a few leads had come in as a result of the media coverage, and there were one or two people whom they were looking at. My mind raced ahead. Were they talking about known paedophiles? I knew there was a register of such monsters, but did the police have the powers to question them in such a case?

More tears flowed, and Jack tactfully withdrew to the lounge while Stephen again held me close. I pulled myself together; today we wanted to bring Elise home. Her presence would help us both and I missed her so much, yet I would have to be strong for my daughter and not give way to my emotions in front of her. Elise was also going through the worst ordeal of her young life.

Stephen went to join Jack in the lounge, returning almost immediately to ask if I was up to talking Jack through our daily routines. Seizing the opportunity to help, even though some of this ground had been covered with DI Duncan, I answered a few questions. We were interrupted only when Jack went into the garden to make a telephone call and again much later when a call came through to him. After the second call, he came in from the garden with a half-smile on his lips. A man was at the station, not arrested but there voluntarily. Could it be the man who had taken her? And if it was, where was she?

It was the longest Monday I could ever remember, partly due to such an early start and my seemingly permanent exhaustion. I felt weak but had no appetite, and my head throbbed continually from the bouts of crying that I struggled to control.

We heard nothing until after lunch, when DI Duncan rang again. This time, Jack didn't go into the garden and we hung on every word he said, attempting to interpret his body language, a futile exercise. When the call ended Jack sat opposite Stephen and me, elbows on his knees and fingers laced together.

'They've got a warrant to search the man's flat. DI Duncan is on his way there now. He's apparently known to the police in Manchester, where he lived previously, but not in relation to any activity with children. He's been cautioned in the past for pestering a woman — emails, texts, that sort of thing — but sufficient for a judge to allow the warrant. The man is denying any involvement, but if he's lying there could be evidence in the flat.'

'Do they think Grace might be there?' Stephen asked.

'It doesn't seem likely. DI Duncan was inside the flat when he made the initial contact, and there was no sign of anyone else there.'

'But he could know where she is, he could have hidden her somewhere?'

'Let's just wait and see, shall we? This man has only come under suspicion because someone noticed him in the park on several occasions. So far, there's nothing concrete to go on.'

'The park — that's why you were asking all those questions!' I wished I had thought about it myself as soon as Grace had been taken, but then we regularly go to the supermarket and several other places, too. My hopes were raised and I knew the next hour or two was crucial and the waiting would be torture.

Fortunately, things were moving swiftly and Jack took a call from Jim Duncan within the hour. I scrutinised his expression, and it took only a couple of seconds to realise that it was not the outcome we would have liked. Grace was not there.

Jack confirmed it when he ended the call. The search had been thorough, and the police took away a laptop computer for further investigation but our hopes were dashed. Perhaps I was naive to have expected such a simple and speedy end to this nightmare. I was beginning to dread each next moment, never mind the hours and days.

The only bright spot was that Elise was coming home. I spoke to my sister on the telephone, briefly telling her about the morning's events and the disappointing search of this man's flat and then asked if she would bring Elise home that afternoon. Bea was concerned for me, whether I would cope with Elise to care for, and expressed concerns that Elise would be upset by the continued police presence. Valid points, which I knew came from genuine concern on Bea's part, but we needed our daughter and I think she needed to be with us, as excluding her would perhaps have consequences at a later date. We would draw strength from each other.

Once it was agreed, I went upstairs into Elise's room. It was a mess. Clothes were strewn over the bed from Saturday, when she had been unable to decide what to wear for the party. I put them away automatically then tidied up her books. Elise loved reading, so much so that we had to check on her at night time to ensure she was actually sleeping and not reading.

When I could find nothing else to occupy me in her room, I moved on to Grace's bedroom and took a deep breath before going inside. Most of the bed was hidden under a mound of soft toys. Like an idiot, I pushed them to the side, unconsciously checking that Grace was not underneath and when she was not I fell across her bed and gave way to tears again.

It took only five minutes for the tears to dry up, and I gazed around at the accoutrements of her three years. Whereas Elise had chosen pastel colours for her room and furnishings, Grace had done the pink thing, big time. Curtains, duvet and even the carpet were pink with tiny fairy lights strung above the bed and the door. Pink bunting was draped around the walls as a frieze, and most of her toys were either pink, or dressed in pink.

We'd laughed as we decorated this room — Stephen complained that he would drown in a sea of pink being outnumbered three to one. Grace, however, loved it — her pink palace she called it. The police had searched it thoroughly, but I could not tell; either they'd been careful to replace everything, or it was so cluttered anyway that it wasn't noticeable.

I left the room to go back downstairs, to keep busy for Elise and for Stephen so that when Grace did come home we would be ready to welcome her back with love, laughter and warm hugs, picking up the threads of our wonderful family life once again.

Bea and Peter arrived mid-afternoon. Typically, my sister brought food: enough lasagne to feed a regiment, a fruit loaf, a batch of scones and a jar of her homemade jam. We embraced, pleased to be together and I thanked them for their care of Elise, who immediately climbed onto my knee, something she hadn't done since turning nine. It felt a little easier having my family around me.

Peter pecked my cheek and shook hands with Stephen, lost for any words to speak. I thanked him for coming; it would have been easier for my brother-in-law to stay away and avoid the awkwardness of being in our home, but they were both here and I was grateful. With nothing new to tell my sister, we focussed our attention on Elise, who had now wriggled in between Stephen and me on the sofa.

'Aunt Bea tells me you have been such a good girl, Elise, well done. Did you play with Jasper?'

'Yes, and he slept with me on my bed. Have the police found Grace yet, Mummy?'

'No, darling, not yet, but they are still looking.'

The answer was not enough, but it was all I had to offer. Naturally our daughter would be missing her sister — they were so close. We were going to have to think carefully about how we presented information to Elise. Our instinct was to protect her, but if she was left out of the loop we might lose her trust.

By early evening, Bea and Peter had left and Jack took another call to say that the DI had released the man they were holding, as there was no evidence to keep him. This was a huge disappointment, but Elise being at home helped us both to accept it and retain a degree of composure. I wondered if there would be other suspects they would bring in for questioning and hoped that if so, it would be quickly. Another day was drawing to a close, and we seemed to be no nearer to finding Grace.

I began to prepare a meal, asking Elise to come and help me. It would be Bea's lasagne with a simple salad; planning meals and shopping for food was the last thing on my mind.

After we'd eaten, the doorbell chimed and Jack went to answer it, returning with DI Duncan and a colleague. My heart leapt again, craving any scrap of good news but it was not to be. Instead, the rather solemn looking DI asked if Stephen would accompany him to the station to answer a few questions. I almost laughed; did they really use those words? But he was serious.

My husband and I exchanged glances, and Stephen attempted a smile of reassurance before moving to the hall to fetch his jacket. Inside I was screaming, *no, no*, but Elise was there and I didn't want to frighten her. Stephen ruffled her hair then kissed the top of her head.

'Goodnight, sweetheart; I might not be back before bedtime so sleep tight.' He then kissed me, whispering, 'It'll be okay, don't worry.' But how could I not worry? I was puzzled too; both of us had answered dozens of questions already over the last couple of days — why more now and why did they have to take him to the police station?

As soon as Elise was out of earshot, I asked Jack, 'They don't seriously think Stephen is involved in this, do they?'

'It's really just what Jim said it was; they want him to go over a few things again. Procedure, Margaret, that's all.'

Jack looked tired and sad. I didn't believe him. Coming at this time in the evening made me doubtful, and the fact that they took him away did too. The DI was again considering Stephen as a possible suspect, just as they had when they searched the house.

Weariness washed over me; in many ways I was unconcerned because I knew that Stephen was completely innocent, but it was frustrating that the police were using valuable time questioning my husband when the person who had really abducted Grace was still out there somewhere.

Jack stayed longer than he might if Stephen had been home, and I was rather relieved when he did leave for the night — there was little more he could do here.

It was half past twelve when I heard a car pull up outside and Stephen turn his key in the lock. Running to the door I hugged him close, words unnecessary; he was home where he belonged.

We did talk, of course, Stephen telling me exactly what had happened, which for the most part was the same probing questions we'd both been subjected to previously. The differences were subtle. He'd been left alone in an interview room for nearly an hour before they began, and the questions were put by someone new to the investigation.

'They told me his name but I can't remember it now. DI Duncan for the most part remained silent, watching me without expression or comment. The new chap began politely enough but very quickly took on a more aggressive manner, and the questions came like rapid fire with no time in between to think or answer. He went over every single minute of that afternoon, asking exactly what they had asked before, but this time the gloves were off. It was almost as if they were pushing me to see if I would crack.

'They asked about our relationship and my relationship with Grace, whether I found her to be a difficult child, did she annoy me, did I lose my temper? Then the questions turned into suggestions, did I snap, was she so excited about the party that she got on my nerves, did I smack her, did I accidentally hurt her? Oh, Margaret, I can understand that they must look into all possibilities, but how could they even think that I would hurt Grace?'

'The police don't know you like I do, and they don't know Grace either. Let's go to bed, you look exhausted.'

We climbed into bed in the early hours, hoping that sleep would bring escape from this interminable nightmare. It did to a point, but I dreamed about my daughter. She was crying out for me and I couldn't reach her; my legs were like lead and wouldn't carry me to her.

I woke early and tried to lie quietly so as not to wake Stephen, wondering what today would bring. Would it be my turn to be questioned or, please God, would they find our little girl, safe and well?

Chapter 6

Jack Priestly

During that first traumatic week, I spent many hours at Lilac House, on the clock and off it too. If there was anything at all I could do, I wanted to be on hand to do it — I'm sure most people would feel the same way. While initially I felt like an unwelcome intruder, a spy almost, by the end of the first week that was no longer the case.

I have to say that both Margaret and Stephen were nothing other than courteous towards me, even at times when I expected some kind of backlash from their frustration, which is probably why we developed a bond. Our common goal of finding Grace united us, and they accepted the practice and methodology of the investigation, even when they did not agree with or understand a particular course of action. Being as upfront and honest with them as possible gave my role and that of my colleagues credibility in their eyes.

When searching Will Hogarth's flat revealed nothing in regard to Grace, the disappointment was devastating. The DI questioned him as long as legally possible but had to let him go without charge as there was simply nothing whatsoever to tie him to Grace.

We were conscious of time slipping by, and other leads that we were following proved to be fruitless in our search for Grace. All available officers were assigned to the case, each working flat out and determined to do their utmost but also aware that with each passing hour, the chances of finding her safe and well were diminishing.

That Monday was a bleak day; to fall from the pinnacle of hope and optimism back to the depths of despair was hard on everyone. I think Margaret and Stephen only survived because it was also the day their elder daughter, Elise, came home from her aunt and uncle's. Elise was a sensible girl, undemanding and with a grasp on the situation that would normally only have been expected of a much older child. Margaret and Stephen both drew comfort from her presence, and Elise was ready to be home even in such harrowing circumstances.

It also seemed fortuitous that she was there when the focus of the investigation turned to Stephen Bryson. I had no warning when Jim Duncan arrived at the house. We had just eaten together when he knocked at about six-thirty. I answered the door and Jim briefly explained that they had had a call from someone who refused to give their name, saying that they had seen Bryson striking his younger daughter on more than one occasion.

I was as shocked as I knew Stephen and Margaret would be, and led my colleagues through to take Stephen away. Naturally there were questions asked after he left. Margaret was stunned and only holding up because Elise was there. I could tell that she didn't buy my explanation of procedure, but I felt it unwise to tell her at that time about the accusations.

Personally, I am always suspicious of anonymous calls. Admittedly, there could be good reasons for not wishing to give a name, but it could also be bogus information given by a vindictive neighbour, colleague or whoever. Hopefully Jim would satisfy himself that Stephen was not involved and would return him to the family as soon as possible.

I stayed longer than I might have otherwise but sensed that Margaret would prefer to be alone, so after an hour or so I went home. I rang the station later that evening to learn that

Jim was still questioning Stephen, so I left a message asking him to ring and update me.

A call from him later informed me that they'd taken Stephen home and for the time being were treating the earlier call as a possible malicious one. It was the best I could hope for, knowing that Jim still harboured suspicions about the father, and of course it was his job to keep an open mind.

During the rest of the first week, we worked round the clock with little or no progress to report. When there is not much to work with, the investigation becomes an exercise in ruling out possibilities in the hope that what is left will be the solution you are looking for. We had ruled out Will Hogarth and many of the known sex offenders in the area. That, however, was a huge ongoing task and as time went by we widened our search parameters and continued to interview those on the register.

We ruled out drowning. On the first day, frogmen dredged the river immediately behind Lilac House, and on the second day they widened their search until it became obvious that Grace was not to be found in the river, a huge relief in one sense, but not in another.

We had tentatively ruled out the parents, although they were always being monitored, mainly by me, and would continue to be so until Grace was found. The main factor that kept them as low priority in the investigation was the lack of motive. As I learned more about the family, their financial circumstances, their history as a couple and individually and their temperaments, I became convinced of their innocence.

DI Duncan, however, remained unsure, occasionally discussing again with me the garden, its access points and the logistics of actually abducting the child and getting her away from the area in the short time before the police were brought in. I thought he was wasting his time, but in actual fact he was probably right in keeping his mind open to all possibilities.

As we entered into week two of the investigation, the mood had shifted somewhat. Most of the officers knew the statistics and leads were not coming in as frequently as before. There were further appeals to the public for information, and calls still trickled in, but none of them came to anything.

The atmosphere was one of disbelief, of metaphorically scratching our heads. Why had no one seen anything? It had been broad daylight in the height of summer. Were people so blind or wrapped up in their own lives that a little girl could be taken from her own garden? If taken by an outsider, the preferred theory, then she would have been shouting or crying, surely. It was an enigma, and we were baffled and frustrated.

My time with the family was slowly reduced. I could not stay indefinitely. Other options for support were offered, in particular Victim Support, but Margaret and Stephen declined. I could understand. They were a private family who had suffered the agony of having their every move recorded by the newspapers and monitored by the police.

During week two, I spent alternate days at Lilac House. Margaret's sister and husband were frequent visitors, and I admired their spirit. Bea Cartwright took on many of the domestic chores, which kept the home running smoothly, and Peter did what he could. Stephen and Margaret could not bear to go into the garden, and he readily took the maintenance of it upon himself.

Each time I called, their eyes asked the question, but they knew the answer by my demeanour. By then, we all seemed to have accepted that we were in for the long haul, and it could be weeks or months before we had any new leads. I could only imagine how the family got through their nights — how they coped with the images in the dark that would surely prey upon their minds. Each evening, I would return to my own home, my wife and children and thank God for them and their safety, offering a prayer for Grace Bryson, too, if she was still alive.

And now today is the anniversary of her disappearance … and also her fourth birthday. What must her parents be thinking? And Elise, too, that sad little girl whose childhood had been so cruelly snatched away with the loss of her sister. If I'm perfectly honest, I would rather know that my child was dead instead of living in limbo. Each new day, each waking thought must bring the same question, 'Will this be the day we find her?'

There is to be another news conference, and we are releasing a projection of what Grace would look like today, although she may not have changed much in a year. These things are supposed to be pretty accurate, and hopefully if Grace is still alive, someone might recognise her.

The Brysons will be at the press conference. I haven't seen them for a few weeks. My role has slipped into that of an occasional visitor, sadly with nothing new to tell them; the case has well and truly gone cold.

Margaret looks so frail and has lost weight that she could ill afford, and Stephen looks so much older than his years. Elise is with them. She smiles shyly at me as I take her hand, leading to the area well behind the cameras; the Brysons do not want her filmed. DI Duncan shows them to a table and the cameras begin to flash. I wonder at the mentality of some of the reporters when they ask such unfeeling questions.

'Mrs Bryson, do you miss your daughter?'

I want to drag the man out of the room and tell him exactly what I think of him! What a ridiculous, hurtful question! Have they no sense? Margaret looks shocked and Jim steps in to begin his spiel asking for information.

The new picture of what Grace might look like today is shown to the cameras, and Jim assures the room that we have never given up hope of finding Grace and the investigation is ongoing. Stephen adds a few words, again pleading for information, however insignificant it may seem. Margaret keeps her head down, crying softly.

The next question comes as a shock to us all, a new low in insensitivity.

'Mr Bryson, do you know where Grace is?'

2014

Chapter 7

Elise McDonald

Closing the front door behind me, I dropped my bag on the hall table and shrugged out of my coat. With legs still weak and hands trembling, I filled the kettle to make coffee. Simon would be home soon, and I couldn't wait to tell him the news. The kitchen was cold, so I headed to the lounge, turning the thermostat up in the hall as I passed through. I nestled into the sofa, seeking warmth and comfort and tucking my cold feet underneath the over-stuffed cushions.

Absentmindedly stirring the milky drink, my brain began to process the afternoon's events and form some kind of plan for the next move. Grace appeared to be a happy, well-adjusted young woman, but she was still my sister whom I wanted back more than anything else in the world. Memories of past hurt replayed in my brain, dancing with hopeful thoughts of a future that could now include Grace.

Sitting motionless, lost in a jumble of possibilities, I gazed onto the garden. It was the end of March, and the daffodils stood like sentinels in the cold black earth. Buds were tentatively showing themselves on the trees with signs of blossom coaxed out by the warmth of the weak spring sunshine. Spring, the season of new birth, of hope.

The sound of a key turning in the front door brought me back to reality. The mug of coffee stood on the table, cold with a milky skin floating on the surface. Simon entered the room, kissing me and then patting my bump as always.

'How are my lovely wife and son today?'

'I found her, Simon, I found Grace!'

Simon held my gaze for only a moment, but long enough for me to see the pity in his eyes. He looked away, saying, 'That's impossible, Elise — what you saw was someone who resembled Grace, or perhaps in some way reminded you of her. But she's dead, we both know that.'

'That's exactly my point — we don't know that! They never found her, alive or dead. But she's very much alive, Simon, and such a beautiful young woman, and she lives just outside the city, at Carlton Wells.'

'Did you approach her?' Simon's tone was slightly accusatory.

'Of course I did! I wasn't going to let her walk out of my life for a second time, was I? Oh, don't look at me like that. I was very guarded with what I said.' As I began to describe the events of the afternoon, Simon listened, expressionless, and only spoke when I had exhausted every last detail.

'Elise.' An almost patronising tone gave an edge to his voice, igniting anger somewhere deep within me. 'This girl may have reminded you of your sister or even yourself at that age. Realistically though, the chances of this actually being Grace are virtually nil. You're vulnerable at the moment, hormonal with the baby coming. Please, try not to get your hopes up — it won't do any good.'

'How can I not get my hopes up when I know it was Grace? I was there. I spoke with her!'

'Darling, it's nearly fourteen years since she disappeared, how can you possibly know for certain? The last time you saw her, she was three years old. Look, I'm going up to get changed now, and if you've no plans for dinner perhaps we could go out?'

Simon dropped another kiss on the top of my head and left the lounge. Subject closed. He might just as well have patted my head and said, 'There, there!' I was left thoroughly frustrated.

Back in the kitchen, I tipped the coffee down the sink and rinsed the mug. Simon's concern was genuine, I knew that, but I'd hoped for some measure of support, not a lecture, kindly though it may have been. I had pictured an evening of planning, working out some kind of strategy together, but it was not to be and I reluctantly followed my husband upstairs to change for dinner.

We'd been eating out a couple of evenings each week of late, taking advantage of our freedom before our son was born. After the birth, we wouldn't have many people to turn to for babysitters. My parents moved to France a couple of years ago and Simon's family lived on the south coast, which was great for holidays but totally impractical for babysitting duties, as we lived in Leeds. Our first port of call for help with the baby would be Aunt Bea, my mother's sister, to whom I had always been close. She and Uncle Peter had no children of their own and Grace and I had been their only nieces, which had made for a strong bond between us, particularly since Mum and Dad moved away.

Managing to avoid the subject of Grace during our meal was difficult as my mind was constantly active, debating what to do next. It was clear that Simon was not going to help.

'You're anywhere but here with me, Elise. I don't need to ask what's on your mind, do I?'

Simon was right. I was in a strange mood, somewhere between reflective and pensive, a mood underpinned by a seed of hope bubbling within me.

'Sorry, love, you're right. I simply can't get Grace out of my mind.'

'I understand, but promise me that you won't do anything without talking it over with me first?'

'Okay, I promise. Perhaps I'll visit Bea tomorrow to talk to her.' I wanted to be transparent with my husband, even though he was convinced Grace was dead. He raised an eyebrow and a look of concern spread across his face.

'By all means talk it over with Bea, and perhaps she can assure you that this girl can't possibly be Grace.'

It would be a lie if I said that Simon's reaction didn't disappoint me. Was it too much to expect some support, or encouragement? In all the conversations we ever had about Grace over the years, I'd assumed that he shared my opinion that she was still alive, out there somewhere, waiting to be found. With hindsight, I could see now that he had never actually believed me — I'd made an assumption, a leap that seemed credible since he always listened and comforted me.

The subject of Grace had mostly been taboo during our evening meal and still seemed a no-go area the next morning by unspoken mutual consent. As soon as Simon went to work, I set off to Bea's. My hopes were now pinned on my aunt and after a twenty-minute drive through the rush hour traffic, my arrival was greeted by the smell of fresh coffee and a comforting bear hug.

'Come in, love, let's get you out of that chilly wind.'

There was a cold breeze, but it was early and the day might turn out better. I was, however, more concerned as to how our conversation would turn out.

'Is Peter around?'

'No, he's off playing golf — probably won't be back until he's hungry, but he said for you to stay for lunch and then he'll get to see you.'

'That will be lovely, thank you.'

Peter Cartwright had been married to my aunt since before I was born. He was a jovial character, everyone's friend, although my mother had never thought him quite good enough for her only sister and viewed him as shallow. It was true that he found it difficult to hold down a job despite having tried several.

Over the years he'd been a van driver, a car salesman, a clerical officer-cum-tea-boy, and even a postman for a while over Christmas one year. I could never understand why these jobs didn't last, but Bea always found excuses for him and uncomplainingly took on the role of breadwinner. I loved her for that sense of loyalty and couldn't help but love Peter too. Perhaps in some ways he wasn't good for my aunt but he seemed to make her happy, which surely must count for a lot.

Presently, Bea was working part time at a newsagents and Peter had begun a new venture selling greeting cards to small retailers. The franchise for this seemed to have cost them more than he was actually earning, but Bea had every confidence that this would prove the most successful endeavour yet. I hoped so too.

With the coffee poured and a plate of homemade biscuits to hand, we settled in the lounge where a coal fire warmed us through.

Jasper, their elderly ginger tom, lifted his chin and opened one eye, lazily stretching his front paws before resuming his morning sleep. Bea and Peter's home was an eclectic mix of styles, or in other words it was furnished from charity shop finds and cheap basement bargains. Somehow, though, it gelled and the overall effect was one of comfortable chaos.

Bea was a hoarder, forever reluctant to throw anything away. A classic example of this being the gallery of my schoolgirl art displayed prominently in the kitchen and including examples of my abstract period (from about three to five years) and the emergence of recognisable figures, houses etc., which although on yellowing paper, crisp from years of sunlight, still adorned an ancient cork pin board.

Although mostly my work, there were a couple of collage pictures that Grace had made for her favourite auntie: sparkly fabric and ribbons glued randomly onto coloured sugar paper, with stars scattered liberally over them all for good measure, each tiny detail firmly imprinted on my mind. I knew for a fact that Bea took these pictures down if Mum was visiting, in case seeing them was too upsetting. They were returned later, however, and I was always glad to see them; they made me think kindly of my aunt, viewing her as an ally in my hope that Grace would return to us one day.

'So, Elise, is everything okay? With the baby I mean?' Trust Bea to have been worrying, even though I had assured her everything was fine.

'Absolutely.' I smiled, my hand moving naturally to the bump that was my son. 'He's doing his best to keep me awake at night, and I'm hoping that's not a sign of things to come.'

'Have you spoken to your mum and dad lately? Are they coming over for the birth?'

'We haven't made any concrete plans, but I thought it might be better if they came a week or two later when I'll be feeling a bit better. Simon gets paternity leave and will be around to help initially, and I rather hoped I could call on you if I need any advice.'

'Of course you can, there'll be no keeping me away! I'm so looking forward to having a baby in the family again.'

We both smiled. The trouble with a family as small as ours is that there aren't enough little ones to go round. After Grace disappeared, I, in effect, became an only child and Bea and Peter had long since given up hope of ever having children of their own. Bea is several years older than Mum and motherhood simply did not happen. These days, she was very much a surrogate mother to me and I knew she'd be as close as any grandmother could be to our son. Her words about a baby in the family preceded a thoughtful silence in which I am sure Bea was thinking about Grace, as was I. I am a great believer in being direct, so I told my aunt what had prompted this visit.

'I saw Grace yesterday.'

'What…? Where did you think you saw her?'

'I didn't *think* I saw her, I did. It was at the shopping mall, the department store at the south end, you know?'

'Yes, yes, well go on, tell me what happened.' Her hand moved in a circular motion to hurry me along. So again I recounted every detail of my meeting with Grace, details that were already firmly embedded in my mind, ready to be recalled as often as I wished. Bea listened in silence with a face revealing both surprise and concern. When every particular had been regaled I paused, holding my breath until a response was given.

'Tell me again why you are so certain it was Grace.'

'Well, the age is about right, although I couldn't ask her directly how old she was. But if you had seen her, Bea, you would just know! Her hair is the same colour as Mum's and mine, but her bone structure is unmistakably from the Bryson side of the family. She has Mum's nose, too, and hair which is cut exactly like mine was when I was seventeen — remember?

Long and straight with a thick fringe, which was always in my eyes? Mum was forever nagging me about it.' Bea was nodding, incredulous, as I asked nervously, 'So, what do you think?'

'I'm shell-shocked! Do you really think it could be her, after all these years?'

'Yes, I am absolutely convinced that this girl, this Jane Solomon, is really Grace and she is so lovely, Bea, wait and see.'

'But what are you going to do? What does Simon think?'

'Simon thinks it's my hormones playing tricks on me. He came right out and said it couldn't possibly be Grace because she is dead. And as for what I'm going to do, I honestly don't know but was hoping that perhaps talking it over with you would give me an idea. Two heads and all that?'

'Oh, Elise, Simon's only concerned for you, but if you are so certain then you have to do something. Just think, our little Grace alive and well after all this time!'

'Well, I know her name, the fact that her "father" is a GP working at Central Health Centre and they live at Carlton Wells, which isn't a million miles away.'

'You weren't thinking of some kind of stakeout, were you?' Bea almost giggled.

'It had crossed my mind, but I might be able to find an address from the internet — the electoral role or something? If I hadn't been so keen to come and tell you, that's what I would be doing today.'

'But what then? You can hardly approach her and tell the poor girl that she's not Jane whatever-her-name-is. What about going to the police — the case has never actually been closed, has it?'

'That's true, but I imagine they might have the same reaction as Simon and write me off as a mad, hormonal woman. In effect, I would be accusing a respectable GP of kidnap, and they will want something a little more tangible than my own certainty.'

Bea was nodding. It was so good to be taken seriously. Simon's reaction had disappointed me more than I realised, but with support from my aunt I felt a little better, bolder even.

'What about your parents — are you going to let them know?' Bea asked.

'I've thought about that, too, and decided to wait until I can find something more concrete to tell them. Neither of them have ever got over Grace's disappearance, and telling them now might just upset them when they're at last building a new life for themselves.'

The front door banged, and Peter's unmistakable voice broke into our conversation.

'Well, where's that beautiful niece of mine hiding?'

He appeared in the doorway, his large frame filling the space and a huge smile fixed on his ruddy face. My uncle was a big man, tall and wide — perhaps a little too wide these days in spite of the hours spent on the golf course. Once black, thick hair was now thinning, combed over the almost bald top of his head, which only served to present a rather comical look. The personification of everyone's favourite, jovial uncle, Peter moved over to hug me, planting a kiss on the top of my head.

'You're home early,' Bea remarked.

'I sacrificed the nineteenth hole knowing Elise would be here. Couldn't miss seeing my girl now, could I?' He looked at me, obviously curious as to why I wanted to see Bea; my visits were usually spontaneous, and it must have thrown them somewhat when I said there was something I needed to talk about.

'Elise has seen Grace!' Bea was as direct as I had been.

'No … you couldn't possibly!' Peter's grin disappeared.

Bea began to answer the questions before they were even asked, concisely paraphrasing what I'd told her. When the tale was finished, there was an uneasy silence. Obviously Peter was not taking the news as well as Bea and seemed to be thinking about a response before giving one.

'Sweetheart…' Peter addressed me. 'This is a difficult time for you, and Grace is bound to be on your mind. Perhaps you only thought you saw her? Sometimes when we want something badly enough, we can imagine things which are not really there.'

All the euphoria of Bea sharing my excitement suddenly evaporated. It seemed my family was to be divided, and Peter had come down firmly on Simon's side.

'But I spoke to her — I know it was Grace!'

His huge hand reached for mine, and he squeezed my fingers with a remarkably gentle touch.

'I understand, Elise, but please don't pin your hopes on this when it's most likely only someone who reminds you of her.'

I pulled my hand away, fighting back the tears.

'I'm only pregnant you know, not mad! It was Grace — how could you possibly know it wasn't?'

'None of us can know for certain, I'll admit that, but look at it logically, love. It's been fourteen years now, so if she's alive and still living near Leeds, why have the police not found her? If this doctor chap had taken her and looked after her all these years, don't you think he would have moved away from the area? Wouldn't someone have put two and two together when there was so much publicity at the time? I just don't want you to be hurt again, Elise, especially now with the baby coming — this should be such a happy time for you.'

'That might be the rational way of thinking, but I know what I saw. I know it was my sister.'

I could not remain with them for lunch as planned. The sadness in Bea's eyes was plain to see — Peter's words had brought an element of doubt to her mind. Could I have lost my ally?

Returning home from my visit to Bea, I felt an overwhelming sense of loneliness. Simon had dismissed my sighting of Grace as some kind of hormonal hallucination, and just when I thought Bea would rise to my side in support, Peter intervened with his sense of the 'rational'. Why were they all so quick to assume that Grace was dead — a thought I'd never seriously entertained? If my sister was dead, I would know.

Fourteen years had passed and now my mind took me back to the beautiful garden of Lilac House, a place much loved by our family until it became untenable to live there anymore ... without Grace. The abduction was most certainly a watershed event for each one of us. For me, it marked the end of a carefree childhood, an endless summer with only the prospect of sunshine and laughter on the future horizon. For my parents, it ended their perfect life.

I did not learn of the miscarriage my mother had suffered until many years later; it was a day that robbed them of not one, but two children. My status of being a sister ended on that day, too. There were to be no more children for my parents, whether because they felt they could never replace Grace, or because they could not risk creating another life with the possibility of suffering another loss, I do not know.

The previous closeness of my mother to Bea became strained, more perhaps because of Peter, who in his bumbling manner expected that there should come a point in time when a line would be drawn and the family would move on. I could forgive him this attitude — he'd never had the privilege of being a parent — but my mother found it hard to accept, well-meaning though he meant such opinions to be.

My understanding of the troubled undercurrents in our family dynamics grew as I did. The innocence that should be every child's birth right disappeared with Grace, and when I returned to school I was a marked child, the object of pity from the teachers and an embarrassment to my friends. Home life was only marginally better.

At nine years old, I still held on to the magical thinking of a child, that if you want something badly enough it will happen and I so wanted to find Grace! In my naivety I pictured her as simply lost, wandering around somewhere looking for the way home. It was inconceivable that she would not come back, and although that expectation remained with me as I grew up, it waned somewhat with each passing year.

My status reverted to one of being an only child, but my parents were so badly wounded that I often felt completely alone. They did their best, I know, but while I needed to keep Grace in the forefront of my mind, they found it easier to do the opposite.

I spent much of my adolescence with Bea and Peter. In many ways, it was easier in their home than in my own with my parents. Bea was always chatty yet a great listener, and when I needed to talk about Grace it was to her that I turned. Rarely did my aunt offer an opinion but then I did not want her to; I needed to keep my own opinions and hopes alive without having them challenged.

I suppose I never quite knew what Bea really thought had happened to Grace, but she never tried to dampen my enthusiasm with negative thoughts. Uncle Peter, however, believed she was dead. I know this, not because he discussed it with me, even when I was older, but because I overheard him chiding Bea for listening to me.

'It's not a matter of giving up hope but of being realistic, Bea. Elise is surviving on dreams and wishes which are never going to be a reality, and I don't think you should encourage her.' His words were spoken kindly yet emphatically. Bea listened to her husband without comment but even then never tried to dissuade me from my belief, and I loved her all the more for it.

As the years passed, my parents began to believe, or perhaps simply accept, that Grace was dead. At what point in time this happened, I do not know; it was probably a process rather than an actual event. I think it was the only way they could cope and begin to rebuild some semblance of a normal life, but I never could accept their view. I cherished and nurtured my hope until it blossomed into certainty, a full blown belief that one day I would find my sister.

The pain of loss grew with me like a heavy weight over my heart, a weight that pulled me back each time I began to enjoy life. At significant milestones, school prize-giving, prom, university, even my wedding day, it was as if I took two or three tentative steps towards happiness, only to be pulled back by this weight, an ever-present reminder that my life could not be happy or complete until I found my little sister, or at the very least found out what happened to her.

Two years ago, my parents decided to move to France. Dad was by this time retired and Simon and I were married, so the timing seemed right. I understood their desire to move away. Within eighteen months of Grace's disappearance, we had moved to another suburb in a different part of Leeds. This coincided with my move to senior school where I could start afresh and make new friends, no longer an oddity or someone to avoid.

Mum and Dad loved France and we had enjoyed a couple of summer holidays there years ago, the four of us, camping and exploring the wonderful little towns and huge palaces. They chose Rouen to settle in, buying a house on the edge of the town, a town they loved and one that very quickly became home to them both.

The last serious conversation I had with my mother was during the week before they moved. She expressed sadness at not being geographically close to me, and before I knew it she was in tears, apologising for any neglect I'd suffered in the past because of her grief and the difficulty she found in being a good mother. Being unaware that she was carrying so much guilt I hugged her close, stroking her hair as she had done for me many years ago.

'You've been a wonderful mother, and I don't want you thinking otherwise. I've always felt loved and cared for, and I totally understand how difficult it was for you and Dad when Grace disappeared. Don't feel bad about moving, Mum, I think this is the right step for you to take now and Simon and I are very settled here. We'll be able to visit often enough, and there's always Skype now that you two have entered the technical revolution!'

She smiled — we understood each other.

'I haven't exactly made things easy for you with my insistence on Grace still being alive, have I?'

Mum bit on her bottom lip and shook her head.

'Do you really believe she's dead, Mum?' I'd never dared to be so direct before.

Mum took in a huge gulp of air. 'In my heart I don't want to, but my mind tells me that she most probably is. The not knowing has made it so very hard, and I feel we've lived in a state of limbo for years. I envy you your certainty, Elise.'

The subject was again closed.

Over the passing years, there'd been a few occasions when I saw someone who reminded me of Grace and hope flooded through my soul, but I'd never been as convinced as I was now about Jane Solomon. What to do about it was the big question; doing nothing was simply not an option, even though I might once again be on my own in my belief that Grace was alive.

Opening up my laptop, I began to do some research. Figuring that Jane, or Grace, was like most teenagers these days I accessed Facebook and typed her name into the search box. Instantly a list of people called Jane Solomon appeared, each with an image beside it.

I scrolled down, hoping she used a photograph rather than a picture of a pet or a cartoon as favoured by many. Suddenly she was there, smiling straight into the camera and I was struck again at the family likeness. Clicking onto her page, I accessed more photographs and read her profile. Grace described herself as a student in sixth form studying for A levels in Psychology, Sociology and Philosophy.

A rush of pride swept over me — my little sister, interested in such academic subjects! Her address was listed only as Carlton Wells, Leeds and there was no email address or phone number.

Moving back to the photographs I clicked on one of Grace, obviously taken at a wedding. She looked so beautiful in a long gown of raw silk with her honey-blonde hair swept up and coiled on top of her head.

Plugging in the printer, I copied the image together with one or two more. An older couple, whom I assumed to be Dr and

Mrs Solomon, were pictured with Grace in between them at the same wedding.

I hit the print button again after enlarging the image. If these photographs had shown that Grace bore no resemblance to either of the Solomons I would have been delighted, but in truth she could have been their natural child. Dr Solomon had short grey hair and his wife had similar colouring to Grace, but it could have been dyed.

Next, I Googled the Central Health Centre in Leeds in search of more information about the doctor. He was the senior partner and had been with the practice for nearly fourteen years. That could fit in, but I knew I needed more. Turning to the good old-fashioned telephone directory I again searched for Dr Solomon, knowing from the health centre's website that his first name was Arthur.

Bingo! Dr A Solomon was listed at Garden House, The Green, Carlton Wells, Leeds. I grabbed a notebook from the desk drawer and began to write down every detail of information I'd discovered, wishing I had done so before going to Bea's — then I would have had something to show her. The task took only minutes, after which I went to the kitchen in search of something to eat. Food was the last thing on my mind, but I was suddenly hungry and my plan to stay for lunch with Bea and Peter hadn't worked out.

As I opened the fridge, nothing more appealing than cheese grabbed my taste buds so I cut a generous chunk of bread, toasted one side then made Welsh rarebit. I was too excited to bother with anything more substantial and would cook later for Simon and me. It was still only two in the afternoon, and I was keen to form some sort of plan.

Going back to Jane's Facebook page, I again began to make notes and print out some more pictures, frustrated that I could not see her full profile unless I sent a friend request — absolutely not the way forward.

Gathering my notes and the photographs together, I placed them into plastic pockets inside a file and then went in search of the few photographs of Grace I possessed. Of course, they were from her very early years, but I'd also kept the image projections that the police had issued over the years in a bid to find new information about her disappearance.

The first of these was put together a year after the abduction using computer-generated imagery and an artist's embellishments. The computer can apparently show the changes in bone structure and growth in a child's face based on data from hundreds of images of children recorded at yearly intervals of their lives. It was not so very different from how I remembered my sister, but future projected images showed more definite changes.

I wished I had older pictures of 'Jane Solomon' to compare. The ones on Facebook were too recent. After gathering and collating my 'evidence', I sat back to think of what my next move should be. I would have loved to brainstorm a plan with Bea but I didn't think that was going to be possible. If all else failed, I would continue on my own.

Chapter 8

Bea Cartwright

When Elise left, I was furious with Peter.

'You could have heard her out before dismissing her like that!'

'I'd heard all I needed to, Bea; she's delusional and always has been.'

'How can you say that? The poor girl's been through hell and needs to feel someone takes her seriously.'

'And do you take her seriously? Do you believe the girl she saw is Grace?'

'I'm not sure. Elise is certainly convinced, and the police never did find a body so theoretically it's possible and she's not delusional — I think she deserves credit for being the only one who never gave up hope. Perhaps we were all too quick to accept that Grace was dead.'

'Quick? It was years! Margaret and Stephen lived in a vacuum for the first year, as did we all. Our lives were overturned too, always helping them out. Elise might just as well have moved in here.'

'Peter, don't talk like that — Margaret is my sister! I had to be there for her and Elise, too. Are you saying you resented helping them?'

'No, of course not. I just didn't expect it would dominate our lives like it did, like it still does at times! Elise is in an emotional state; her judgement at the moment can't be trusted.'

I listened to my husband and wavered in what I thought. Elise was so sure, so excited, but Peter was, as always, a voice of reason. Is it a man thing, to believe the worst? Maybe ... and now I didn't know what to do. Perhaps I would ring Elise later — I hated there being ill feeling between us, and she needed support with the baby coming so soon. I set about making lunch. I would give Elise time to calm down and ring later, when she'd had time to think.

At the beginning of this nightmare, none of us could have predicted that Grace wouldn't be found. The hours turned agonizingly into days then weeks, then years. I couldn't do enough for Margaret; she was still my little sister and I'd always looked out for her. Peter too, despite his little outburst, had been so supportive, particularly with Elise. We took her on holidays with us — nothing fancy, just the caravan at the coast. The sea seemed to calm her, and she loved to walk along the beach even in the rain; in fact, Elise preferred the bad weather. The brooding clouds seemed to suit her quiet, pensive moods; the constant lapping of the tides were soothing, particularly as she grew older. At times, I secretly pretended she was ours; the hurt of childlessness never really diminishes.

Margaret and Stephen appreciated our involvement with Elise, particularly in those early years. It was hard for them to live normally, and any happy times brought with them a weighty sense of guilt, as if they had no right to a life of their own while Grace was still missing.

People asked me over the years whether it would be preferable to know what happened to Grace, even if that meant knowing she was dead. I would have to say, for myself, yes — and I think as time moved on Margaret and Stephen might have agreed, although it was never discussed with us. I thought that when they sold the house they might pick up the threads of life again, and outwardly that appeared to be the case, but I know they found it difficult to actually 'live' again.

This of course impacted on Elise. Children pick up the vibes and undercurrents of adult moods and emotions, and Elise was an intelligent girl — nothing of any significance escaped her. She rarely commented on such matters to her parents and only occasionally confided in me. I know it was a relief when they moved to a new area and she began senior school. She'd always felt marked because of the attention Grace's disappearance brought on the family, and attending a new school brought a degree of release — she was just another pupil there, no different from the crowd.

The three of them remained close but never quite as carefree as when they were a family of four. The symmetry of their family life had been destroyed and evidenced itself in the mundane details: setting the table for only three, only one child in the back of the car. Simple, seemingly insignificant things, when thrown into the melting pot, upset the very heart of a family, bringing unexpected painful memories just when life was beginning to run smoothly again.

And as for my relationship with Margaret, it was never quite the same. Previously, we'd shared the same sense of humour, laughing at things others could not understand; at times we communicated with just a look, words not always necessary, things that a shared childhood bring to siblings. After the abduction, those untroubled times were gone — it was like living life at a permanent wake where we felt that our behaviour should reflect the tragedy of the situation, which it did, and still does at times today, fourteen years later.

Of course, the move to France affected our relationship, too. When geographical locations separate you, it's bound to affect any closeness there once was. The telephone is not the same, nor any of the newer methods of communication, emails or Skype. Not that I was against the move. I think we all realised that for Margaret and Stephen, it was the only way left that they could possibly enjoy their life without Grace.

Elise visited when she could, and so did Peter and I. Their new home in Rouen felt right, and it was a beautiful town — I could have lived there myself. They became happier than I had seen them for years — fourteen years, to be exact.

I wondered again if Elise would tell her parents about this girl, and if she did, what the effect on them would be. After lunch, I picked up the telephone and dialled Elise's number.

'Hello?' Her voice was quiet. I wondered if she'd been sleeping.

'Elise, it's Bea. I'm really sorry about this morning. We didn't want to upset you, but this sighting seems so incredible — we just don't want to see you get hurt again, especially with the baby coming.'

There was a moment's hesitation before she spoke.

'It's fine, don't worry about it.'

I could tell she was still annoyed with me.

'Look, shall I drive over and we can talk?'

'No, Simon will be home by the time you get here and he doesn't believe me either.'

'Darling, it's not a question of not believing you — we're concerned and don't want to see you getting hurt again. Have you decided what to do?'

'I've already got some information on the family. Are you interested, Bea, or just humouring me?'

'I'm interested. Haven't I always been on your side?'

'Yes, but I still don't know what you actually think.'

Perhaps I had sat on the fence for too long.

'I'd like to believe that Grace is alive, that she has lived a happy life with people who care for her. On the other hand, if I believe she is still alive, what if she's living some kind of horrendous existence, some kind of slave … oh, Elise, I really don't want to go there!'

'It's okay, I know. I've battled with the same demons, fought off the same disturbing images, but I really believe I've found her!'

'What can I do, Elise, to help you, I mean?' I made a snap decision to stand by my niece, even if Peter thought us both insane.

'Do you mean that, Bea — will you really help me?' She sounded so hopeful, so young and optimistic.

'Yes, I mean it!'

'Well, you can start by dusting off that computer you so rarely use. I'm sending you an email with some information I've found. Have a good look at it, then get back to me and tell me what you think.'

I said goodbye and quickly went to do as she asked. By the time our slow old desktop started up, the email was waiting for me and I found myself gazing at the girl Elise was so certain was her sister. I could see why, and I could very easily accept that she was right if it hadn't seemed so absurd that Grace could have been living only ten miles away, alive and well. Would the three-year-old Grace not have had memories, I wondered?

I closed my eyes and spent a few unproductive minutes trawling through my own mind to find the earliest memories I could. Starting school should have been in there somewhere, along with other milestones for a young child, but I had no recall of that actual first day, just snatches of school life in general. To be honest, my brain was a mess, a hotchpotch of disconnected snippets with absolutely no chronology at all. Rather like my home, I thought, looking round at my treasured clutter.

I sent Elise a reply: *Tactics meeting at ten tomorrow, my place or yours?*

Smiling as I hit the send button, I imagined Elise's delight at having me back on board.

Chapter 9

Elise McDonald

Bea's simple email had lifted my spirits, and I hastily replied before there was time for a change of heart. My suggestion was to meet at my house, as there was less chance of being disturbed here — Simon would be at work and we would have the morning to ourselves.

Filled with new hope and energy, I decided to avoid the subject of Grace that evening and try to relax with my husband. Our baby was certainly making his presence felt, perhaps sensing my excitement and erratic mood swings. I made a cup of peppermint tea and found an old CD of The Carpenters, which I put in the player before settling down with my new file, a dossier of sorts with everything I knew about 'Jane' and the Solomons.

Tomorrow could not come quickly enough, and knowing now that Bea would be considering our next move, too, it was going to be so much easier. I found myself singing along with Karen Carpenter to *Close to You*, mentally changing the words to apply to my sister. Could I really be close to finding Grace after all this time? I was certain now that I was.

Bea was early, always one to allow extra time for a journey due to their ancient and unreliable car. It amazed me how it ever got through its MOT tests, never mind getting from A to B. But she was here and I couldn't wait to get started.

The kettle was boiling; Bea looked in dire need of a warming drink. It was the first day of April and a cold start to the month. Seated in the lounge, the warmest room in the house, I passed the file over and sat back to watch her reactions as she read it. Her eyes widened then narrowed as she scrutinised the photographs, which were laid side by side against the very last projection image the police had made four years ago.

'Well, what do you think?' Patience deserted me; I was fired up.

'You've certainly been busy — where did you get all this stuff?'

'Off the internet, mostly; you just need to know which buttons to press.'

Bea was looking at the street map of Carlton Wells on which I'd enlarged and circled the Solomon's house.

'Are you up for it then?' my aunt asked, a twinkle in her eye.

'What, Carlton Wells?'

'Yes, isn't that what you wanted?'

'Of course!' My grin matched Bea's and within thirty minutes we were on the ring road, skirting Leeds city centre and heading north to the village of Carlton Wells.

Bea insisted on driving but we took my car — it was much more reliable than my aunt's old one and had a full tank of petrol, which I doubted hers ever had. I tried to relax during the journey but my heart was racing, even though this was simply a scouting operation and we had no plan to approach the house or any member of the Solomon family.

For the first time I wondered if 'Jane' had other siblings, although having assumed that this doctor or his wife had taken Grace because they could not have children of their own, it seemed logical that she would be an only child. Why else would they abduct her and then bring her up as their own?

Entering Carlton Wells, I glanced at the mileage we'd covered: twelve miles from my own home and only fifteen miles from Lilac House, but it might have just as easily been the other side of the world. Who was it who said that the best place to hide something was in plain view?

Bea slowed down to the required thirty mile speed limit and we headed for the heart of the village, parking at the edge of a large central green. During the journey we spoke very little, both focussed on our own thoughts. Now Bea switched off the engine and turned to face me.

'What now?' she asked.

I scanned the well-tended, pretty village for inspiration. It was a world away from the clamour of Leeds city centre — a desirable commuter area with large, individually designed houses, probably built over a century ago yet maintaining their character and charm. And my sister lived in one of these houses, ignorant of who she really was or how much she was missed!

A tea shop stood on the opposite side of the green, so I suggested we walk over to have a coffee and talk strategy. The wind had whipped up on the short walk across the green and I felt cold right through to my bones, but the interior of the tea shop was warm and welcoming with only a few other customers huddled in pairs or groups at the back of the room. We took seats by the window and were almost immediately approached by a friendly waitress who took our order for tea and scones. In only a few minutes, she was back with the drinks and a ready smile.

'Girls' day out, is it?' she inquired idly, while setting fresh scones and jam before us.

'Something like that,' Bea answered, 'I've never actually been here before; it's such a pretty little village.'

'That it is; I've lived here all my life and never wanted to leave.'

'I think my doctor lives here, Dr Solomon — do you know him?' Bea lied with a smile.

'Oh yes, I used to babysit for his daughter, Jane. They live in the big house opposite, the one with the wisteria climbing up the walls; you can just see it above the privet hedge.' She pointed across the green, where we could easily pick out the large detached house outside of which was my car. We had unwittingly parked right outside of the Solomons' home!

There was little more we could find out from the waitress; to ask more personal questions about the doctor or his family would arouse suspicion. Bea smiled and thanked the woman, who then left us to our tea.

I shifted my chair to an angle to give a better view of the house and for a while stared blankly through the window.

'Penny for them, Elise?' Bea's voice brought me back from my musings.

'It's so strange to think that Grace has been living here, well and presumably happy, while we've endured years of agony, hoping for something like this but fearing the worst. How could someone do that, Bea — take a child from another family just because they wanted her?'

My aunt reached across the table and squeezed my hand.

'Let's not jump to conclusions too soon, shall we, love? We've had a look at the place and had confirmation of where the girl lives. Isn't that enough for now?'

'It will never be enough until Grace is back with us.' Tears were welling in my eyes; this was proving to be a very emotional experience.

Bea topped up my tea from the pretty china teapot.

'I know, Elise, but we've accomplished all we came here for. It's too early to make an approach; we must think things through carefully now.'

She was right of course, so I turned my attention to the scone in front of me, adding generous amounts of butter and jam. I would have loved to sit and watch the house all day, but Bea wisely insisted we left for home. Staying would almost certainly have made me feel more melancholy than I already did, so I reluctantly agreed.

It would have suited me to remain quiet throughout the journey home, but Bea had other ideas.

'We need to decide how to pursue this, Elise. We have some basic information now, but nothing which tells us conclusively that this girl is Grace. I think we should go to the police.'

Bea was right. My instinct was to move swiftly, to approach Jane and her 'parents', but I could see the pitfalls of such an impulsive move. But what if the police refused to take action, as we had no solid evidence to give them?

'Jack Priestly!' I said aloud. 'He would look into this, I'm sure.'

'Is he still working in this area, or working at all? Policemen retire early, don't they?'

'The last time we heard from him was a couple of years ago, before Mum and Dad moved to France. He always kept in touch — a phone call a couple of times a year and a Christmas card. He was still working then. I'll ring the police station later and ask for him.'

This seemed to satisfy Bea. I spent the rest of the journey anticipating a future that could reverse all the heartache and pain of the past and finally bring Grace home where she belonged.

Chapter 10

Jack Priestly

As I returned from lunch, the memo on my desk bearing the name Elise McDonald and a request to ring took me by surprise. It set off a chain of thought that threw me back fourteen years, then bounced swiftly through those incredibly sad days to my last contact with the Bryson family.

It must have been two years since Stephen and Margaret moved to France, and our relationship now was reduced to the exchange of Christmas cards scrawled with a few 'catch up' words inside. They were the only family I worked with whom I'd felt compelled to keep in touch with, probably because the case was never closed — Grace had not been found. Fourteen years' worth of memories flooded back at the sight of Elise's name, memories that remain frustrating as they had no conclusion to enable me or the Brysons to wrap them up and move on.

The case was relatively active for the first year after the disappearance, although the initial manpower was reduced to a much smaller team. My own involvement also diminished as it became clear that we'd exhausted all the normal channels of investigation, and I was no longer serving the original purpose of liaison. I did, however, make a point of calling round or telephoning every week or two, regrettably with nothing new to report.

On the first anniversary of Grace's disappearance, I attended the press conference to support the family. There was, however, very little new information forthcoming and during the following week, as we investigated every call prompted by the appeal, the familiar frustration returned. This little girl seemed to have disappeared off the face of the earth. If anything, the ridiculous question from the reporter directed at Stephen, suggesting that he knew his daughter's whereabouts, hampered any effectiveness the appeal might have produced. Through that reporter's insensitive question, the general community were fed a seed of doubt, and I could almost picture Joe Public and his wife shaking their heads and agreeing that it was most likely the parents who had done something to their daughter.

I never doubted Stephen or Margaret. Jim Duncan, the SIO, maintained reservations — particularly concerning Stephen — but there was never any evidence to suggest culpability and certainly no motive. When the police search inevitably scaled down, I knew for a fact that Stephen Bryson went into Leeds city centre every Saturday, handing out leaflets with his daughter's photograph on them, appealing for information. He continued this practice for almost two years, which to my mind is not the action of a guilty father, but a devoted one.

After the first anniversary appeal, my contact with the family became less frequent until eventually I could not justify the time spent with them and began to visit unofficially, in my own time. I was welcomed into their home, and it seemed that in some strange way I became their last link to Grace. My relationship with the family began on that fateful day, and our connection was solely concerned with that little girl.

Over time, however, we talked of other things; they enquired about my wife and family, and I followed Elise's landmark achievements as she grew up. Whenever I thought of the Bryson family, a degree of guilt niggled at the back of my mind. I had two happy, healthy children and the pleasure of watching them grow up, whereas they did not.

Witnessing the overwhelming sadness of Stephen, Margaret and Elise made me appreciate my own boys even more. Jake, my eldest son, was about the same age as Grace and as he grew and we celebrated each birthday, my thoughts often turned to the Brysons. Perhaps I brushed their enquiries about my boys off too quickly, as if talking about them might be construed as boastful. Yet as I came to know them better, I knew they were genuine, and if they did make any unspoken comparisons between our respective children it would only be to be pleased that I was not going through the heartbreak they were suffering.

So now, after fourteen years, the memo from Elise intrigued me. I knew she had married shortly before her parents moved to France, and in their last Christmas card they mentioned that she was expecting her first baby, an event that would hopefully bring joy to the family. As to why Elise wanted to speak to me I had no idea, so I picked up the telephone to find out.

'Thank you so much for getting back to me,' Elise said, and hearing her voice reminded me that she was now a grown woman. I found the passing of years a somewhat strange phenomenon and often mentally viewed people as they were when I first met them, though Elise was now expecting a child of her own.

'I wasn't sure if you were still working or not.'

'Retirement's still a few years away for me yet. How are you, Elise? It's so long since I've seen you.'

'I'm well, thank you; expecting a baby in a few weeks, a little boy. And you and your family?'

'All fine, thanks. So what is it I can do for you?' I was curious.

'I've found Grace. She's alive and well and living only a few miles out of Leeds!' Elise was suddenly animated, so sure of herself while I was stunned at her words.

'What makes you think it's Grace — have you talked to her? Where did you see her?'

A long story followed, told rather breathlessly and more than a little vague in places. When she had finished, I asked a few questions and from her answers gathered that this was all a recent development and that Elise and her aunt had been to the village that very morning.

'Is Bea with you now?' I asked.

'Yes, we're at my house.'

A quick look at the clock on the wall told me that it was one-thirty, plenty of time to go and see Elise and Bea; this suddenly took priority over my other plans for the afternoon.

Scribbling down the address, I left immediately, replaying the details of the call in my mind and trying to make sense of them. Was it really possible that Grace could be alive, that she'd been taken and looked after for the last fourteen years? If it was true, it seemed incredible. A string of questions danced through my head, but I was wary of making any judgement until I'd seen Elise and Bea.

The address I arrived at was in a leafy suburb, not unlike the area in which Lilac House was situated and not far from it either. A row of Victorian terraced houses stood behind walled forecourts, each one built with rich red bricks and boasting large bay windows, exactly the kind of house I would have imagined Elise to be living in.

The door opened before I had a chance to ring the bell and Elise stood before me, a picture of healthy expectant motherhood with a face reflecting a mixture of emotions. Excitement and apprehension played in her eyes, and I realised how important my opinion was going to be. She took my hand while at the same time reaching up to kiss me gently on my cheek.

'It's good to see you again, Jack.'

I was led into the hallway, a long narrow space off which the reception rooms lay to the right. We headed towards the kitchen at the end of the hall where Bea sat at a large pine table, nursing a mug of coffee. She rose and smiled, offering a hand to welcome me.

'Thank you for coming. I know you must be busy, and we really appreciate your time.'

I was offered coffee and took a seat at the end of the table, Elise and Bea on either side of me. Bea was right; I was busy so I asked them to explain again what exactly had happened to make them believe they had found Grace. As Elise began the story of recent events she pushed a document file towards me, which I opened as she spoke. Still listening, I scanned the contents of the file and automatically sorted them into two groups, one the historical photographs, the other new images, mainly copied from the internet.

Elise finished her tale and looked hopefully at me.

'So this has all come about because you saw this girl, Jane Solomon, in the shopping centre?' I asked.

'Yes. I know it doesn't sound like much to go on, but I'm absolutely positive. I spoke to her and had a chance to study her face, and I'm certain that she is Grace.'

My heart was heavy — after all this time Grace was still dominating her sister's life.

'You realise that there's no evidence of any kind to back this up? It all boils down to seeing a girl who you thought could be your sister.' I hated being the one to disillusion Elise, but I was used to dealing with solid evidence and proof; gut instinct came into play occasionally, but to proceed with anything I needed facts.

'But that's why I wanted to tell you, in the hope that you can get some proof! Visit this family and ask them — do something, Jack, please!' Elise was desperate.

'I'd need a good reason — something more concrete than this — before I could approach the family. Think about it, Elise — what could I say? "Is your daughter really your daughter or did you abduct her?" It's not enough, not nearly enough. We're talking about a respected doctor here; there are no grounds to question him about something so personal.'

'Couldn't you approach the girl herself, ask for a DNA sample or something?' Bea added.

'Absolutely not. Put it the other way round, Bea; if the police came knocking on your door to say that they thought a family member was not really part of your family and could they have a DNA sample, what would you think, especially as such a suggestion implicated you in a serious crime?'

Bea nodded. Elise looked close to tears.

'I know this is upsetting for you both, and I'm sorry. What do your parents think about it all?'

'I haven't told them. They've been through so much that I was going to wait until we'd spoken to you and found out what you could do.'

I nodded, understanding. 'That's probably very wise. Look, I really am sorry but there's nothing we can do.'

I felt as if I was breaking their hearts all over again; the effect of my words was obviously devastating. If there was something I could do, I would gladly have done it, but what they were asking was impossible. Looking again at the contents of the file, I could see how Elise could think this was Grace, but there were probably hundreds of teenage girls who looked just like this and the girl also bore similarities to both the doctor and his wife.

'I can understand how you thought this was her, but this is a difficult time for you with the baby coming soon; your thoughts are bound to turn to Grace and your own childhood. You'll probably feel differently when the baby arrives.' That was one of those moments when you wish you'd kept your mouth shut. I sounded patronising even to myself and the look Elise gave me, somewhere between disappointment and frustration, confirmed it.

'You sound just like my husband and Uncle Peter. Being pregnant doesn't impair my judgement, you know. I'm not an emotional wreck or hormonal, Jack. I know it was Grace!'

I felt suitably chastised and mumbled an apology, and before I thought it through found myself saying, 'Look, I could go round unofficially if you like and ask for their co-operation. Their response might tell us something — would that help to ease your mind?'

Elise became animated again, hope replacing the previous disillusionment.

'That would be wonderful — when will you go?'

'Maybe tomorrow when I finish my shift; I'll try to make it soon, but please don't get your hopes up — this may all come to nothing.'

'I won't but thank you so much — we're very grateful.'

They looked it too. Had I done the wrong thing in raising their hopes? I couldn't tell, but I was committed now. What on earth I was going to say to the doctor and his family I didn't know, but hopefully something would come to mind. Probably an edited version of the truth would be best — the man was a doctor; he would surely understand the anguish this family had suffered.

I said goodbye to Elise and Bea and headed back to the station. Jim Duncan, who'd been the SIO on the Bryson case, had retired recently and his replacement was a complex character, a man who didn't seem to have as much soul as Jim and I hadn't fathomed him out yet, so it was probably best not to tell him. Visiting the Solomons would not be easy, but it was probably best done as soon as possible in the hope that this could be resolved swiftly, for Elise's sake.

It had been a long and tiring day, and I was looking forward to the weekend that came at the end of an eight-day shift. Overnight, I thought over what Elise had told me. I was impressed with her tenacity and unswerving belief that Grace was still alive. In a fair world such determination would be rewarded, but the world is not fair, and I was afraid that I would be the one to dash her hopes again, the harbinger of bad news.

Carlton Wells was a picture postcard village, one that I had occasionally driven through but more often passed around on the bypass. It didn't take any great detective skills to find the Solomons' residence; the clue was in the address Elise had given me, 'The Green'.

I parked at the side of the large open square and took in my surroundings. Bea had mentioned a tea shop, which I noted on the opposite side to my parking spot, closed now — but then it was six-thirty on a rather cold April evening, and any tourists would be long gone by now, with regular customers probably in the warmth of their own homes. Garden House was easy enough to find: a large double-fronted home, neat and well cared for, on the outside at least.

Ringing the bell, I tried to remember exactly what I had planned to say; my intention was to keep things light and appeal to the compassionate nature of the Solomons. I was planning to speak to the doctor alone, a man-to-man chat in the hope that we could get things cleared up immediately without upsetting Mrs Solomon or their daughter.

I was in luck; Dr Solomon himself answered the door. Force of habit made me show my warrant card as I smiled and asked if he had a few minutes to answer some questions. The doctor looked momentarily puzzled but stood aside to allow me into his home, showing me to a reception room on the right-hand side of the hallway. A large oak desk stood under a window, offering a view of the garden. A large brass angle-poised lamp was lit over a screen on the doctor's computer, which he switched off when he showed me into the room.

'Is this about one of my patients?' A reasonable question, I thought.

'Actually no, it's rather more personal than that.' Now he did look perplexed, especially when I paused for a moment to take in his reaction. 'I'm reviewing an old case, one which has never been closed. It concerns events which happened fourteen years ago.' My words elicited only a brief nod from Arthur Solomon as he waited for further explanation. 'It concerns the abduction of a child, a little girl, who went missing from home and has never been found. Perhaps you remember it; there was considerable publicity at the time?'

'Yes, I do seem to recall a local abduction, but I hadn't realised it was never resolved. But how can I help you with this, DS Priestly?' A frown was set on the doctor's face, unsurprising really; his question was certainly valid and one I would ask myself if our roles were reversed.

'We've actually had someone who was closely connected to the case come forward to say that there has been a sighting of the missing girl. I realise that this must seem rather strange, doctor, but the information we've been given suggests that the missing girl is living here as your daughter, Jane.'

The doctor's eyes widened in surprise, and I was unsure whether he was going to react angrily or not. He measured his words before answering. 'That's absurd, and fourteen years is a long time for a fresh sighting in such a case, surely?'

'Yes, it is, but the witness is insistent that Jane is actually this missing child. I do apologise, but as a doctor I feel sure you will understand the trauma this family has experienced. If it's not too impertinent, could you perhaps let me see some proof that Jane actually is your daughter, then I'll be able to leave and not trouble you again.'

'I'm assuming this witness is a family member, so yes, I can see how devastating this must have been. I do, however, feel rather perturbed that you should take this sighting seriously and that it appears someone has been watching my daughter and possibly my wife and me too?'

'That's more than understandable, sir, and I do apologise for such personal questions, but we have an obligation to pursue any new information, even so long after the event. Perhaps you could show me your daughter's birth certificate and possibly some early photographs you might have to hand? It would help enormously.'

Dr Solomon remained silent for a moment then rose and left the room with only a nod in my direction. His reaction was hard to read, but then what would be a normal reaction to such a request? I could hear muffled voices and presumed he was explaining to his wife what I was doing there.

After a few minutes, the door to the office opened again and a middle-aged lady entered. I recognised her as Mrs Solomon from the photographs Elise had shown me. Taller than she appeared in the photographs and with a surprised expression, she entered the room and stared directly at me.

'I'm Elizabeth Solomon.' Her voice was flat, monotonous. 'My husband tells me you have some strange idea that our daughter isn't really ours but some girl who was abducted years ago. What sort of people do you think we are, detective?'

I stood up. 'Good evening, Mrs Solomon. I know this must seem an unusual request, but any new leads have to be followed up in such a serious case. I thought an informal visit now would enable me to clear the matter up quickly, and then hopefully I'll not have to trouble you again.'

Doctor Solomon returned, carrying a photograph album and a piece of paper. The paper was a birth certificate, which he handed over for my inspection. It looked like the real thing, dated in July 1997 with details of their daughter, Jane Frances Solomon, all seemingly genuine. The condition of the certificate was as would be expected for a piece of paper that was seventeen years old, and as I read each detail carefully there was nothing to arouse suspicion.

'This was issued in Newcastle upon Tyne. Did you live there in '97?'

'Yes, I worked at a practice in Jesmond and Jane was born there.'

Both the doctor and his wife remained solemn, two pairs of eyes watching for my reactions.

'When did you move to Leeds?' I tried to sound casual, wanting them to relax.

'Not until 2000 — the summer, I think. We wanted to move further south to be closer to my elderly mother, so I took a position as a locum, which allowed me the chance to search for a suitable home. Elizabeth and Jane joined me later, when we bought this place.'

I nodded and smiled; everything seemed to check out.

Elizabeth Solomon took the album from her husband and offered it to me. I sat down to look through its pages and found a comprehensive record of their small family unit, each parent smiling into the camera with Jane being held in turn by her father and mother. It chronicled a happy family life, clearly showing Jane from birth to a teenager, a babe in arms to a toddler, a child and finally a young woman. I felt almost foolish, as if I had intruded on this respectable couple insinuating, without proof, an involvement in a kidnapping years ago.

'You have been very kind and helpful.' My words seemed hollow. 'I'm sorry to have turned up like this without warning, but I won't be troubling you again. As parents yourselves, I'm sure you can understand what this family has gone through over the years. Their little girl would have been about Jane's age now, and we have never found out what happened to her.'

Arthur and Elizabeth Solomon seemed to soften as they listened.

'I'm sure it must have been dreadful,' Arthur replied. 'Naturally your visit has come as a shock, and I'm sorry if we seemed a little unhelpful at first; we were just thrown off balance by what you seemed to be suggesting.'

'Is Jane at home?' I asked.

'No, she's at a friend's house. You don't need to question her, do you?' Elizabeth's worry lines deepened.

'No, I don't think that would serve any purpose. I'd better be going now. Thank you for your help.'

I had barely been in the Solomon's home for half an hour but had seen enough to convince me that Elise was mistaken. Jane Solomon was not Grace Bryson.

Chapter 11

Elise McDonald

'No, you're wrong; they've somehow managed to deceive you!' This was not the outcome I was expecting. Jane is Grace — surely Jack could see that! 'Did you meet her?' I asked.

'No,' Jack said. 'She was out, but I spoke with both parents and saw Jane's birth certificate and the family photographs. There's no way this girl can be Grace. I'm sorry, Elise, I know this isn't what you wanted.'

'Too right it isn't! But you're wrong, Jack, and if you won't help me prove it, I'll do it myself.' My tears were from anger and frustration — why would they not believe me? I'm Grace's sister; surely I could be trusted to have known it was her.

Simon put his arm around my shoulders, embarrassed at my outburst. 'Jack's done everything possible, Elise; he's been there and even seen photographs. I'm sorry, love, but you'll just have to accept that this girl isn't Grace.'

'Don't patronise me! I don't have to accept that she isn't … because she is — I've seen her, spoken to her; I know!' Exhaustion swept over me like a thick, dense blanket. It was eight forty-five p.m.; Jack had come straight round from Carlton Wells and I should have been grateful. Taking a deep breath, I offered an apology. 'I'm sorry, Jack; you've done your best when you didn't have to do anything, and I'm grateful.'

Jack and Simon exchanged a look that I wasn't supposed to see.

'Elise.' Jack's voice was gentle, concerned. 'Promise me you'll not do anything stupid now?'

'Define stupid?'

'I don't need to; you know what I mean.'

'Yes, but you have to understand that this is something I need to follow through. Although I'm grateful for your help, I'm convinced that the Solomons have somehow deceived you.'

Neither Simon nor Jack spoke, and there was a few moments of embarrassed silence until Jack rose to leave.

'Keep in touch, Elise. You can always talk to me, you know that,' Jack offered before heading towards the door.

As I watched him leave, he somehow didn't seem as tall as I remembered from childhood; his shoulders were slightly hunched and his bearing was that of a much older man. Maybe even Jack Priestly had been affected by Grace's disappearance.

Following to the door, I reached up to hug Jack, perhaps as a way to apologise. He seemed surprised by the action but kept his hands on my shoulders and said, 'I do understand, more than you think, Elise, and I would have dearly loved for this girl to be Grace ... but she isn't. No matter how many times you insist on it, it's just not possible, so think about it carefully before you decide to do anything else, please?'

I nodded and then watched him move to his car and drive away.

Simon was waiting for me in the lounge; I could hear him pacing the room. I almost bottled out and ran upstairs to bed, but we needed to talk and it was as good a time as any. Feeling like I'd been summoned to the headmaster's room, I braced myself for a difficult conversation, but he would have to open the dialogue — I wasn't going to make it easy.

'Sit down, Elise; we need to talk.'

I quietly sat in my favourite armchair and looked expectantly at my husband.

'This can't go on. I'm getting worried about you.' Remaining silent was not what Simon was expecting of me, and he reluctantly continued. 'The Solomon girl is obviously not Grace, and Jack Priestly has without a doubt confirmed this. It's time to let it go now, love, for your sake and the baby's. Stress is the last thing you need at the moment — it can play havoc with your blood pressure and that puts the baby at risk as well as yourself.' Another silence. 'Elise, are you listening to me — are you taking this in?'

I shrugged — not a very mature response, granted, but I was not in the mood for lectures. All I wanted to do was to ring Bea and update her, then collapse into bed and sleep for a full twelve hours.

'Please, darling, promise me that you'll drop this now so we can get back to looking forward to our baby?'

'Why is it that everyone wants me to make promises? I'm still sure this is Grace so no, I can't promise anything.'

Simon flopped down on the sofa.

'Look, I know that I didn't experience the terrible time you went through all those years ago, but I can't help that. If you want to talk about it, I'll gladly listen.'

'Talking won't help; it's time for action, but it appears I'm on my own in this.'

'You're not on your own, I'm here. Just because I can't believe this girl is Grace doesn't mean I'm not on your side. I love you, Elise, and for your sake I wish she *was* Grace, but there's plenty of evidence to prove that she is Jane Solomon.'

We were going round in circles and I knew I was being unreasonable. The strain was showing in Simon's face. Simon went into the kitchen to make cocoa, and I rang Bea to tell her of Jack's findings.

'Oh, that's such a disappointment!' Bea sounded deflated. 'Are you happy with that, Elise? Do you think you could have made a mistake?'

'Right now I don't know what to think. Jack saw the girl's birth certificate, but these things can be forged, can't they? And photographs can be tampered with, too, they could have simply pasted the earlier photos in.' My head was spinning.

'That sounds rather complicated, love. And where would they get early pictures of Grace? Now, if there were no pictures from before the age of three then that would be suspicious, but I suppose that's what DS Priestly was looking for.'

'Yes, he seems to have been thorough and asked all the right questions. Oh, Bea, I feel so weary and honestly don't know what to do next.'

'Right now, you need to do nothing except get yourself to bed and sleep. The Solomons aren't going anywhere, and now you've put Jack Priestly in the picture that adds another mind to the melting pot. Even if you have to wait until baby arrives before you do anything, it will be better than rushing headlong into an action you might later regret.'

'You're so sensible, Bea, thank you. And you're right; I do need sleep. Maybe tomorrow the next step will come to me.'

We said our goodbyes, and I went back into the lounge where Simon waited with cocoa and chocolate biscuits.

The next morning, I awoke to a sinking feeling, knowing that something was wrong, and I felt miserable but for a few moments could not remember why. It didn't take long for the events of the previous evening to come back to mind, and I instantly wanted to snuggle down under my duvet, shut out the world and go back to sleep. I resisted; the alarm clock told me it was already after eight, and I could hear Simon pottering in the kitchen downstairs. He would be going to work soon, and I wanted to see him before then.

'Good morning.' I forced a smile as he turned and saw me.

'Elise, I was going to let you sleep in.'

'Thanks, but I need to be up. I can't spend the rest of this pregnancy lying around like a beached whale.'

I kissed my husband, wanting things to be right between us. I needed harmonious living and had never been good at coping with atmospheres or half hidden moods. Simon's arms wrapped round my waist until we were as close as our son would allow us to be.

'How are you feeling today?' He kept hold of me, waiting for an answer.

'A little sad, disappointed perhaps, and I'm sorry if I behaved rather childishly last night.'

'It's okay, understandable really. I worry about you, Elise; you've been through some very bad experiences in life, but we're on the cusp of an adventure into parenthood. It's an exciting time, and I want us both to enjoy it to the full! Have an easy day today; chat to Bea if you like, but please try to focus on our son rather than Grace, okay?'

He was right, and as no other plan had come to mind I resolved to do just as Simon asked. A relaxing day might do me some good. I would start with a long leisurely bath then settle down to read.

Once again, my sister was pushed to the back of my mind and I was at a loss to know what to do for the best. Simon poured coffee for me then went off to work, and I was left alone with my very confused thoughts.

Chapter 12

Bea Cartwright

If ever a couple were made for each other, it's Elise and Simon. From the day I met him, I knew he could make her happy and heaven knows she could do with some happiness. Their wedding day was special, but even then Grace was somehow in the shadows. It was Grace who should have been the bridesmaid, her sister's confidante and support. Her absence from the celebration was palpable, and I saw in my niece's face only a restrained happiness.

Oh, she was in love all right and I was delighted for her, but Elise never quite allowed herself to be totally happy; there was always a part of her that still grieved. True, we all felt like that at times and still do, but it's different for us. We were adults when Grace disappeared and had already lived happy lives, years during which we fulfilled our dreams and enjoyed life to the full. Elise was barely nine when happiness was snatched away from her, and the years ahead would always be tainted with the sadness of separation from the sister she adored.

Of course, at the time we didn't know that Grace wouldn't be found, and still today the not knowing is one of the hardest things to bear. The human imagination can weave some terribly disturbing images and there were many times, particularly in the darkness of a sleepless night, when such disturbing thoughts would not let me rest. In the light of morning, I always tried to tell myself that the reality of what happened to Grace could surely be no worse than what my imagination tortured me with during those vulnerable times, but still the images haunted me.

None of us converted those nightmares into words; it was as if speaking of such things would somehow breathe life into them and make them real. We became adept at sidestepping around them, desperately trying to search for positive issues to talk about and good things to hope for. Over the years, the positives thinned out to almost zilch — we lived in hope of something fresh to hope for, something that never came.

Peter was my rock through those very worst of times, proving invaluable in the early days to Stephen and Margaret, as well as Elise and me. Our niece frequently stayed with us, occasions when we tried so hard to make life as normal as possible. Peter always seemed to go that little bit further for Elise, making an extra effort to raise a smile or distract her with silly jokes and antics. Between Peter and Jasper, there were sporadic episodes when Elise appeared to be relatively content, which went a long way to helping us as well.

Although Peter was denied the opportunity to be a father himself, I could not fault the way he treated Elise, and he didn't appear to resent the time I spent with her. He readily joined in with family occasions too, occasions that were inevitably tinged with sadness and a sense of loss, yet ones we celebrated in an attempt to pursue a relatively normal life.

My husband was not always the most patient of men, and this recent talk of Jane Solomon quickly began to irritate him. He declared my support and encouragement to be a cruelty, to be offering false hope where, in reality, there was none. The news from Jack Priestly seemed to concur with Peter's thinking. Jack was convinced that Elise was mistaken, but would she accept this or not? I was unsure.

By ten a.m. I decided it was suitably late enough to ring Elise, and the phone was answered almost immediately by my niece, declaring that she'd been on the point of ringing me. Wisely, she had gone to bed early and slept well. After initial pleasantries, the conversation returned again to Jack's findings, or rather the lack of them.

'I do trust Jack's judgement, but that makes it particularly hard because he found nothing to prove that Jane is Grace.' Elise spoke quietly, obviously confused. 'But I was so certain, Bea, and now I don't know what to think. Simon says I should put it all on hold until the baby's born, and he's probably right. That would be the sensible thing to do.'

'I'd have to agree with that, love. Try to concentrate on yourself and the little boy who's coming soon. You both deserve to be relaxed and happy at this time.'

My niece was silent for a moment, as if thinking.

'Last night, Bea, for the first time since seeing Jane, I actually thought I might be mistaken. I want her so much to be Grace, but perhaps I'm being arrogant in my conviction and it really is time to listen to others and admit the possibility that I'm mistaken?'

'Well, the advice of those who love you is certainly given with the best of intentions. Why not leave it for a few days, or even until after the baby comes like Simon suggested? Then we can think again and look with fresh eyes at whether there is anything we can do.'

I could hear Elise's slow breathing and knew how hard it was to admit that she could be wrong.

'Yes, that's what I'll do. At least Simon will be relieved, and I have been feeling exhausted and don't want to put the baby at risk.'

'It'll be for the best, Elise. Put your feet up and read a few good books; you'll not get much chance after the birth.' I felt relief that she was at last heeding advice. 'And of course, you know where I am if you need me. Perhaps we could go out for lunch one day next week? That's something else you'll not be able to do soon, without a bag full of nappies and bottles.'

'That would be good, Bea. I'll ring in a day or two and we'll fix a time.'

Elise hung up, sounding resigned. At least Simon would be relieved and Peter, too, when I told him.

Chapter 13

Jack Priestly

It had been a week since I visited Dr and Mrs Solomon — a week during which I had been the one to squash Elise's newfound hope that her sister was alive. In quieter moments at work, my thoughts drifted to that visit and I wondered if I could have conducted it differently. But Jane Solomon clearly was not Grace Bryson.

I also tried to think of anything else we could possibly do to reactivate the case. Would it be worth taking it to the new DI to see if it could be reviewed? Many old cases had recently been re-opened due to advances in technology and particularly DNA. Unfortunately, in this instance there was never any tangible evidence; the little girl disappeared from her own garden and had never been found. Still, it was bugging me like no other case had ever done, and the look of dejection on Elise's face haunted me.

My wife, Sarah, took a keen interest in the case at the time it happened and followed events through the press. She, too, felt the heavy disappointment at the lack of answers and took a personal interest in the search. Perhaps it was because we were of the same generation as the Brysons with young children of our own that made it all so particularly pertinent.

I told Sarah that Elise had been in touch after 'seeing' Grace and how I'd visited the home where she thought the girl was living. We talked about Elise, Grace and our own boys, feeling so blessed that we had healthy, happy children. Sarah was dreading Jake moving on to university — it had been our experience with friends that when a child flies the nest, they very rarely come home again.

'Unlike Margaret and Stephen Bryson, at least we still have our son,' she said, 'and only a text away! Oh, I almost forgot, Jake is bringing his latest girlfriend home for a meal tomorrow night.' Sarah shook her head. 'Another indication of how quickly he's growing up. Where has the time gone?'

Jake was a good kid and we were very proud of him and his brother, Dan, who was also doing well at school. Dan was an academic year behind Jake and would be going to university the following year. Sarah would certainly feel it when they were both away, and I had to admit that I would too.

The next day, I spent the afternoon washing the car as Sarah prepared the meal. At five-thirty p.m., as I was closing the garage door, Jake pulled up and proudly introduced me to his girlfriend. On reflection she must have thought me quite strange, as all I could do was to gaze mutely into the pretty face of Jane Solomon.

It took me several minutes to get over the shock of meeting Jane face to face, and throughout the meal I had to stop myself from staring. Sarah was unperturbed by the girl, but then I hadn't told her the name of the family I'd visited in Carlton Wells. Generally I left small talk to Sarah, who was far better than me on such occasions, but I listened carefully to each answer Jane gave, slipping in the odd enquiry myself by way of making conversation.

When Jane told us where she lived, I asked how long they had lived there and if she had any memories of her home before that. Sarah gave me one of her 'looks'; perhaps I wasn't being as subtle as I thought. Naturally the answer was no, but, I was reminded, she'd only been three years old. Next I enquired if she had any siblings.

'No, I'm the only one. Mum was apparently quite ill after I was born, and they decided not to have any more children.'

'So you don't remember much from your days before you were three? No close friends you had to play with, anything like that?' My attempts to delve into this girl's memories apparently were again lacking subtlety, as Sarah shot me a warning look.

'What an absurd question, Jack. Do you remember your first three years of life?'

'No, I suppose not. Sorry, Jane, but it's interesting to find out when we first begin storing memories don't you think?' I tried to make light of my strange questions.

'Dad's a detective, Jane, and I think he's been on some sort of psychology course recently. Don't encourage him and become his guinea pig!' Jake laughed.

There was no reaction from Jane to the news that I was a police officer, so presumably her parents hadn't mentioned my visit.

'There's probably very little crime in a village like yours, Jane, so a sighting of a police officer must be a rare occasion?' I was fishing again.

'That's true, but I'm not sure we'll be living there much longer. Mum and Dad have decided to move back to the Newcastle area — they've put the house up for sale.'

Jane seemed a little sad at this, whereas I was shocked. How strange that the Solomons had decided to move within a week of my visit to question them about Grace Bryson. Was this simply a coincidence, or were they trying to hide something? I went fishing again.

'Oh that's a shame. How do you feel about moving? It's right in the middle of your A-level studies, isn't it?' My curiosity earned another reproachful look from Sarah.

'Well, I am quite surprised really, and it will be hard to switch to another college in the middle of studies, but apparently Dad's been thinking about it for a while now. They miss being in Newcastle.'

I nodded sagely but had no time to pursue the conversation as Sarah asked me to help her clear the plates ready for dessert. When we were alone in the kitchen, she asked, 'What on earth are you doing giving that girl the third degree? You're off duty, remember, and she's not one of your criminals.'

'Sorry, love, but I'm just trying to make conversation, make her feel at home, you know.'

'Well it sounds more like an interrogation to me! Mild curiosity is one thing, but you sounded downright nosey.' She poured cream into a jug and passed it to me. 'Take this in and ease off on the questions, Jack.' Sarah smiled when I adopted my 'suitably chastised' face. Perhaps I'd tell her later; my wife is one smart lady and her opinions are always worth hearing.

The rest of the evening passed uneventfully. Jane sat beside our son, holding his hand as we finished the meal with coffee in the lounge. If this was the kind of girl Jake was drawn to, I would be more than happy with any future relationships.

I concentrated on every word Jane said that evening, hoping to pick up bits of information that could prove useful but there was nothing, and knowing that Sarah was watching I stopped acting like a police officer and relaxed into the role of husband and father.

Perhaps I would talk to the DI on Monday. Another point of view usually helped, and George Wheatley would be able to look at the case with fresh eyes and no prior knowledge to bias him in any way. Whether he'd think it was worth another look remained to be seen. Elise's sighting and the Solomons' sudden decision to move hardly amounted to solid evidence, but I was feeling uncomfortable about Jane's family now and more inclined to take Elise seriously.

Monday morning was perhaps the brightest day of the year so far. An early promise of spring was now visibly being fulfilled, and the sun quickly warmed the morning air, suggesting a fine day. I drove to work having decided to approach DI Wheatley as soon as possible to try and interest him in reviewing the Bryson case. Obviously, this would mean admitting my previous visit to the Solomons, an action I judged reasonable and wasn't too concerned about, but one he could take issue with if he so wished.

The opportunity came mid-morning, when the DI returned from a meeting and was alone in his office. Having gathered together the details of the case and refreshed my own memory of certain points, it was time to request a review, so I knocked on Wheatley's door.

Our working relationship was good but still not fully formed. So far I had found the new DI to be fair and reasonable and hoped he could say the same about me. I was offered a seat; he must have realised it was more than a minute I needed, probably from the sheaf of papers under my arm.

The DI's office was warm, too warm for my liking but comfortable, having been refurbished a couple of months ago. If it was a reflection of George Wheatley's personality, then I would say he was a meticulous and methodical man. Everything was tidy, even current files were shuffled into ultra-neat piles and set exactly at right angles to the edges of the modern wood and steel desk. There was nothing personal on display, no family photographs or certificates of commendation, no plants or sporting trophies, which gave the room an almost clinical feel.

When seated opposite my boss, I began to air my thoughts. 'Are you familiar with the Grace Bryson case from 2000?' I began.

'The little girl who was abducted?'

'Yes, it was my first FLO case involving a child.' The DI nodded, understanding, so I continued. 'There was an older sister, Elise, grown up now of course and expecting her own child soon. She contacted me a few days ago to say she had seen Grace in Leeds city centre.' I paused, not for effect, although the DI's eyebrows did rise in mild surprise. 'Elise is very resourceful and surreptitiously managed to find out this young woman's name and address then asked me to look into it.'

A slight frown appeared above the eyebrows now. 'And did you?' Wheatley asked.

'Yes. I visited the house informally and spoke to both parents. They live in Carlton Wells, a very nice village north of the city; he's a GP, Dr Arthur Solomon.'

'When you say informally, Jack, what exactly do you mean?'

'Well, I used my warrant card to introduce myself and told them I was making some inquiries about a historic case due to recent new information.'

'And did you tell them what that information was?'

'Yes, a sighting by someone who'd been closely involved with the case and who believed their daughter was the missing girl. I tried to keep things light and friendly and asked if they could clear the matter up by showing me some documentation to prove their daughter's identity, which they did.'

'So, why are you telling me now rather than before your visit?'

'Well, I didn't think it would come to anything. The missing girl was only three at the time and will be seventeen now so will obviously have changed considerably over the years. The doctor did produce the birth certificate and photographs from their daughter's birth up to present day, which all looked pretty genuine to me. I told Elise all of this and that I was satisfied the girl was not her sister, which of course was upsetting news. However, over the weekend I've learned that the family concerned have suddenly put their house up for sale and are leaving the area.' DI Wheatley gave nothing away in his expression, so I went on. 'I don't like coincidences and this one made me wonder, so I thought it might be prudent to have another look at the case in the light of this.'

'A decision to move house is hardly new evidence.' He paused for a minute to think. 'Leave that with me.' The DI pointed to the paperwork on my side of the desk. 'I'll have a look and let you know. Come back after lunch when I've had a chance to read it.'

'I'm in court at twelve today, hopefully for only an hour, two at the most. Will after then be okay?'

Wheatley was already flicking through the files. 'Fine, that's fine,' he muttered and I left the room.

My time in court turned out to take the full two hours. I was giving evidence in the trial of a serial joyrider, who decided to play ignorant and came up with a story that the car had been loaned to him. It was frustrating listening to his solicitor weave pathetic excuses, which he thought to be plausible reasons for leniency towards his client. My thoughts were elsewhere and I was impatient to find out what the DI had decided.

By three p.m. I was seated for the second time that day opposite George Wheatley, waiting for his decision.

'There was very little to go on, wasn't there?' he asked.

'Absolutely. We proceeded as quickly as we could with door to door enquiries and had as many personnel as were available combing the area, but it seemed as if the girl just vanished into thin air.'

'The suspect from the park — what happened with him?'

'Hogarth? We had to let him go. There was nothing at all to connect him with the abduction. His reluctance to let us search his flat was because of pornographic magazines and rather iffy downloads on his computer, which we found when we eventually got a warrant. He wasn't into children and visited the park to watch the joggers and young mothers there. After him, there were never really any other suspects.'

'And the father, Stephen Bryson?'

'Yes, we received an anonymous tip-off that he physically abused the girl. Again, there was nothing concrete to prove the allegation, and I have to say that my involvement with the parents left me with nothing other than respect for them both. I put the call down to a malicious time-waster.'

I would hate to think that the DI was considering interviewing Stephen again, but if we were going to review the case it was a strong possibility.

'Apart from yourself, who else is still here from the original team?'

'Only Dave Bennet; the rest have moved on or left.'

'Right, we'll review this one, Jack. You and Bennet can take it, other personnel only when and if necessary. Obviously this Dr Solomon is as good a place as any to start, but I'd like you to re-interview the parents of the other children who were at the party. They had access to the garden, and some of the previous interviews are a bit sketchy to say the least. You'd also better inform the Brysons that we're looking at the case again, simply as a matter of courtesy, but we may need to interview them too. I know you've got other cases on the go and I trust you'll not neglect those. Keep me posted on any developments.'

I left the DI's office trying to suppress a smug grin. If he hadn't agreed to my request, I would certainly have been tempted to do a little digging on my own, but this approval made it legitimate and I headed straight to Dave Bennet's desk to set the wheels in motion.

'Dave, we're reviewing the Grace Bryson abduction, just you and I for now, and I want you to start with a comprehensive search on Dr Arthur and Mrs Elizabeth Solomon, Garden House, The Green, Carlton Wells. Dig deep — they are possible new suspects, but tread carefully.'

Dave was delighted at the news; no one likes an unsolved case, and he was as eager as I to have a second chance at resolving it.

Leaving him to begin a computer search, I was tasked with phoning Elise to let her know that we were re-examining the case and to get a contact number for her parents. I knew Elise would welcome the news but feared she would pin all her hopes on it. I had already decided not to tell her about the Solomons' house being up for sale, thinking she may do something silly, like approaching them herself. I didn't like holding things back, but we would tell her in time when we knew more.

I picked up the phone and dialled her number. As expected, she was delighted that we were taking her seriously and readily gave me a phone number for Stephen and Margaret, but asked to be allowed to ring them first. I had no problem with that and agreed to delay my call until the evening. Before I rang off, Elise made me promise to keep her informed on anything that turned up, no matter how trivial it seemed.

Chapter 14

Margaret Bryson

At what point do you abandon hope? Fourteen years is a long time to grieve and to hope, a long time to ponder, to regret and to torture yourself with 'what if'. What if we had never had a birthday party that day? What if I had watched my daughter more closely and not blindly trusted the security of our own garden? What if I had not taken the easy way out and swallowed those sleeping tablets?

You try not to go down these roads, to discipline your thoughts and feelings, but it is not possible to do so. I will always have regrets, even if hope has now deserted me. Regrets centred on that fateful day when Grace was taken from us and which reach from that moment of time throughout the following years, still able to chastise me today.

I regret the way that I subsequently neglected Elise, that she grew up sensing the heavy burden of loss and I failed to provide her with a carefree childhood. Nine years old is too young to be faced with such stark reality, to learn that everyone in the world is not kind and loving. Elise deserved better, but I was so consumed by grief and guilt that I could not offer it. That bright summer afternoon should be remembered for its happiness, its celebration, but instead it marked the end of all the good things it should have represented.

I could no longer trust myself to be a good parent after Grace disappeared; I felt guilty and unworthy of the role of a mother. Like ripples in a pond, the effect of that awful day widened and grew, affecting my sister and her husband, our relationship with them and with our friends. At some point almost all of our friends and neighbours were interviewed, which alienated some of them, almost as if we had cast suspicion on them by directing the police to their door.

Our true friends stood by us, understanding that everyone in our circle came under police scrutiny, even Stephen and me. Bea stood by us, loyal and faithful, and quite honestly I could not have gotten through those first months without her. She and Peter provided practical help with day-to-day tasks and especially the care of Elise. It's hardly surprising that the bond between Bea and Elise is as strong as it is between me and my daughter. Bea took over the mothering role that I should have fulfilled, yet remained a wonderful sister, never impatient or angry, keeping opinions to herself and simply being there when needed.

Peter, too, did not complain, or at least not in my presence. He seemed to accept his wife's support of our family and also rallied round to help where possible. I wondered if on occasions Peter's support became a trial, a duty almost, and if he was jealous of the time Bea spent with us? After that first awful year, Bea did confide that Peter thought the time had come to put the whole incident behind us and move on. I'm sure he was not alone in this opinion, but even after a year, two years, three and more, the pain was still raw. Each summer, we anticipated reliving that fateful day.

Grace's birthday became a day of mourning rather than a celebration. This was particularly hard on Elise, who even refused to celebrate her own birthdays from then onwards. We wondered why this should be — a fear that the same fate might befall her perhaps, or a desire not to upset us? During that first year, Elise asked many questions that I felt so totally inadequate to answer. 'When' was the most regular enquiry, when would Grace come home? When would the police find her? And 'how' too: if we moved to a new house, how would Grace know where to find us?

Our family had lost its symmetry. Three seemed such a lonely number, which we were reminded of every mealtime. Grace's chair was empty, as was her bed. Her toys were left unloved, tidy when they should have been strewn around the house for someone to trip over.

I eventually had to dispose of her clothes, telling myself that when she came back they would no longer fit and we could have such fun buying new ones. Even moving her toothbrush from the mug in the bathroom was such a difficult action to take. It took over a year to complete these simple tasks, with such reluctance, as if I was finally admitting that she was never coming home.

In some ways, moving away from Lilac House helped; it no longer held any charm for us. A new home was found for only three occupants, who moved in devoid of enthusiasm or excitement. Elise began a new school, which I'm sure was so much easier for her. No longer marked out as a child to be pitied or an oddity to stare at, she immersed herself in the academic side of school life, eagerly doing homework and applying herself one hundred percent to the challenge of learning. Perhaps it was an effort to make up for being the only child we had left, a kind of 'survivor's guilt' they call it, don't they? Or maybe it was simply her way of coping. Her questions had dried up by then, but I know that Elise's hope never diminished.

In leaving Lilac House, we also lost some of our friends, particularly Christine and Harry Robinson. They did their best to remain loyal but in time they and others tired of the situation, as we were certainly not good company at any occasion. We became an embarrassment, and I know that Harry in particular resented being questioned by the police, which happened on more than one occasion. I heard a couple of years later that Christine and Harry had divorced, which was a surprise, as they seemed so happy. The children they longed for never arrived, and perhaps their separation was something to do with that.

So, at what point do you abandon hope? When did I cease hoping to see my baby girl again? There is no day or hour that I can pinpoint; it happened gradually, over time, a slow drip, draining the heart of all emotion. I would dearly love to say that I still hope to find Grace, but I'm weary and tired and probably need to accept that the truth is Grace is dead!

The call from Elise struck like a physical blow. Her unwavering insistence that she had seen Grace threw our world into turmoil, and the news that the police were once more looking into the disappearance brought such bittersweet emotions. Would we again come under the intrusive microscope of the police investigation? Would we be questioned relentlessly and mentally poked and prodded? Would our quiet existence be intruded on by the press, eager for some scandal and always wanting to believe the worst about people?

It was impossible to put my feelings into words. Would that seed of hope reawaken somewhere deep inside of me, or should I again apply the logical thinking that had robbed me of such hope in the past?

For two years, Stephen and I have lived a quiet but contented life here in Rouen, a beautiful, tranquil town. We have improved our grasp of the language and been accepted into the community. The anonymity is a blessing; we tired of being continually in the glare of publicity, of having our lives raked over by the press on each anniversary or every fresh 'sighting' of Grace. We had clawed back a degree of normality and expected to live out our lives in relative peace and quiet.

Stephen barely commented on Elise's news. His thoughts may possibly reflect my own — the same fears, the dread of further disappointment, perhaps? We're waiting now for Jack Priestly to call, thankful that he is the one to reopen the case, a friendly face in what could be the start of another nightmare situation.

Elise was so sure, so buoyant, and I feel we must support her. Simon is sceptical, but he was not around at the time and sees only what the rest of the world sees and hears: is it plausible, or at all likely that Grace is alive after all this time?

Now I am the one with questions for my daughter. We will travel back to Leeds, find a house or flat to rent for a while and remain until after the birth of our grandchild. I failed Elise in my role as a mother; perhaps I can somehow make it up to her in my role as a grandmother.

Chapter 15

Jack Priestly

DC Dave Bennet was never happier than when he was sitting behind a computer screen, pressing keys at an alarming rate and collating information about every topic under the sun. I had done the odd training course; none of us could escape the advance of technology, but my heart wasn't really in it. I knew the basics of a computer, emails, word processing and that kind of thing but much preferred to get someone to do the tricky stuff for me, and Dave Bennet was just the man for that.

Before the day was over, Dave presented me with a complete background file of Dr Arthur Solomon from date of birth, through school, university and on into his working life. There wasn't much information about his activities outside of work, other than being the chairman of a local hospice and having a passion for golf. The printouts detailed previous addresses where the doctor had lived, his National Insurance number and his only transgression: a speeding offence for which he'd opted to take a speed awareness course rather than a fine and points on his licence. Otherwise, Solomon was the fine upstanding citizen he appeared to be.

Dave had put together similar information on Mrs Solomon. The couple were married in 1994 in the Parish Church of St. George, Jesmond, which was Elizabeth's home parish. Arthur was born and brought up in Bamburgh, a village on the northern stretch of the Northumberland coastline, and one I had heard of only because of its famous castle. There was nothing in the file to indicate that the Solomons were the kind of people who would abduct a child, but another visit to Carlton Wells was in order and this time I would take Dave; it always helped to get another viewpoint.

Evening was the best time to catch the doctor at home, but first I needed to ring Margaret and Stephen Bryson. They were expecting my call, having spoken to Elise earlier in the day. It was difficult to gauge Stephen's mood as he spoke; there was almost a resigned anticipation that the whole case was going to be dragged up, and they would once again be subjected to the same ordeal they had suffered after Grace's disappearance. I tried to reassure him that it would be different this time, but in reality I could make no promises.

After a few minutes' conversation, he told me that they were making plans to come back to the UK in the next few days and stay at least until Elise's baby was born. I thanked him; it would certainly make things easier for the investigation. After putting the handset down I went to find Dave, and at six-thirty p.m. we found ourselves on the road to Carlton Wells.

'Are we doing the "good cop bad cop" thing?' Dave asked. Obviously he needed to get out more and away from his computer.

'It's still softly softly for the moment. I'll ask the questions; you chip in when you feel it's appropriate. I'd like another look at that birth certificate — it looked genuine, but perhaps I didn't look closely enough.'

I'd been quietly pondering how to handle things if Jane was there; she was bound to recognise me and would certainly ask questions. Yet that would present the Solomons with a problem too, and would create an opportunity to gauge their reaction. Would they tell her the truth of why two detectives were making house calls? It could prove to be very interesting.

'Nice place,' Dave commented when we drew up outside Garden House. 'I wouldn't want to move if I lived here.'

An estate agent's board advertised that the house was for sale; the doctor was certainly acting quickly. Mrs Solomon answered the door this time and was visibly shocked when she saw me. Dave and I both flashed our warrant cards and I asked if we might go inside to talk.

By the time we were over the doorstep Arthur Solomon appeared, a frown on his face as he led us again into the study. Before the door was closed, I heard the sound of someone running down the stairs.

'Is Jane here, Dr Solomon?' I asked.

'Yes, she's busy studying.'

'If you wanted her to be here as we talk, that would be fine by me,' I offered.

'No, there's no need to involve my daughter. Perhaps you can tell me why you are here again. I thought things had been cleared up on your last visit?'

'Ah, yes, since then we have re-opened the Grace Bryson case, so this is perhaps a more official visit than last time. I would appreciate seeing Jane's birth certificate again, and the photographs, if you have them to hand.'

'This is ridiculous! Do we look like child abductors?' Anger was simmering below the doctor's controlled expression and his wife looked pale, as if she might pass out at any time. Their reactions were only confirming to me that we had found Grace Bryson. The doctor made no attempt to move, and his wife was watching him, taking her lead from him.

'Do you have a warrant?' Dr Solomon asked.

'No, I didn't think we needed one. You were very helpful last time, and I assumed you would co-operate today as well.'

'Well, I don't think I shall. Quite frankly, I am appalled that you are wasting your time by insinuating that we have committed this crime when you could be chasing real criminals! This is tantamount to harassment, and as a point of principle I will not show you the documents you have already seen unless you return with a warrant, or arrest me.'

Elizabeth Solomon let out a gasp of air when she heard this then clamped her hand over her mouth. Arthur shot a warning look in her direction, but I hardly thought she was going to go against what he said.

'We can certainly come back tomorrow with a warrant.' I spoke with confidence, when I really didn't think there was much chance of getting one with such flimsy evidence. Then I thought I would give them one last chance. 'Of course, there is a conclusive way we can prove that Jane is your daughter, and that is by a routine DNA sample, from Jane and you.'

Solomon's face was deep red, his eyes almost bulging out of his head as he tried to control the anger he so obviously felt. 'I have given my last word on the subject and would like you to leave now.'

'Thank you for your time, doctor. We'll be back tomorrow with a warrant — would the same time suit you?'

Dave and I moved towards the door, which Dr Solomon held open for us. In the hall I caught a glimpse of Jane at the top of the stairs, crouching down, trying to see what was happening.

'Good evening,' I said to Dr Solomon as we left the house, unsure whether Jane had seen me or not. The door was closed swiftly and firmly, and I almost expected to hear the thud of bolts shutting us out.

I dropped Dave off then headed home after another long day, making a quick call to Elise to keep her in the loop. There was little else that could be done that evening. Tomorrow, I would have a word with the DI to get his okay on applying for a warrant.

Sarah warmed a meal for me; she'd eaten earlier with the boys, something that happened often and something she uncomplainingly accepted as part of the package of being married to a policeman. As I began to eat at the kitchen table Jake appeared, a frown warning me that something was wrong.

'I've just spoken to Jane. She says you've been round to see her parents, but they refused to tell her what for. What's going on, Dad? Are they in some kind of trouble, because if they are I'm sure Jane has nothing to do with it!'

'You know I can't tell you anything about an active case, but you don't need to worry — it's nothing that Jane has done.'

'So you are investigating them? Is that what all those questions were about over dinner, using Jane to find out about her parents? Becauseif you were, I don't think it was very fair!'

'No, Jake, it's not like that. I was surprised to meet Jane, that's all, and you're quite right; I shouldn't have been so inquisitive and I'm sorry.'

This was new, being chastised by my son, but he was correct; sometimes I forget that I'm off duty.

Jake turned away, still unhappy, but he accepted that I could tell him nothing more. Now I knew that Jane had seen me and wondered how her parents would explain my visit. Perhaps tomorrow I'd return, with or without a warrant and earlier in the day to hopefully catch Mrs Solomon alone and see what she had to say on the matter without her husband there to lead her.

Chapter 16

Elise McDonald

It is now two weeks since I saw Grace, two weeks in which I have questioned my judgement and even doubted my own sanity. From being so certain and elated at the prospect of having found my sister, I fell into despondency and was almost persuaded that I'd been mistaken. But now things have changed again, and I am at last being taken seriously.

Mother and Father arrive tomorrow. Strangely, they had not welcomed the news of the case being reopened, but perhaps they can only see the negative side of the situation. As a child, I was shielded from most of the early investigation and perhaps even now can hardly imagine what my parents went through during that most horrendous time. Most people would expect this recent development to renew their hope, but in allowing themselves to hope they would also become vulnerable to fresh pain.

Things are moving quickly, and with Jack's voice now added to mine people are at last taking notice. Simon still finds it difficult to accept, but is certainly more open-minded now that a police officer is supporting my sighting of Grace. Naturally Bea is delighted too; she was always inclined to believe me, whereas Peter is remaining quiet on the subject, waiting to see the outcome of the investigation.

Jack rang to update me earlier this evening, on his way home from Carlton Wells. He doesn't tell me everything but is doing his best to keep in touch, and from what he did say I could sense that now he is seriously considering the possibility that Jane could actually be Grace.

I was sitting in the lounge, looking once again at the folder of information I'd gathered on the Solomons, when Simon arrived home. Making no comment about the photographs I was studying, he produced a huge bunch of flowers from behind his back. After hugging my thoughtful husband, I took them to the kitchen to find a vase; they were beautiful, predominantly white with an extravagant mix of chrysanthemums, carnations and narcissus, a promise of good things ahead. Serving the casserole I'd prepared earlier, we ate at the kitchen table and over our food I told Simon about Jack's latest call.

'The Solomons are being obstructive, which makes Jack even more suspicious that their "daughter" could be Grace. Just think, Simon, it might only be a matter of days before we know! Grace could be with us when our baby is born!' I'd indulged my thoughts that day and allowed myself to picture the amazing reunion we would have. Mother and Father would be here, Bea and Peter and of course Simon. 'You'll love her, Simon, I just know you will, and she'll love you too; it's going to be so wonderful!'

'Elise, don't get carried away with all this, please. It could take longer than you think. The police aren't going to simply march into this family's home and bring Grace here to you. And have you thought about how this girl will feel? If she is Grace, it will come as a life-changing shock. She's grown up as Jane Solomon, and it will almost certainly be a traumatic experience to learn that she is not the person she's always believed herself to be. To her, this doctor and his wife are family; she will love them and may even want to stand by them.'

I didn't want to think about what he was saying, sure that my sister would want to be reunited with her true family and I told him so.

'Elise, you're assuming that Grace will have memories of you and Stephen and Margaret, but think about it logically; she was only three years old. You remember her because you were so much older, but the reality is that the only life she knows is that of being Jane Solomon. Can you remember much about your first three years of life? I certainly can't. To this young woman we will be strangers; most likely she'll have no memories of you or your parents. This isn't going to be easy for anyone, but particularly not for Grace.'

I concentrated on my food, pushing a cube of beef around the plate with my fork, suddenly not hungry anymore. Admittedly, some of what Simon said had crossed my mind in the last couple of weeks, but they were unwelcome thoughts that I pushed away, avoiding dwelling on them and preferring to think in a more optimistic manner.

Surely Grace would have some memories of her first three years? We would remind her, tell her about our idyllic childhood and the love we shared as a family, about the years since then when we've lived in sadness without her and how much we have missed her.

Grace probably did love the Solomons and would have very mixed feelings when the truth was known. The Stockholm syndrome came to mind, although in this case Grace would not realise that her 'parents' were kidnappers and the bond built with her abductors would seem a totally natural one.

I forced myself to meet Simon's eyes and acknowledge the sense of his words.

'I do know that it's not going to be easy, and I have thought about some of what you're saying. The truth is that having lived all my life not daring to be happy, now when we are so close to getting Grace back I want to think only of the goodness and happiness it can bring. I'm not so naive as to expect her to slot into our family without a period of adjustment, but for now I simply want to enjoy the knowledge that we've found her, that she is still alive. I think we all deserve to enjoy that, and we'll cross all those other perilous bridges when we get there.'

Simon nodded, not wanting me to be hurt again. We spent the rest of the evening snuggled together on the sofa, watching an old black and white film on television. My mind was not really on the film; I was anticipating the events of the following day. Jack had intimated that he may be going back to Carlton Wells with a search warrant, and my parents would be arriving in the evening.

I'd missed them more than I realised, and if there was good news waiting for them when they arrived, all the better. They were bringing their car over on the ferry and had booked into a Travelodge for a couple of nights, intending to look for a flat or house to rent for a few weeks. We would happily have let them stay with us, but Mum insisted that Simon and I needed our own space, particularly after the baby was born.

Sleep took a long time to come that night as my mind raced with all the possibilities the future could hold. For fourteen years our family had been incomplete, but now we were so close to ending the heartache of the past and writing a new chapter in our family history — a happy, positive chapter.

I lay still, listening to Simon's deep, even breaths and allowed my imagination to invent such a future, one with endless possibilities, one with my sister at its heart.

Chapter 17

Jack Priestly

Sunshine streamed through the window when I woke. Sarah was already up and dressed, and I could hear the boys getting ready in their rooms. After showering, I went downstairs in search of food and company. The smell of coffee from the kitchen was beckoning and my wife smiled at me as I entered, offering a cheek for a kiss.

'You should have woken me,' I said to Sarah, glad that she hadn't.

'Why? You worked late yesterday, and I know you didn't sleep well. Someone has to look out for you.'

My phone rang; it was Dave Bennet. He was already in the office and obviously had been for some time.

'I've found out more about Elizabeth Solomon. It appears that she spent several weeks in a psychiatric unit in the spring of 2000. I tracked down some of their old neighbours in Jesmond, who were certainly more helpful than the health centre her husband worked in ... and guess what? She was admitted with severe depression after their three-year-old daughter died of meningitis!'

'Dave, if I was there with you now I would kiss you! Why on earth didn't we cotton on before —? Grace was abducted as a replacement for their own daughter! Check the register for deaths in Jesmond, will you?'

'Already done: they're faxing a copy of Jane Solomon's death certificate as we speak.'

'Great work, Dave — is the DI in yet?'

'Yes, been at his desk for an hour or so, not like some detectives I know!'

'Okay, very funny. Can you go and let him know these latest developments? I'll be there in half an hour.'

As I put my phone away Sarah looked inquisitively at me, having heard only one side of the conversation. I quickly filled her in on Dave's findings, admitting that I'd perhaps been somewhat slow in concluding that Jane Solomon had actually existed. As I talked, Sarah filled a thermos mug with coffee and buttered a slice of toast, which she put into my hand. I took the mug and toast with me for the short journey to the station, excitement rising within me as I anticipated how the day might work out.

Dave Bennet was waiting and quickly briefed me on his conversation with George Wheatley. The DI had not only authorised a search warrant but also arrest warrants for both Dr and Mrs Solomon.

After making sure everything was in place, we left the station late that morning. First stop was Central Health Centre, where the doctor worked, to arrest him before moving on to Carlton Wells and arresting Elizabeth Solomon too. My excitement was tempered with a degree of concern, mainly for Jane, or Grace, or whatever we should call her. Presumably the girl would be at college, and after her parents were safely in custody we would find her to break the news, which would certainly be devastating.

Dave drove through the busy city centre, chattering excitedly about the case.

'I honestly never thought we'd find this girl alive. Who would believe that she's been living so close as the daughter of her abductors? It's surreal. I wonder if she remembers any of it.'

'I doubt it — it was her third birthday, and no one remembers much about those early years. Grace will have to be told what happened to her, though.'

We arrived at the health centre — a modern purpose-built single-storey building which, despite its age, looked to have seen better days. The car park was full and we parked on double yellows outside the main entrance — perks of the job. Inside, a reception desk was manned by two harassed-looking receptionists. When one of the receptionists was free, I showed my warrant card and asked to see Dr Solomon. The woman looked puzzled as she shook her head.

'There's a waiting room full of patients who'd like to see Dr Solomon too, but he hasn't turned up today.' She looked past me to the next person in line.

I shifted position to block her view and asked, 'Have you heard from him? Did he call in sick?'

'No, he didn't call in and we can't reach him on his home number or mobile. Sorry I can't help; as you see we're very busy.'

She was right — she couldn't help. We left and jumped back in the car.

'What are you thinking?' Dave glanced at me.

'Probably the same as you. Has the good doctor done a runner?'

Albert Einstein once said that logic will get you from A to B, imagination will take you everywhere. Being a policeman, I was trained to think logically but there were times when it was more productive to think outside the box. This was one such case. I should have seen this coming. Perhaps I played my hand too soon and scared the Solomons away. Both Dave and I were quiet as we drove to Carlton Wells, expecting to find nothing more than an empty house. Dave broke the silence.

'Unbelievable isn't it, that they would go out and steal a child to replace the daughter they'd lost? I wonder how they went about it.'

'I should have anticipated this, should have thought to check the register of deaths sooner.'

'Hey, don't start the blame game, Jack. No one would suspect a doctor; we're all conditioned from birth to trust them, which put him at an advantage from the start. And the stats show that children are mostly abducted by paedophiles for unspeakable purposes, not by a respectable couple who wanted to replace a dead child!'

I sensed that the house was empty as we pulled up outside. We went through the motions of walking up the path and ringing the bell, but there was no answer. Stepping back and looking up at the bedroom windows confirmed our thoughts; the curtains were drawn and no one was home.

Dave went around the side of the house to double check for any signs of life, and I went to the house next door to speak to the neighbours. The door was answered by an elderly lady who was obviously struggling to walk. I apologised for the disturbance and showed my ID before asking if she had seen her neighbours that morning.

'Oh yes, they were up ever so early packing the car up for a holiday no doubt, although they usually tell me when they're going away.' As she spoke, the lady walked slowly back down the hallway and I followed, hoping to learn more. The lounge was dark and badly in need of some TLC — it also smelled of cat pee.

'Do you know where they might have gone?' I knew the answer before the words were delivered.

'No, my dear — as I said, they usually tell me when they go away, but not this morning.'

The lady sat down on a sofa of indeterminate colour, moving a sleeping cat, which leapt down with an angry yowl.

'And was Jane with them?'

'Yes, she was in the back of the car with a face like thunder, not like her at all; she's such a lovely young woman, but I think there had been some kind of altercation between her and her parents. When I let Monty out last night I couldn't help hearing them shouting, which is most unusual; they are generally such a quiet family. Still, Jane's getting to that awkward age, I suppose; they'll probably have a few more tiffs before she's much older.'

'Is there anywhere they usually go — a caravan or a favourite place, perhaps?'

'Oh, all over the place, abroad sometimes, or Scotland and I know they like Devon too, but this time who knows? Can I give them a message for you when they come back?'

'That's very kind, thank you, but it's not necessary. If I could leave a card with my number on, would you ring me when they return?'

She reached out an arthritic hand and took the card, smiling.

'Are they in any trouble?'

'Nothing for you to worry about. Thank you for your help. I'll drop the latch on the way out, shall I?'

Dave was leaning against the car, waiting for me.

'Nothing, Jack. The house is secure with no sign of life anywhere.'

We climbed despondently back into the car and headed to Leeds.

'I suppose it's pointless trying the college for the girl?' Dave asked.

'She's with them — the neighbour saw her.'

'So, what next?'

'Back to the station. I'll have to report to the DI, who isn't going to be very happy with me.'

I was right, he wasn't. I think he would have liked the kudos of clearing up an old case so early on in his appointment, but I hadn't yet given up hope. I gave Dave the task of circulating the Solomons' details and the car registration, hoping they wouldn't attempt to leave the country. The only positive side to the investigation now was that we had no concern for Grace's safety; if they'd brought her up as their own daughter they were hardly likely to harm her now, but I'm sure she would be asking difficult questions and I wondered how the doctor would answer them.

It was early afternoon, and there was one more thing to try before I went to tell Elise what was happening. I rang Jake's mobile number. He answered almost immediately.

'Hi, Jake, can you talk?'

'Yeah.'

'I don't suppose Jane has turned up at college today?'

'How do you know that? She didn't ring in sick or anything, and she's not answering her phone. What's going on, Dad?'

'I'll explain later, but can you give me her number? We need to get in touch with her parents.'

Jake recited the number from memory. It amazed me how these kids could remember such long phone numbers but forget to put the rubbish out when they were asked. I said thanks and left him in a totally bewildered state, promising to talk to him later that evening. I took the number in to Dave Bennet to add to the system, telling him to ring a few times during the course of the day to see if he could get an answer, which neither of us really expected. I had the unenviable task of calling at Elise McDonald's.

Elise opened the door, smiling. I could tell there were others in the house from the noise behind her, but she reached for my hand anyway and pulled me inside. The noise was from Stephen and Margaret Bryson.

'They caught an earlier ferry,' Elise explained, and I found myself being greeted like an old friend, which made me feel terrible. Bea and Peter Cartwright were among the group, and suddenly they all went silent and gazed expectantly towards me.

'Have you been to Carlton Wells today?' Elise asked, eyes bright with anticipation.

'Yes, but it appears that the Solomon family have gone away.' I hated myself for having to say those words, for bringing disappointment to each person in that room.

After a moment's silence, Stephen asked, 'What do you mean, Jack, gone away?'

'Exactly that, I'm afraid. A neighbour confirmed that she saw them packing up the car very early this morning, and no one seems to know where they've gone. We tried Dr Solomon's place of work and apparently he didn't turn in this morning, and they haven't been able to contact him. I'm so sorry about this, but we are doing all we can to find them.' I was very conscious that what had been a happy reunion was now spoiled by the news I'd just delivered.

'Jack, is this girl really Grace?' Margaret was pale, worry lines defining her face.

'We can't say definitively at this point, but everything we've found out so far indicates that she is.'

'And can you tell us what you have found out?' Stephen Bryson spoke again, but everyone's eyes remained on me.

I took a deep breath. 'As I'm sure Elise will have told you, on my first visit to the Solomon household the doctor was co-operative and showed me a birth certificate and photographs of "Jane" from birth to present day. Everything seemed to be in order, and I felt confident that we were on the wrong track and the girl couldn't be Grace. Then later, from another source, I learned that the doctor had suddenly put his house up for sale, a coincidence which didn't sit comfortably with me.

'At this point, the DI gave the go-ahead to officially reopen the case and DC Dave Bennet was assigned to assist me. We paid another visit to Carlton Wells but were made most unwelcome this time, with the doctor refusing to help. We had no option but to leave, and I told him we would return with a warrant. Dave began to research the history of both Solomon and his wife. He discovered that Elizabeth Solomon was an inpatient at a psychiatric unit in the spring of 2000, following the death of their daughter, Jane, from meningitis.'

Margaret gasped at this point and I could hardly begin to understand what must be going through her mind. Glancing round the room, I could see the effect my words had on each person. Tears were welling up in Elise's eyes, and Simon slipped a protective arm around her shoulders.

'So, we've found Grace, but now she's been taken away again!' Elise spoke the words that everyone was thinking, and there was nothing at all I could do except nod in agreement.

The local newspaper ran the latest developments. There were photographs of Dr Solomon, his wife Elizabeth and Jane, with the question posed, '*Is this girl really Grace Bryson?*'

I'd told Jake everything about the investigation the night before, feeling it was only fair for him to hear about it from me rather than read the sensationalised account in the papers. At first he found it hard to believe, then he questioned me and I tried to give as many answers as I could. Jake had met Dr and Mrs Solomon on only two occasions, but they were very welcoming and pleasant; therefore, it was difficult to accept that they could have actually abducted a child to bring her up as their own daughter.

'But wouldn't Jane remember? It must have been quite a traumatic event in a child's life?' he asked.

'Well, I'm no psychologist but she was only three, and I don't think she would remember that far back, or if she did perhaps she somehow blocked it from her mind? You're not that much older, Jake — can you remember your third birthday party?'

'Did I have one?'

'Exactly, and you will have seen photographs of your early years to keep memories alive. Jane would have nothing to remind her of those years.' I understood how difficult this was for my son to understand.

'What do you think they'll do, leave the country?' Jake looked concerned.

'Possibly, but we've alerted the ports and airports, so unless they have false passports we'll be notified immediately. The likelihood of them having forged documents is very slight. They only knew we were looking at them as suspects in the last few days — hardly time to put something like that in place. I'm sure they thought they'd gotten away with it after all these years, which they would have done if you hadn't brought Jane here. Do you know what kind of relationship she has with her parents?'

'A pretty good one, I'd say. Jane occasionally complains that they're a bit old-fashioned and overprotective of her. There was a trip to Gibraltar from college last year, which they refused to let her go on. It wasn't the cost either — that would be nothing to them. She's never been anywhere without her parents, which is a bit odd, don't you think?'

I nodded. It's funny how people's actions have new meaning when you know their history. I could certainly understand why the Solomons never let Jane too far out of their sight, and now Jake was putting two and two together as well.

'I keep trying her phone, but it just rings out — no voicemail, which she always keeps on. Perhaps they've taken it from her?'

'Possibly, but keep trying, son, and let me know immediately if you get a reply.'

Phone lines were in place in anticipation of the influx of calls the media coverage would almost certainly bring, and by the time I got to the station, there was already a long list of callers — mostly the doctor's patients who were panicking that they had entrusted their health to a kidnapper. There was little we could do for them, so I instructed the officers on the phones to refer them to the health centre.

Dave took a uniformed constable to do house to house enquiries in Carlton Wells. The case was in the public domain now, and we could ask pertinent questions without the need to obfuscate the issue. We were meeting for a lunchtime 'catch up' and I was hoping for good news. Dave came in with a smile on his face.

'Isn't it amazing how people always thought there was something not quite right about the family but never did anything?' We heard plenty of those types of comment.

'Any clues as to where they might have gone?'

'The lady who works in the tea shop thinks they have a holiday home somewhere in Northumberland. It would tie in with the doctor's roots; he was born in Bamburgh, if I remember correctly.'

'That's as good a place to start as any. Can you do a land registry check on the area? I shouldn't think there'll be too many home owners called Solomon. I'll ring the local station and see if they'll do a bit of leg work for us. If they do have a place there, they'll probably be known to the locals. With a bit of luck we'll find them before the story and photos hit the national papers and scare them away.'

I was confident of finding the Solomon family soon. It would surprise me if after all this time they had a solid back-up plan, and they may well be floundering in their decisions. Then there was Jane herself. They wouldn't be able to keep the truth hidden for long, and I couldn't see them locking her away indefinitely.

Chapter 18

Jane Solomon

This is scary — something really weird is going on, but Mum and Dad won't tell me anything. They've clammed up ever since Jake's dad visited them. I've been whisked off to Stable Cottage in such a hurry that it feels as if they're hiding, but surely they would never do anything that would get them into trouble with the police?

Mum told me to pack last night and that we would be away indefinitely. She said she would square things with college and I could use the time away to revise for my mocks, which are in another two weeks. I tried arguing — there are a couple of lectures coming up that I really should attend — but she was insistent. There was no choice; they wouldn't entertain the idea of me staying in Carlton Wells on my own. When I was alone in my room I decided to ring Jake, but I couldn't find my phone and the landline appeared to have a fault.

Now here we are in our cottage, but the mood is anything but a holiday one. It's a rather miserable day, overcast with the threat of rain. Mum and Dad are keeping very quiet and that scares me. I know I'm lucky to have such great parents, and we generally have quite a good relationship, always able to work out some kind of compromise when we disagree. But they were both so quiet in the car — an uneasy silence unlike our usual journeys, when we plan what we'll be doing and look forward to relaxing at the cottage.

When we arrived, Mum went through the motions of unpacking in the kitchen, storing the hastily packed fridge and freezer stuff, again in silence. I asked if I could borrow her mobile phone, as I couldn't find my own.

'I didn't bring it with me.' She was a little too quick to reply, snappy almost, but then she softened. 'That's not a bad thing, though, is it, love? We can enjoy the peace and solitude without interruptions for a change, and you know the signal here's a bit iffy anyway.'

Her face looked strained; it was obvious that something was very wrong.

'What's going on, Mum?'

'Nothing, darling — we just needed to get away for a few days, that's all.'

'How many days?'

There was no reply, and Mum turned away, gathering up the groceries brought from the cupboards at home to fill the cottage's empty larder. My question was completely ignored.

'I think I'll walk into the village to phone Jake. He'll think it's odd that I'm not at college.'

Mum turned back to me, panic in her eyes.

'No, Jane, please don't!'

'Why on earth not? Are we hiding from something?'

Before there was a chance for her to reply, Dad came into the kitchen — he'd obviously heard our conversation.

'Jane, I know all this must seem rather strange to you, but we need you to trust us. There are things we can't tell you at the moment, decisions we have to make, but whatever happens please know that we love you. Trust us, please?'

That was no comfort at all. What on earth was going on that they couldn't tell me about, and why did they not want me to go out or contact my friends? I didn't believe for one minute that Mum had come away without her phone; she would never do that. Something was driving my parents into hiding, and my mind was turning somersaults to try and work out what it could be.

I lay on the bed listening to their muffled voices below. If Dad was in some sort of trouble at work, why couldn't they share it with me? He'd never been one to run away from problems before, and I couldn't imagine it was financial trouble. I spent the evening in my room, feeling claustrophobic, and only going down to eat, a meal that we had in an uncommon silence. What frightens me most is that Mum and Dad seem so anxious. They're jumpy at the slightest sound and constantly looking out of the window.

After our meal, Dad told me that we were going to go abroad for a while, probably somewhere in Spain.

'Where in Spain and why the hurry, Dad? What is it that you're not telling me?'

'Please just trust me, Jane. I've never let you down before, have I?'

'No, but this is frightening me. If you tell me what's wrong, at least I can understand.'

'I'm sorry, darling, but for now it's better if you don't know. Maybe when things have settled down we can talk, but not yet.'

That was the day before yesterday, and the atmosphere this morning is no better. Mum looks as if she hasn't slept at all and Dad is edgy, almost as if he's expecting something to happen. I made another attempt at asking if I could go to the village, but the answer was the same, an emphatic 'no'.

As I rummaged in the kitchen cupboards to find something for breakfast, Mum's handbag slipped off the worktop. I stooped to pick the bag up and found not only Mum's mobile phone but my own too.

'You lied to me! And you hid my phone! What is going on?'

I was sick of asking and getting nowhere. I ran out the front door and made for the road to the village. Dad came after me but gave up after realising that I was much faster than he was. It was rather blustery with the salty breeze from the sea blowing all around me, but running warmed me up.

Slowing to a gentler pace I headed to the village. I had no bag or coat and only a five pound note in my jeans pocket. I planned to buy a coffee at the café, then use the change to ring Jake from a payphone. It would be so good to hear his voice. I was missing him, and the thought also crossed my mind that his dad might have told him why he'd visited our house.

The café was only just open with no customers yet, but the smell of fresh coffee was good. I took a window seat and picked up a laminated menu. The waitress and the cook were laughing over some private joke in the kitchen and were in no hurry to serve me, but I wanted to get my coffee and some change to ring Jake.

'Excuse me,' I spoke up, 'Could I order please?'

The waitress ambled over to my table, pulled a pair of glasses down from the top of her head and found a notepad in her pocket. There was no eye contact, and I felt like a nuisance, unwelcome.

'Just a coffee and a slice of buttered toast please.'

'Jam?'

'Yes, thank you.'

She moved back into the kitchen to get my order. The bell on the door jangled as another customer entered: an elderly man who shouted a greeting to the ladies in the kitchen. My coffee was placed unceremoniously in front of me, together with the overdone toast and the waitress moved on to the other customer, bestowing a smile upon him.

When she went to get his order, the man pulled a copy of the *Daily Express* out of his overcoat pocket and placed it on the table in front of him. After a few moments, he looked up and gave me a nod. I smiled and said good morning, and his attention returned to the waitress and his breakfast.

As I gazed through the window, my thoughts were of Jake. I finished my coffee and stood to pay. The waitress was sitting with the customer now and their voices were low, almost conspiratorial. She rose when I went to the counter and stared at me with wide blue eyes.

'You're her, aren't you?' she said.

All three were gawping at me now.

'I'm sorry, I don't know what you mean.'

'The girl in the paper ... the one that was kidnapped — it's you, isn't it?'

When I realised they were serious and this wasn't a joke, I felt quite faint and sat down on the nearest chair.

The man came over and showed me the front page of the paper. My head swam as I looked at the photographs of Mum, Dad and me and the caption, 'Could this girl be the missing Grace Bryson?' I almost collapsed on the table. Kidnapping seemed impossible. I'm their daughter, aren't I?

'Have you escaped, love?' The waitress was kindly now and put a comforting arm around my shoulders. 'Should we ring the police for you?'

'No, it must be a mistake. I need to call someone...' As I stood to go to the phone, the elderly man offered me his mobile.

'Sit there to do it, love — you look all done in.'

Trembling, I dialled Jake's number, silently praying that he would answer it.

He did.

'Jane, where are you?' He sounded anxious.

'Bamburgh, in a café. I've seen the paper, Jake — what's going on? Who is Grace Bryson?'

'We think it's you. Look, don't panic, we'll talk it through later. Where are your mum and dad?'

'In the cottage — Stable Cottage in Bamburgh.'

'Is anyone with you?'

'Yes, another customer and the staff.'

'Can I speak to one of them?'

I passed the phone to the man beside me and watched as he nodded and made a few noises then gave the phone back.

'I've asked him to call the police. They've been looking for you, but don't worry; my dad's in charge of the case and we'll get you back here as soon as possible. I'm going now, Jane, to ring him. Wait there until the police arrive, and I'll see you very soon.'

Jake rang off. The waitress put another cup of coffee in front of me and the man sat down beside me.

'The police are on the way, love. Your young man seems very capable and has asked me to stay with you until they arrive. How are you feeling?'

I couldn't answer. I stared at the photographs again and wanted to read the report, but tears were stinging my eyes, blurring my vision.

'What does it say?' I whispered.

'It seems that this doctor and his wife kidnapped you when you were three and have brought you up as their own daughter.'

He patted my hand. For a brief moment, I thought about running back to Stable Cottage to see Mum and Dad but I didn't have the energy. There was so much I wanted to ask them. Could it really be true?

Chapter 19

Jack Priestly

I was in the DI's office when Dave Bennet poked his head around the door.

'Your son's on the phone, Jack, says he's heard from Jane Solomon.'

George Wheatley nodded towards the door and I almost ran to speak to Jake.

'Has she rung? Where is she?' This was the kind of break I'd been hoping for but perhaps a little sooner than I had expected.

'Bamburgh — she's in a café. Dr and Mrs Solomon aren't with her; they are in a cottage, Stable Cottage, Jane said.'

'Is she all right?'

'Not great; she's seen the newspaper and is shocked and confused. I told her to stay in the café until the police get there, and I asked one of the customers to phone the police and stay with her until they arrive.'

'Well done, Jake!' I felt suddenly very proud of my son. He'd acted sensibly and done exactly the right thing.

'Will you be going up to Bamburgh, Dad?'

'As soon as I know she's with the police, yes.'

'Can I come with you? Jane's really scared and a friendly face might help.'

'You're right about that, son — I'll be glad for you to come. I need to speak to the police up there first and then I'll let you know what we decide.'

'I'm heading home; you can pick me up from there.'

Dave was standing beside my desk and had caught the gist of the conversation.

'Comes to something when your lad's solving our cases for us!' he laughed.

A couple of phone calls later, I learned that Grace had been safely picked up from the café and was heading towards Kelso Police Station. I arranged for local officers to go to Stable Cottage in Bamburgh and arrest Dr and Mrs Solomon on a charge of abduction. We set off in separate cars and I swung by our home to pick up Jake.

Kelso was a small border town and one of the nearest places to Bamburgh with a police station at about twenty-seven or twenty-eight miles away. It would be a good three and a half hours' drive from Leeds. I was unsure what man power they had in the Kelso force, but the sergeant I spoke to assured me that they could handle the arrest of Dr and Mrs Solomon and keep Jane out of harm's way in the meantime.

At home, Jake was anxiously waiting for me with a couple of thermos mugs full of coffee. He was quiet as we set off, only asking if I'd heard whether Jane was safe or not. Thankfully I could tell him that she was, largely due to his quick thinking. My son lapsed into silence, knowing this would be a long journey and refused my offer of putting on a CD.

The first hour dragged. Travelling always seems to take longer when you are anxious to arrive at your destination. I thought Jake had fallen asleep, but then he began to ask questions.

'What will happen to Dr Solomon and his wife?' Jake went straight to the heart of the matter, a chip off the old block there.

'They'll both be charged with abduction. Hopefully the Kelso police will have found them by now and have them in custody.'

'And Jane?' His voice trembled. This wasn't such an easy question to answer and was most certainly one of the strangest cases I'd ever worked.

'Well, that's difficult to predict at the moment. Jane herself will of course have a say in what happens next. I know the Bryson family are keen to meet her, but I think we'll have to take things slowly. It must have come as a tremendous shock and will undoubtedly take time for her to understand and accept the situation. Social services will probably have some involvement too because of Jane's age, but what she wants to do will certainly be taken into account.'

'I can't begin to imagine how she must be feeling. The Solomons have always been so close, and Jane really loves them! Do you think she'll stop loving them now because of this? And will she ever be able to accept a whole new family who are really nothing more than strangers to her?'

Jake seemed to have a pretty good understanding of what Jane must be going through. I was suddenly really glad that he was with me, for Jane's sake — she certainly needed a friend at this time. We tossed a few more thoughts around on the immediate future without reaching a conclusion, because really the only one who could decide was Jane herself. There was a whole bundle of 'what if's' in the equation that would take time to work through, not least of which was, would she want to be called Jane or Grace?

My thoughts also turned to the Brysons. They desperately wanted Grace back, but this was no longer their little girl — she was now a young woman on the verge of becoming an adult, and in her own eyes she was Jane Solomon. Knowing

Stephen, Margaret and Elise, they would want to enfold her into their family and make up for all those lost years, but would Jane want that, or would it be overwhelming?

For myself and Dave, the case was finally coming together and we were keen to interview the doctor and his wife to find out who had helped them, as I was certain they did have help. It seemed highly unlikely that Solomon just walked into the Brysons' garden and took Grace without being seen or heard.

Eventually we arrived at Kelso police station without having stopped at all on the way, and I needed to use the bathroom and hopefully find some coffee and a sandwich. Jake was more concerned with seeing Jane, but we made a quick bathroom stop as the desk sergeant rang to inform his colleagues we were there.

Jane looked pale and confused, the dark streaks on her cheeks betraying the fact that she'd been crying. When we entered the room, she ran straight into Jake's arms and I watched in awed silence as he held her, speaking soothing words and holding her tight. It was most certainly a good move to bring him. Jane must have felt so very alone, and my son was perhaps the only constant in her life at that moment.

The room we were directed to felt warm and comfortable; the powers that be in the Force had at last begun to appreciate that a comfortably furnished, pleasant room was an asset in dealing with sensitive and vulnerable victims.

A young female PC brought in coffee and biscuits and stayed with us as I began to question Jane, who squeezed herself as close as possible to Jake on a two-seater sofa, taking comfort from his presence and holding his hand so tightly that her knuckles were white. It was impossible to understand what the poor girl must be going through, and my questions were phrased simply to find out exactly what she knew and how she'd been treated during these last few days.

As expected, no harm had come to her at her 'parents' hands, but no explanation as to why they were apparently running away was forthcoming either. Jane knew the bare facts from the morning's newspaper reports, so I tried gently to fill in the blanks in her understanding of the situation.

During the next hour or so, Jane asked more questions of me than I did of her, and I tried my best to enlighten her. We were interrupted once by the desk sergeant, who asked to have a word with me, and as I left the room he made sure we were well out of hearing range before he told me two things: firstly that their duty medic was in the station and ready to examine Jane, a formality in all such cases, and secondly that his colleagues had found Stable Cottage and Elizabeth Solomon, but that Dr Solomon was dead.

Dave Bennet reached Kelso before Jake and me and was on his way to Stable Cottage, expecting to find Dr and Mrs Solomon already under arrest. I managed to reach him on his mobile — no small achievement in this part of the world — to inform him what had transpired in the last hour.

Dave was only minutes from Bamburgh and arrived shortly after our conversation, greeted at the cottage by the two Kelso officers and an ambulance crew who were on the point of moving Dr Solomon's body. The local officers had rung for the ambulance, and the paramedics confirmed that Arthur Solomon was dead.

Dave acted swiftly and declared the cottage a possible crime scene, and working with the Kelso PCs he began to preserve any evidence that may be pertinent as our investigation unfolded. He later told me that Elizabeth was sitting in a chair beside the window, arms wrapped tightly around her body as she rocked to and fro. She seemed to be staring at nothing, and when Dave asked a question it didn't register. Mrs Solomon appeared to have retreated into a private world, oblivious to reality.

Dave made the decision to dispatch the ambulance crew with Mrs Solomon, accompanied by one of the local officers, to the hospital. Then he called in the scene of crime officers. Elizabeth Solomon obviously needed medical help, but it was too late for the doctor. The paramedic's initial assessment was that the doctor had possibly suffered a massive heart attack, or a stroke. The SOCOs would still make a thorough search of the cottage, but it was expected that the autopsy would confirm the paramedic's initial opinion.

Jane was our priority now. After all she'd been through, I wondered how the news of Solomon's death would affect her. I need not have worried; she simply nodded as if the news was expected, but I suppose Solomon had suddenly become a stranger, someone who'd gained her love and loyalty by false means.

When Dave was back at the Kelso station, we prioritised our next moves. Elizabeth Solomon was safely at the local hospital, where a police officer would remain for the time being. His account of her state of mind suggested that a possible transfer to Leeds and admittance to their psychiatric unit was likely. There was little danger of Mrs Solomon absconding; we would talk to her in due course when a medical evaluation had been completed. I tasked Dave with ringing the DI with an update on the situation, while I could no longer put off ringing the Brysons.

Elise answered the phone, and as her parents were also there she switched to speaker mode so they could all hear my news.

'We have Grace, and she's fine! They'd taken her to a cottage in Bamburgh and from what I gather intended to go abroad from there. Dr Solomon appears to have suffered some kind of fatal heart attack, and Mrs Solomon is at the local hospital receiving treatment.' As I paused for breath there was an audible gasp from Elise, and Margaret groaned.

'When can we see Grace?' Elise asked.

'I understand how keen you are, but Grace has only learned the truth about her past this morning and it's been a tremendous shock. We'll be heading back to Leeds soon, where a social worker will be on hand to talk to her, then what happens in the short term will be Grace's decision. There's so much for her to take in that you'll have to be prepared to wait a while longer, I'm afraid. Meeting you might simply be too much at this time.' I could imagine how difficult this was for them and their patience would once again be tested, at least until Grace felt able to meet them.

Jane was given the all clear from the police doctor and was ready to return with us to Leeds. Jake sat in the back seat, with a protective arm draped around her shoulders and I was aware of occasional soft crying. We travelled in almost complete silence, and at one point I could see through the mirror that Jane was sleeping. The journey felt every bit as long as it had been that morning, possibly even more so as we contended with the rush hour traffic.

Having spoken to DI Wheatley, I knew that a social worker would be at the station to meet us and interview Jane. Just what the poor girl would want to do, I couldn't guess. The house in Carlton Wells was no place for her to go alone, and to take her to the Brysons' — who would justifiably argue that she belonged there — was also not an option. Putting her in some sort of care facility seemed totally inappropriate but might be what the social worker would suggest.

Eventually we arrived, and as I led the two young people through the station there were smiles and nods from colleagues; the news had spread quickly. We had at last found Grace Bryson, alive and well!

Finding a comfortable interview room, I took Jane inside and dug into my pocket for some money, giving Jake instructions to go to the canteen and buy sandwiches for all of us. Within ten minutes, a female social worker tapped on the glass panel of the door and entered, introducing herself as Lillian Simpson. Lillian was probably in her early forties, rather plump, with unruly greying hair that seemed to be recovering from a bad perm. However, she had a wide, genuine smile and her soft brown eyes were intelligent and friendly.

'Do you want me to leave?' I addressed my question to either or both of them.

Jane looked anxious and immediately replied no, and Lillian nodded encouragingly to show her willingness to my presence during their interview. Jake appeared in the doorway and gravitated towards Jane, who reached out to grasp his hand once more. I introduced my son to Ms Simpson and we sat in a little huddle, none of us at ease, with the exception perhaps of the social worker.

Lillian spoke softly to Jane, explaining that because she was only sixteen the social services child protection team had a duty to make sure that any provision initially made for her care was deemed suitable by them. She continued, 'Now, if you think you could tell me something about what's been happening over the last couple of days, it would be really helpful, and if you have any questions I'll try to answer them.'

Those smiling eyes punctuated her words, very caring, very maternal.

Jane briefly described how her 'parents' had suddenly put the house up for sale, then hurriedly packed up to go to Bamburgh, their holiday retreat.

Having declined to have the interview recorded, which would perhaps have been too intimidating, I was making mental notes. Jane recalled the events of the morning from the point when she found her mobile phone and the argument that ensued. Tears streamed down her cheeks as she described seeing the newspaper in the café and phoning Jake. Considering what a long, harrowing day it had been, Jane spoke clearly and accurately. It was almost seven in the evening.

Lillian glanced at the clock on the wall then said, 'You've had a difficult and tiring day, and I think our priority now is to find somewhere safe for you to stay tonight. I'm going to pop out for a few minutes to make some phone calls, then hopefully we'll get something sorted.'

Lillian left just as a constable was arriving with tea and coffee. I left the room briefly too, seeking out Dave Bennet. Unsurprisingly, he was at his computer.

'They bought the cottage in Elizabeth's maiden name — that's why I didn't find it!'

'Go home, Dave. You've done well today — we couldn't have solved this without you.' We'd all had a long day; I'd be glad to get home too.

'Will she be alright?' He waved his hand in the direction of Jane.

'In time I would say yes, but there's a lot for her to process — her whole world has just been exposed as a lie, and the poor girl doesn't know who she is anymore.'

Dave left and I returned to the interview room. Jake and Jane were eating sandwiches, and I grabbed one too.

'Dad, could Jane come and stay with us?'

The request didn't surprise me and the same idea had occurred to me, but I was unsure of the protocol in such a situation. I knew Sarah would have no objections, but what would Lillian Simpson think of such an idea? She soon returned and shuffled her ample rear end into a plastic bucket chair, as we were occupying the comfortable seats. I offered her mine, but she dismissed it with a wave of the hand.

'Well now, there's a bed available at a hostel not too far away. You could maybe have a few nights there until we can think of something more permanent.' Lillian was still smiling.

'What do you mean by more permanent?' Jake spoke up.

'It depends what happens really. There's no precedent for this rather unusual situation. Jane may want to move in with a member of her family, her real family that is, or perhaps remain in care until she's older, a foster home perhaps?'

I think we all balked at the latter option. Jake was itching to speak again but looked at me for permission. I nodded and he said, 'Jane could come and stay with us — we have the room, and I'm sure Mum won't mind.'

Lillian's eyebrows raised and she looked at me.

'We'd be delighted to have her with us. She's been a visitor to our home before, and we'll give her all the support she needs.'

Jane was sitting on the edge of her seat, nibbling on her nails, waiting, hoping.

'Is that what you want, Jane?' Lillian asked.

'Oh, yes, please. I don't want to go to a hostel ... or somewhere strange.'

'It is somewhat unusual, but I presume you've had a criminal records check, DS Priestly, and what about your wife?'

'Yes, everything's in order there too. Sarah helps at the local primary school, and they did a CRB check at the end of last year.'

'Well, if you'll excuse me, I'll just have to make another call.'

Lillian left the room again and I followed. I thought it prudent to ring George Wheatley for his approval before actually taking Jane home with us. Having absolutely no idea of what he would say, I was delighted when he declared it to be a great idea and actually thanked me. Another brief call alerted Sarah to the possibility of a guest and, as expected, there was certainly no objection to the idea.

Nearly an hour later and with everyone's approval, the three of us entered our home to a warm welcome from Sarah and Dan. Sarah showed our visitor to Jake's room, which she'd hastily prepared, and as I passed by on my way to the bathroom I heard loud sobbing and caught a glimpse of Jane being held by my wife as the fears and tensions of the day finally caught up with her.

Chapter 20

Margaret Bryson

The day I had never dared to hope would come has done so, and I can hardly believe it's true — Grace is alive! Jack Priestly rang to tell us they have found her; the girl living with the doctor and his wife really is our daughter, but we have to wait a while longer before we can see her. DNA samples will be taken from us to compare to Grace's, but Jack seems to think there is little doubt, that it is simply a formality.

My instinct is to seek out our daughter and hold her so tightly that she'll never be taken away again, to look into those eyes and be able to say how much we love and have missed her! But I know we must wait. The poor child has no memories of life with us. Dr and Mrs Solomon indoctrinated her with the belief that she really was their daughter. Such a despicable act of cruelty is beyond understanding; to steal a helpless child simply to replace their own dead daughter is abhorrent. I would normally feel empathy for a couple who lost their child, but their actions were utterly selfish and undeserving of any pity.

When I think of the years of despair we suffered, the agony of not knowing, thinking our daughter was dead, or imagining my beautiful Grace suffering at the hands of some monster, anger threatens to consume me. But I refuse to let it rule me, knowing that unchecked anger brings with it such ugly bitterness. I should at least be grateful that Grace's fate was not as wretched as we so often imagined.

I expected that this would be the best day of my life, but it is tainted by sadness and worry, anticipating the days to come. Questions intrude into my new-found happiness, and I am acutely aware that there is still a journey ahead, which could be fraught with all sorts of problems. I can only pray that we'll be able to bond with Grace and that she will grow to love us as we have always loved her.

And as for Elise, it is patently evident that motherhood will suit her: she is radiant and looks as if her world is now bathed in brilliance! The baby is due in three weeks' time. Hopefully we will have formed some kind of relationship with Grace by then, which would complete Elise's happiness as well as my own.

Being back in Leeds feels so strange; it is a place we were once so keen to escape from, but at least now there will be no suspicion hanging over our lives. It's so sad that people are always prepared to think the worst of you in a situation like ours, and at times it hurt bitterly.

Stephen and I have spent hours talking about what we should do if Grace wishes to live with us, which we hope will be the case. Although we're happily settled in Rouen, we would give it up in a heartbeat to move back here if that is what our daughter wants. The reasons we left are no longer valid, and the future holds so many more possibilities than it did only a couple of weeks ago.

As well as being closer to Elise and our first grandchild, I would also love to be nearer to Bea and Peter once again. Throughout the years they have been stalwarts, never doubting us as others have done, and understanding and caring for us at those times when we most needed them. Seeing them again these last few days and catching up with other friends has been a joy. I even seem to have reclaimed some of my past enthusiasm for life and hope it's not too late to build a new, happier one.

Jack promised to ring tomorrow, when hopefully he will have had a chance to talk to Grace and determine how she feels about meeting us. We will need to move slowly, and common-sense dictates that for our first meeting there should only be Elise, Stephen and me. Bea is dying to see her niece again, but the last thing we want to do is overwhelm her; so much has happened in a relatively short time frame, and Grace must surely be emotionally drained. We need to get to know each other all over again, slowly and without pressure or expectations. I don't even know how she will feel about us calling her Grace. Maybe she will wish to remain Jane?

Tonight I will sleep well, a rare occurrence for me, but I can relax completely now, knowing that my daughter is safe, and I pray that she too will be able to rest and regain strength for whatever tomorrow brings.

Chapter 21

Grace

I awoke in a strange room, and on opening my eyes the events of the last two days came flooding back, washing that awful sense of fear over me once again. Reluctant to get out of the warm mass of duvet, I gazed at my new surroundings. It was Jake's room, which somehow made it familiar, comfortable. A cork notice board displayed a handful of family photographs and memorabilia from a cup final he'd been to with Dan and their father.

What today would bring was impossible to imagine; this last week has been totally unbelievable, and there's a part of me that would like to opt out of the coming weeks, but I know that's not possible. While trying to sleep last night, my head was full of so many incomprehensible thoughts.

Dad is dead. How I feel about that I honestly don't know, because apparently I've never known the real Arthur Solomon. To me he was a loving father, kind and generous, a father who always made time for me, and I never doubted his love. But that father died even before I was told of Arthur Solomon's death. In fact, that man never existed at all; it was all a lie, a complete sham! And my mother was no better.

It's so good of Mr and Mrs Priestly to let me stay here, as we'd only met once before. But I feel adrift, and Jake is probably the only true friend I have — at least he doesn't lie, and I know he cares about what happens to me. Dan's okay too and didn't even blink an eye when it was suggested that Jake shared his room so I could sleep in here. They must have a pretty good relationship. I used to wish for a brother or a sister, and now apparently I have one. In fact, there's a whole family whom I have never been aware of! Jack says they are keen to meet me, but truthfully I'm a little afraid of meeting them. What if I'm a disappointment or we don't get along?

I don't even know what will happen to me in the future. Will I have to go and live with them just because I'm their daughter, even if we don't like each other? And will everyone start calling me Grace, which is apparently my true name? It's like being lifted out of one life and dropped into someone else's. I can understand the Brysons wanting me back, but I'm not the three-year-old they knew. Will they expect me to call them Mum and Dad?

A gentle tap on the door broke into my thoughts and Sarah quietly opened it, peering in to see if I was still sleeping. She smiled when I lifted my head from the pillow.

'It's nine o'clock, Jane, but you can sleep in if you like?'

'No, I'll get up, thank you. I don't want to be a nuisance.'

'You're certainly not that. I'm pleased to have you here, and you can stay as long as you like.' Sarah sat on the edge of my bed. 'The boys have left for college and Jack's off to work, so there's just the two of us and I have nothing planned for today.'

'Sarah, do you think I should call myself Grace now?'

Sarah smiled. 'I'd wondered that myself, but it's entirely your choice. I suppose we think of you as Jane because that's how we were introduced, but your family think of you as Grace. What would you prefer?'

'Grace, I think. From what Jack's told me, there once was a Jane Solomon who died — that's when they took me to replace her … and I don't think I want to have a dead girl's name.'

'Okay, Grace it is. That will please your family, but you'll have to forgive us when we forget and call you Jane, okay?'

'Do you know my real family, Sarah? What are they like?'

'I've met them once by chance. It must have been a couple of years after you disappeared, when Jack and I were in the city centre. We were introduced and Margaret, your mother, asked after our boys. I suddenly felt terribly guilty that my family was complete when they were so obviously still missing you. I saw them on the news broadcasts too of course, Stephen at the first appeal and both of them a year later. They seem to be lovely people. Jack has always had a soft spot for them and a tremendous respect for the way they handled themselves during those horrendous days when suspicion and accusations were flying all around them. We do actually still exchange Christmas cards — they were very appreciative of the way Jack handled the case.'

'I have a sister, too, don't I?'

'Yes, Elise. I've not met her, but she was the one who recognised you and started the search again.'

'How on earth did she recognise me? It's fourteen years since she saw me last.'

'I know, it's incredible, isn't it? She was in a department store in the city and saw you shopping. Elise followed you to the store entrance and spoke to you. You then apparently helped her when she felt a little unwell. Do you remember? It was three or four weeks ago?'

'Yes, of course! She was pregnant and I helped her to a seat and sat with her a while. So she's my sister?' I remembered the incident clearly, and the impression Elise left me with was certainly a good one. 'Do you know if she's had the baby yet, Sarah?'

'No, but it's imminent, I think. Elise came to Jack for help, and he went to Carlton Wells to visit the Solomons. They convinced him that you were Jane, which was easy really as they had a genuine birth certificate and photographs of a baby and a toddler; apparently you look very much like their little girl did.'

'Perhaps I ought to feel sorry for them, but I don't. They brought such pain to the Bryson family and although they treated me well, it was all lies. I honestly don't know how I feel about them.'

'Are you sure learning all this isn't too much for you? You can take a few days to process all these events, you know. Jack has plenty of other things to do at work.'

'No, I want to know everything. I need to know who I really am, and although it's a bit scary I'd like to meet my family soon. It's almost as if I know Elise, and I did like her when we talked.'

'That's a great start. Jack will be pleased. He's going to ring at about ten this morning to see if you're up to talking to him, but you don't have to do it today?'

'I think I do. Can I have a shower now? Then I'll be ready for his call.'

'Of course, help yourself. There are clean towels folded on the seat for you. I'll get the kettle on, and we can have a late breakfast.'

Jack and Sarah are such amazing people, and I think their offer of staying here as long as I like is genuine. Inside I feel quite torn, and I'd like to stay with Jake's family but I also have a strong desire to meet my real family. I wonder if we could do that today?

Chapter 22

Jack Priestly

Jane was still sleeping when I left for work. She must have been shattered after the events of the previous day, and there was no point in disturbing her. The questioning can wait a few more hours; after all, this case has taken fourteen years to solve and there are still gaps to fill in. The first task of the day is to update the DI on the details so far.

Wheatley was in his office when I arrived and greeted me with a smile, something he's not known for giving away readily.

'How are things with the girl, Jack?'

'She was sound asleep when I left, but I'll ring at about ten when I hope she'll be ready to answer some questions.'

'Good, but if you say Jane has no memories of the past, or what happened, she'll probably be of little help.'

DI Wheatley is right — Jane obviously has no memory of who she really is, so it's unrealistic to expect her to recall any details of the actual abduction.

'There may be a few clues from the years spent with the Solomons, things Jane would have thought irrelevant at the time, but might now have a different meaning.' I was grasping at straws. Dr Solomon was dead and his wife would probably be unable to answer any questions, for a while at least. When the DI was satisfied that he knew everything, I went to my desk to ring the Kelso police station and find out what had happened with regard to Elizabeth Solomon. Dave Bennet was again glued to a computer screen but looked up when he saw me.

'Message there from the lads at Kelso,' he told me, eyes already back on the screen. A post-it note was stuck to my desk with all the information I needed from them. Impressive for a small country station; I'd expected them to be fairly laidback, but they were certainly on the ball with this.

The note told me that an officer stayed most of the day with Elizabeth Solomon, but she was in no fit state to speak to anyone. The officer stood down when the hospital decided to move the patient to a secure unit at a hospital in Leeds, where I can attempt to question her myself. It seems unlikely, however, that I'll gain any useful information as the doctors initially talked about her withdrawing into some kind of psychotic state. My understanding of this is very basic, but I do know that it involves losing a grip on reality, something that didn't surprise me in the least. I'd ring the hospital later and try to arrange a visit.

It wasn't quite ten, but I decided to ring home to see if Jane was awake. Sarah answered and gave me a potted version of their earlier conversation. Jane was in the shower. It seemed that she wanted to give a full statement as soon as possible, and Sarah said she was also keen to meet the Brysons.

'She's tougher than you think, Jack. Shall I bring her down after we've eaten?'

'If she's up to it, yes, that'll be great. I'll ring social services — they'll probably want to be in on the interview, so perhaps we can get one of their child protection team to be here as the "appropriate adult".'

As luck would have it, Lillian Simpson took the call and was free to come herself. I was pleased to maintain the continuity for Jane's sake, and also I liked Lillian's manner; she was efficient while being realistically down to earth.

Things pulled together nicely, and by eleven-thirty that morning, Jane, Lillian, Dave Bennet and I were assembled in an interview room, coffee in front of us, to begin taking a formal statement. Before the tape was switched on, Jane informed us that she no longer wanted to be called Jane; her preference was to take her true name of Grace. I smiled inwardly, knowing exactly what that simple change would mean to the Brysons.

We began with routine questions, skipping over the name issue and the date of birth. The real Jane Solomon was born in July, but we were now dealing with Grace Bryson, who had no idea that she was actually born in August.

Grace confirmed that she'd been living in Carlton Wells and had no memories of any other home. She answered questions about Dr and Mrs Solomon, all the while her pale face reflecting the pain this caused. They'd treated her well and appeared to be a happy family, but because of what Grace now knew, those memories were marred by the fact that they'd been living a lie.

It was unlike any interview we had ever conducted, mainly because Grace asked almost as many questions as we did, but I was okay with that. She needed to know who she was, and the interview took the form of a conversation with each person contributing at times, even Lillian.

At one o'clock we took a break for lunch. Lillian asked if she and Grace could use the staff canteen, a shrewd move that would give an opportunity for her to talk to Grace alone. I pointed them in the right direction before going back to my desk to have a working lunch and catch up on some paperwork. I rang Sarah, who wanted to know when to come back for Grace, but as she'd expressed a desire to meet her family I suggested that Grace could come home with me, via Elise's house.

We resumed our interview at two and altered the focus to look at the future. Technically speaking, Grace was no longer a police concern, but there was no way I was going to hand her over to social services and forget about her. For me, this was not simply another case to work and solve. Over the last fourteen years it had become personal, the three-year-old Grace Bryson never completely out of my mind.

Now I'd been presented with a second chance and was determined to see this through to its conclusion, even if it was on my own time. It was strange how Grace had eventually come to me, through Jake of course, but it seemed as if fate intervened.

'Grace, do you have any thoughts on your immediate future?' Lillian asked. 'Someone you would want to go to, perhaps?'

'There's no one really.' She looked questioningly at me, and I smiled reassuringly.

'Grace can stay with us as long as she likes. It's a delight having her around, and I know Jake wants her to stay. Would you be happy with that?'

Grace nodded and smiled as if a weight was suddenly lifted from her shoulders.

'I'm grateful for your offer, Mr Priestly, and would certainly like to stay with you for a while. But perhaps when I meet my real family, they might expect me to stay with them?' The latter part of the sentence was formed as a question and one I could easily answer.

'Your parents are desperate to see you, and I know without doubt they'll want you to be with them. But we can take it slowly, give you all time to adjust and get to know one another before decisions are made. You do have options, Grace.'

The interview was rounded up before three that afternoon, and when I suggested that she might like to meet her family, Grace jumped at the chance. A quick call told me they were at home and overjoyed that their daughter wanted to meet them so soon. Before we left, a swab was taken from Grace and sent away to be compared to one already taken from Margaret and Stephen Bryson. It seemed a formality now — there was very little doubt that we had found their daughter.

On the relatively short journey, Grace asked countless questions, only some of which I could answer, before lapsing into a thoughtful silence until we pulled up outside Elise's home.

Chapter 23

Elise McDonald

Jack's phone call had an ambivalent effect on us all. Naturally, we welcomed the news that Grace wished to meet us so soon, but a nervous tension seemed to electrify the room. Would we disappoint her, would she like us? With only half an hour to prepare, we were all in a spin! Mum and Dad were still with me, Bea and Peter had gone home, and Simon was still at work. It was perfect, exactly how we wanted it; meeting three family members was more than enough for a girl whose whole world had suddenly been tipped upside down.

That half an hour seemed so much longer than thirty minutes, and I became an unashamed curtain twitcher, my attention shifting from the window to the clock and back again so many times that my neck ached. Mum and Dad were anxious too. Earlier in the day, we'd covered all the 'what if' questions we could think of, and now that Grace was actually on the way to meet us we'd exhausted all reasonable possibilities regarding how this meeting would go. I suppose I had the advantage of having met Grace before, but I wondered now how she would remember that incident. With hindsight, it would almost certainly seem contrived, and she may possibly resent my duplicity. Soon … we would know very soon.

'They're here!' I shouted. My voice sounded strange, croaky and raspy.

Jack's car pulled up in front of the house, and I watched as he and Grace got out. My parents were peering over my shoulder, straining to catch the first glimpse of their long lost daughter. I felt my face colour up, whereas Mum's had gone pale. Dad was unreadable, his expression grave, worried about the outcome.

I let the curtains drop back into place, not wanting Grace to see us staring. Jack steered her through the gate and down the path, where I opened the door to welcome what would surely be a complete new chapter of our lives!

Grace appeared tired, although she attempted a smile when our eyes met. Three weeks ago, when I first saw my sister, she was a picture of health and happiness, but now the events of the last few days were reflected in a different, rather jaded appearance. Dark circles outlined those blue eyes, and the confidence and energy of youth appeared to have deserted her.

As I opened the door wider to allow them to enter, Grace moved slowly into the hall where Mum and Dad were waiting. No one knew what to say. Tears were glistening in Mum's eyes and I could tell she longed to hold Grace in her arms, yet restrained herself as we all did, trying not to be overwhelming.

I watched as Mum and Grace held each other's gaze, two pair of identical eyes saying more than any words could at that tender moment. Grace moved closer to Mum and then suddenly the two were in each other's arms, tears flowing from them both. A lump in my throat prevented me from speaking. I think Dad felt the same, and even Jack looked as if he was holding back tears. He was the one to speak first.

'I'm going to wait in the car, Grace, to give you all a chance to get to know each other again. I'll be there if you want me.'

Jack returned to the car. I don't think any of us would have minded him staying — he was very much a part of our lives and we owed him so much, but I appreciated his sensitivity.

Having prepared a tray for coffee, I brought it into the lounge to serve my family. 'My family' — the words had an almost melodic sound to them, well rounded and finally complete. For the last fourteen years, I'd only referred to 'my parents,' and it is so satisfying being a family again. The three of us are now four; our symmetry is restored.

Conversation was rather stunted at first, polite but certainly not flowing. I think we all wanted to drink in the moment, look at each other and simply enjoy being together. It was probably most difficult for Grace, who had questions but initially was wary of asking them. My first question to her was to ask if we should call her Jane or Grace. The reply came without hesitation and delighted us all. In adopting her real name, she was identifying with us and I hoped this good start would bode well for our future relationship.

'Would it be too painful to tell me what happened on the day I disappeared?' Her question was directed at Dad.

'Now that we know you're safe it's not a problem, but we can really only tell you what happened from our experience. We still seem no nearer to finding who actually took you from the garden, and I don't suppose you have any memories?'

'Sorry but no, I can't remember that far back, or anything from before I started school really. I think Jack's working on that now, but if they couldn't find out who it was at the time it's probably even harder now.'

Dad began to relate the details of that horrendous day, giving a very brief account, which Grace had probably already heard from Jack. I think we all wanted to discuss the future, but none of us were brave enough to address that particular subject.

'How is it staying with the Priestlys?' I asked.

'Fine — they're great people. I'd only met them once before, when Jake took me home for a meal last week. I think that's when Jack knew who I really was, when I told him that we were putting the house up for sale and how suddenly it had all happened. Sarah says I can stay there as long as I like, but I wouldn't want to take advantage of their kindness. Tomorrow Jack's taking me to Carlton Wells to get some clothes and things. I've still got my key.'

'I have some photographs, Grace, if you'd like to see them?' Mum looked hopeful as Grace nodded enthusiastically. They were in a large box — photographs of me as a child and of Grace in her first three years. Mum passed them over one at a time and watched her daughter's reaction as she held them and studied each one. Perhaps they were both too emotional to comment. For almost five minutes, there was complete silence in the room.

After all the images had been seen, Dad was the one to break the silence.

'We know that this is still very strange for you, Grace, and we don't want to push you into any decisions until you're ready, but have you thought about your immediate future?'

'I've been thinking of nothing else! It seems sensible to stay with the Priestlys for a few days at least, but after that I honestly don't know. I want to get back to college soon before I've missed too much, and obviously I can go with Jake. Tomorrow, after we've been to Carlton Wells, I'm meeting the social worker again, supposedly to discuss my future. On Thursday, I have an appointment to see a doctor to see about a referral for counselling. Everything's happening so quickly.'

'You don't have to do anything you're not ready for, or comfortable with. I only asked because we want you to know that there's a home for you with us, should you feel you would like that,' Dad said gently. 'We've spent fourteen years wishing you were still with us — naturally we love you and want you back. But you are also a young woman now, not the child we lost, and the decision is yours.'

I felt compelled to make a similar offer. 'There's a room here for you, too — you will always be more than welcome.'

Tears welled up and began to spill down Grace's face. Mum instinctively put an arm around her and Grace leaned onto her shoulder. A relationship was now not simply a distant hope but a strong possibility, and the seed was growing already. My sister was home where she belonged.

Chapter 24

Jack Priestly

While Grace was visiting with her family, I took the chance to make a couple of phone calls. The first one was to Dave Bennet, who was co-ordinating the details of a search of both the Carlton Wells property and the cottage at Bamburgh. There would be nothing tangible relating to the actual abduction fourteen years ago, but we were looking for documentation, anything from the past that may throw light on the logistics of how Grace was actually abducted and whether or not they had an accomplice.

The search would be early the next morning, when Dave would take a uniformed constable to the Bamburgh cottage and I would co-ordinate another team at Carlton Wells. If Solomon had paid an accomplice, there may be paperwork that would help to identify him, or her, I suppose. It was often the case that abductors used a woman to help, as children tend to be more trusting of women.

Dave also told me that the DNA results were in, and as expected Grace's DNA matched Margaret and Stephen Bryson. After a brief progress report, the next call was to Leeds Infirmary to enquire about Elizabeth Solomon's condition and the possibility of an early interview. From the switchboard I was directed to the sister in charge of the mental health department, a self-contained unit within the grounds of Leeds Infirmary. Elizabeth was an in-patient and, the sister told me, currently unable to have visitors. I did, however, get the name of the consultant in charge, whom I could ring later to explain what we needed. This wasn't going to happen immediately, and it was obvious that even if Elizabeth was fit to answer questions, her fragile mental state would make those answers unreliable.

Glancing at Elise's home and wondering what was happening inside, I couldn't begin to imagine how I would feel in the same predicament as Grace. She would have to 'learn' to be Grace Bryson now that it was clear she is not Jane Solomon. Such a massive change is thoroughly daunting, and although Grace appeared to be a very intelligent and strong young lady, it was going to take time and tenacity to get through the next few weeks.

Events were moving quickly, and I was aware that Grace would go through so much turmoil and would be pulled in one direction and then another. When the story hit the newspapers, it would bring an avalanche of media interest and everyone would want a piece of Grace Bryson. It was understandable really — a girl who was kidnapped and believed dead suddenly turns up alive and well fourteen years later; even I would want to read about that one.

While looking at the house and imagining the conversations, or lack of them, inside, the door opened and Grace came out, followed by the Brysons. I jumped from the car and went to meet them and give the news that the DNA samples matched. It was the seal on what we already knew and ruled out any alternative explanations. The family said their goodbyes with hugs that seemed perfectly natural, and as we drove away Grace watched and waved to her parents and sister until they were out of sight.

'How did it go?'

'Quite well, I think. They are lovely people; I really like them.'

I smiled, relieved for them all, and then left Grace to her thoughts for the rest of the journey.

Jake was waiting anxiously for our return and almost knocked us over in an attempt to hug Grace. I was proud of my son — he was looking after her in such a responsible, mature way. Sarah had a meal ready. I was incredibly hungry and sure that Grace would be too. As we ate I was determined not to ask any more questions, and my family seemed resolved to do the same. The atmosphere was pleasant with only general conversation, and some of the tension seemed to disappear from our guest's demeanour. She briefly once again became an ordinary teenager, having a meal with her boyfriend's family.

As the following morning dawned, the respite of the previous evening dissipated and the tasks and duties of the day crowded in once more. I left early to meet a couple of officers at Carlton Wells, and Sarah was bringing Grace there later on. Her reaction to going back to Carlton Wells was difficult to gauge. Over breakfast, she asked me what sort of things she should get from the house and if this would be the last time she would ever go there. I suggested getting only essentials for now, as we could go back again another day. Obviously Grace needed fresh clothes, having been wearing Sarah's borrowed ones for the last two days.

The next question was about what would happen to the house. When there's no precedent for a case, it's difficult to give an answer. I asked who the Solomons' solicitor was, and she gave me the name of a legal practice in the city. Another task was now added to the lengthy list, as I added contacting the solicitors to advise them of the doctor's death and Elizabeth's incapacity. I told Grace not to worry, as all would be taken care of in time. Secretly I was hoping that the solicitor held a valid will for the doctor and would be able to assist in the practical issues of the property and the care of Elizabeth.

Approaching the village, my thoughts were jumping about on all the loose ends this case had thrown up. It was certainly a learning curve for me, and I wondered how much more so it would be for Grace, who was burdened with all the emotional baggage too.

After parking outside the gate of Garden House, I sat for a few moments to collect my thoughts. A police car pulled up behind me with a couple of uniformed officers, and we left our cars to begin the task in hand. Grace had provided keys and I opened the door to begin the search.

Starting on the first floor, we found a box room containing a small desk and a few shelves full of books, everything neat and tidy. The decor was rather chintzy with wallpaper covered in huge peony roses, which to me felt overpowering, almost oppressive. A woman's room for certain, but was it Elizabeth Solomon's or Grace's?

I asked one of the PCs to begin there in the hope that we'd be done with the upstairs before Sarah arrived with Grace. The second PC I tasked with a sweep of the bedrooms. I took the downstairs study, the doctor's sanctuary, expecting that to be the likely source of the material we were looking for.

The doctor was certainly methodical. I began with the desk. From a cursory glance around the room, it seemed pretty much the same as it did on my last visit, maybe with a few photographs missing but nothing else of importance, other than a laptop computer, which was previously on the desk.

I sat in Dr Solomon's chair and pulled open the top drawer on the right-hand side. It was a shallow space filled with pens, paperclips and other office essentials. The drawer below it was locked with no key in sight. Trying the left-hand side, I found two deeper drawers that were also locked. I left them for the moment and picked up a desk diary for 2014. Reading it proved no help at all; it was a social diary with dates for future golfing days and a few work-related entries.

I moved next to some box files on the shelves, pulling out two, one marked 'Finance' and the other 'Receipts'. The financial one contained bank statements going back about ten months, and the second held mainly utility bills. Everything seemed up to date and methodically filed away. Another box file was filled with paperwork relating to investments, shares and saving accounts.

I stacked all three boxes near the door to take back to the station for closer scrutiny. At least we now had the name of Solomon's bank, although Grace could probably have told us that.

PC Garret returned from the box room.

'It appears to be the daughter's room, sir. Homework assignments, exercise books, that kind of thing. Where next?'

'Have a scout around the downstairs rooms and gather up any documentation to take back to the station.'

Garret went off to the reception rooms and PC Drayton appeared in the doorway.

'Out buildings next,' I told him. 'Anything out of the ordinary that catches your eye, bag it and bring it here.'

Once alone, I turned my attention to the desktop computer. It was an old model, and there was little doubt in my mind that we would find more interesting and recent things on the doctor's laptop. I didn't even bother to switch it on. Dave could have the pleasure of searching it.

After a couple of hours, we'd almost finished the search when Grace arrived with Sarah. I could sense that it was difficult for her to be in the place she'd once called home, the house in which she'd felt safe and happy. She was viewing it with different eyes now. Sarah stood close and squeezed Grace's arm.

'Do you want me to come up with you?' she asked.

Grace shook her head. 'I'll be fine.'

'Before you go, would you know where Doctor Solomon kept the keys to the desk drawers?'

Grace went to the windowsill and turned a little blue jug upside down, and a set of keys fell out. I thanked her, and she moved quietly to the hall and up the stairs. Instinctively, I knew there would be nothing of interest in the drawers if he kept the keys in such an obvious place and one that Grace knew. Still, I went through the motions of a search as Sarah moved back into the hall, admiring the house.

'If you wanted a house like this, you should have married a doctor, not a policeman.' I grinned at my wife.

'That's just what I was thinking!' Sarah returned my smile.

Grace packed two large suitcases in ten minutes flat and I went upstairs to carry them down for her.

'Have you got everything you need?'

'Yes, I've put a few books in too, school stuff, you know? My laptop and iPad aren't here. I suppose he took them to the cottage.'

'Dave Bennet's over there now; he'll bring them back with him, but we'll have to check the laptop out before you can have it back — sorry.'

I could tell by the weight of the suitcases that there was more than just a few clothes inside, and I got Garret to take them to Sarah's car. We were done, but I asked Grace if she wanted to see anyone before we left, the next door neighbour, perhaps? She shook her head without even considering it; meeting people now as Grace Bryson was going to be awkward to say the least.

Chapter 25

Grace

I think the part of the brain that handles emotions must have stopped functioning for me. Going into the house left me feeling cold. I have a strange stillness inside, as if detached from reality. Not that I even know what reality is anymore.

The events of the last few days have been incredible, and all I feel is numb. Getting out of bed each morning is an effort — Jake's bed, which has perhaps now become my one place of safety, where I go to shut out the world and try to work out who I really am. But DNA doesn't lie, and I know in my head that I truly am Grace Bryson and that I was taken from home on my third birthday to be brought up as Jane Solomon.

In my heart I'm confused. Do I have to learn how to be Grace? Will my new family have expectations? They keep saying they love me, but as yet I can't say that I love them because I don't know them. Margaret and Stephen seem like great people, and I know they've suffered years of agony because of me. Elise is really nice too, but my love for them simply doesn't exist yet and I feel it's expected of me.

And then there's the Solomons. A couple of weeks ago, I would readily have said they are my parents and I love them, but now I'm no longer Jane Solomon and never have been, except in the Solomons' crazy fantasy world. Arthur's dead. A couple of weeks ago, this would have been devastating — I'd be shedding tears, genuine tears of sadness. But now it's hard to define my feelings. It's hard to grieve for a man I never really knew, a man who lied to me for the whole of my life.

And then there's Elizabeth, a woman I thought was my mother, who was kind and affectionate and whom I loved more than anyone else! But she must have been in on all these lies from the beginning; she was the one to stay with me and care for me, feeding me those daily lies to keep up the pretence. Perhaps her love was genuine, but it was certainly not for me — it was for her daughter Jane *and I am not Jane!*

You can't have love at the expense of someone else. Couldn't they see that? How could such intelligent people put another family through so much pain, especially as they knew first-hand what it is like to lose a child?

So, here I am, Grace Bryson. A name that makes me part of a family I don't know, an unfamiliar name. But I never really was Jane Solomon. It was pretence, a sham; my whole life was a lie. The real Jane Solomon is dead, and I have only ever been a replacement to her parents.

Things feel a little more settled now that I have some of my own clothes and Jake has emptied a few drawers for me to use. The Priestlys have been wonderful, and I don't know what would have happened without their generosity. I would probably be in some kind of hostel or children's home, and they really seem to mean it when they say I can stay as long as I like.

It's probably time to go back to college now, but even that seems a bit daunting; everyone will know what's happened to me, and the last thing I want to do is answer all their questions. It's been so strange having those photographs splashed all over the papers, but thanks to Jack and Sarah the press don't know where I'm living. That suits me fine; I don't want to be an object of curiosity, or someone to be pitied and whispered about. I know not everyone will treat me like that, but I'm still going to feel self-conscious going back to college, even with Jake by my side.

After the outing to Carlton Wells, Sarah took me shopping in Leeds and we had lunch out together. No one recognised me, which was good, and for a couple of hours I felt quite normal. But now I have a new dilemma. Jack has asked me to consider visiting Elizabeth with him. Apparently he spoke to the consultant at the infirmary and was told that she may never be able to answer his questions. The consultant suggested she may open up if someone close to her was to visit, and sadly there's only me who fits into that category.

Jack asked on returning from work, and he also had my iPad with him. DC Bennet has finished with it and hasn't found anything that would be useful to their investigations. I could have told him that — no one uses it except me. So, I feel connected again. The laptop may take longer. They won't find anything on that either, but I suppose they have their procedures.

The first thing I did after dinner tonight was to check out Facebook. There were so many messages from friends — true friends who want to help. It was slightly overwhelming, and the only thing I could do was to post a general message to thank them all for their concern and let them know I'll be back at college soon.

Several of the messages asked what I wanted to be called, so I changed my name on my Facebook Profile to make it clear that I was going by my true name, Grace Bryson. Perhaps this is the start of a new life for me, and time to let Jane Solomon rest in peace.

Chapter 26

Jack Priestly

Before going to bed last night, Grace agreed to come with me today to visit Elizabeth Solomon. It can't have been an easy decision, and it's a brave thing to do for someone who's been through so much. The hospital suggested that late morning was probably the best time to visit, but they also warned that it was unlikely we would get any answers to our questions.

Parking at the infirmary was horrendous, not to mention expensive, and it took three laps of cruising around the huge parking area before we saw someone driving out of a bay and nipped into it.

Grace was quiet throughout the drive and rather pensive, but after getting out of the car and heading for the psychiatric unit she asked what information I was hoping to get from Elizabeth. I noticed that she now referred to the Solomons by their names; it appeared that to Grace they were no longer parents, and I silently agreed that they certainly did not deserve those loving, intimate titles.

'What I'm trying to do is piece together the events of the day you were taken. I've always thought that the doctor must have been working with an accomplice, but perhaps it was only Elizabeth, who at the very least consented to the abduction. It doesn't feel right that this was an opportunist crime, and the fact that your age and appearance matched their daughter's so well rules that out in my book. It must have been planned.'

Grace nodded, thoughtfully. 'It would make your life so much easier if only I could remember, wouldn't it?'

'You were only three; hardly anyone has memories that far back, at least not complete ones. It may be that one day you will remember something, but don't worry about it — I'm sure we'll find out everything in time.'

The unit was well away from the huge sprawling hospital, an attractive, newer, single-storey building set in its own small garden. A notice on the doors asked us to ring the bell for attention, and then a crackling disembodied voice asked who we were. The doors were unlocked and we walked in. Although it was not part of the main hospital, there was still that distinctive smell of an institution, which I suppose was very hard to overcome. Grace seemed a little apprehensive and nervous.

'You don't have to do this, Grace; I can still go in alone if you like?'

'No, I'll be fine. I think having me with you might encourage her to talk, and I want to help.'

I squeezed her shoulder. She was a strong young woman, and I found myself hoping that the relationship with Jake would survive and blossom.

The four wings of the building were set out around a square courtyard area with floor-to-ceiling windows on the inside of each of the blocks, a design that offered as much natural light as possible. The first block housed the main entrance with a small reception room, where we waited to state our business. A young woman looked up from her keyboard and came toward us.

'Mr Thompson would like a word before you see Mrs Solomon. He's in the office on the right there. Please just go in; he'll be expecting you.'

I knocked on the door, then opened it a fraction. The consultant was indeed expecting us. Grace tugged my jacket as I walked inside.

'Should I wait out here?' She looked rather apprehensive now that we were actually about to see Mrs Solomon — understandable really, after everything that had transpired over the last few days.

It was probably a good idea for me to see the consultant alone, so I nodded and Grace moved away to wait in the corridor, sitting awkwardly on a red plastic chair, hands in her lap and head down. It did cross my mind that she might have a change of heart and run out of the building, but I should have known better. Grace would keep her word and go through with this, difficult though it might be.

The consultant was a wiry little man, no more than five foot five I would guess, and prematurely balding, which seemed to make his head look almost too large for his body, but his smile was genuine as he offered me a seat. The room was uncomfortably warm, and Mr Thompson was in shirt sleeves that had wet patches under the arms. He got straight to the point and asked me what I was hoping to achieve from this visit, just as Grace had asked a few minutes earlier. My reply was pretty much the same as before: to find out exactly what had happened on the day of the abduction, fourteen years ago.

Mr Thompson nodded thoughtfully, his arms resting on the desk, fingers laced together. He was well versed in the details of the abduction, both from what I'd shared previously and from the media. There was probably not a household within a fifty-mile radius that did not know the story of the abduction and subsequent finding of Grace Bryson.

'Mrs Solomon has said nothing which could pass as coherent since arriving. True, she is more stable now that we have her on medication, fluoxetine, a mild antidepressant, and lorazepam, an anti-anxiety drug. It's still early days, and the medication may be increased or even changed when we see how effective it is.'

'Grace is with me, Mr Thompson; I'm hoping her presence might prompt a reaction from Mrs Solomon — is that okay with you?'

'Yes, it's probably a good idea, but I would like to be present too. If there is a reaction, it may help us in making a more accurate diagnosis, although having read her medical history I am almost certain that she is suffering from post-traumatic stress disorder. That was the diagnosis last time she was an in-patient, in Newcastle I think it was. It seems to have returned, prompted no doubt by the death of her husband and of course the other related events. It seems likely that the previous PTSD was never fully addressed, and this episode is a recurrence or a regression into the same state as before.'

The doctor stood to go and I followed him from the office, relieved to see Grace waiting for us. Mr Thompson shook hands with her.

'It's good to meet you, Grace, and I admire your bravery in helping DS Priestly. I'll be attending the interview as well, and hopefully Mrs Solomon will be a little more lucid than previously.'

The consultant led the way down the corridor with short but purposeful strides as we followed on. Turning a corner we began to pass by a series of rooms, some occupied, some empty. The last door on the right was ajar, and Mr Thompson paused to smile at us before pushing it open and entering the room.

Elizabeth Solomon sat in a chair by the window, arms wrapped tightly around her body, rocking slowly backwards and forwards. She didn't register our entry into the room but remained in her own silent world, even when addressed. Her appearance had changed quite dramatically since I last saw her. Hunched shoulders and unkempt hair gave the impression of one so much older than her years, nothing like the woman I'd encountered at Carlton Wells.

Grace's eyes widened as she too noticed the change.

'Elizabeth, there are some visitors here for you.'

The doctor moved two chairs to the other side of the window, at an angle where we could see and be seen by Mrs Solomon. I took one chair and Grace the other. Mr Thompson moved back to the door to observe and be on hand if needed.

'Hello, Elizabeth, how are you?' My words were not acknowledged. 'Jane has come to see you.' Still no response. We remained in silence for a few moments, and then I tried again. 'Is there anything we can get for you, a drink perhaps?'

I looked at the doctor who shrugged; it was as he expected. Another silence was broken by Grace, who leaned over to touch Elizabeth's arm.

'How are you, Mother?'

I was a little surprised; we hadn't discussed what we would say, and I realised that Grace called her 'mother' in an attempt to reach into Elizabeth's solitary world. A few more minutes of silence passed before Mr Thompson came closer.

'Shall we have a little walk to the day room, Elizabeth?'

He took her hand and she stood obediently, allowing him to manoeuvre her out of the room as we followed in a slow procession. Elizabeth shuffled — there was no other word to describe it — and it made her seem even older. She didn't seem to notice anyone or anything about her surroundings and complied with the doctor like an automaton.

Again, we sat in a group of chairs in one corner of the room, but although there was no window for Elizabeth to stare out of she still avoided eye contact, looking down into her lap, arms still hugging her body with fingers clawing into her arms. I tried to get her attention and Grace did too, but there was nothing; she didn't even register that we were there.

It seemed pointless to stay, so we stood to leave. I wondered if the medication contributed to that distant look and if she might improve in the future. I would ask Mr Thompson before we left.

As the three of us began to move away, Elizabeth suddenly said, 'I'm so sorry, Jane.'

I looked at the others to see if they heard it too. It seemed they had and were as surprised as me. Elizabeth had spoken, but still there was no eye contact. The words were addressed to Grace, but she was unable to look her in the eye.

Grace sat down again and taking the older woman's hand asked, 'Why are you sorry, Mother?'

There was no answer. The only response came in the form of tears, which slowly trickled down Elizabeth's cheeks.

Chapter 27

Elise McDonald

Events have been moving swiftly, and my son decided he did not want to be left out. The afternoon after being reunited with Grace, I knew that labour had begun. Dismissing the first few pains as cramps, I laid down to rest after lunch, but when the pain increased Simon rang the maternity ward for advice. My due date was almost another two weeks away, so they told us to wait a few more hours to see if the pain eased and if it didn't to make my way to the hospital.

Almost as soon as Simon put the phone down my waters broke, confirming that this was really it! As my husband dashed around collecting together the things I should have prepared days ago, I rang my mother. Naturally, Mum wanted to come to the hospital with us, but thinking it could be tomorrow before anything happened I put her off, promising that Simon would keep them posted.

We clambered into the car and I concentrated on breathing correctly to control the pain and let Simon do the panicking, as he seemed to be anxious enough for both of us. Surviving Simon's erratic driving, we arrived at the hospital at around five-thirty.

After booking in and an initial examination, we were told that it could still be several hours before our son made an entrance into the world. Simon went to the hospital restaurant to buy sandwiches and coffee and to ring both sets of parents to update them with the news. I was alone in a two-bedded room right next door to the delivery suite. The room felt clean and comfortable without that strong antiseptic smell hospitals so often have.

I could hear the patient in the delivery room shouting, apparently at her husband, and when Simon came back he grimaced at the noise and asked if I was going to be that bad. I had no idea and told him so, just as a nurse put her head round the door to see if I was alright.

'Take no notice of the noise — some mothers find that a good old shout helps. Of course, if it was men who had the babies, there would never be more than one child in a family!'

Simon rolled his eyes. At that point, I think he was more apprehensive than me.

A doctor came to check on my progress, and I was wired up to a monitor while Simon ate his sandwich. He did offer me one, but I'd have probably thrown it at him if I took one. The contractions grew steadily stronger and more frequent, and at eleven-thirty I was moved into the delivery room with Simon holding my hand and looking decidedly pale. So far, I'd managed to control the pain with the breathing techniques learned at ante-natal classes but was grateful for the gas and air to help.

Undignified is hardly the word to describe childbirth; being flat on my back with my legs raised up in stirrups was an embarrassing pose to say the least. The midwife kindly suggested that if I was uncomfortable, I could try turning over on all fours. The pain was certainly a bittersweet experience, and I tried to focus on the fact that very soon we would meet our son and it would all be worth it.

At three thirty-five in the morning, our son was born. The midwife asked Simon if he would like to cut the cord, which seemed to surprise him, but he did as she directed and then beamed with pride. I didn't think I could ever feel so happy —

not only had our longed-for son arrived, but Grace had been found too. Life couldn't get much better than this; we couldn't stop grinning like a pair of Cheshire cats.

Thinking there was still a couple of weeks to go, we hadn't decided on a name so the nurse wrote 'Baby McDonald' on the tags. Simon decided to ring our respective parents, even though it was so late, or should that be early? I was sure they would be waiting for news and even if they had managed to sleep, would certainly not mind being woken up.

When Simon came back, bringing our families' love and good wishes, I'd decided on a name other than Baby McDonald and hoped he would agree.

'How do you feel about calling our son Jack?' I searched his face for a clue to his thoughts.

Simon paused for a moment before saying, 'I like it. I presume it's after Jack Priestly?'

'Yes, he's done so much for our family, and if our son grows up to be like his namesake, I'll be very proud.'

Simon agreed and then kissed me. Tiredness was catching up with us both, and my husband left the hospital to try and grab a few hours' sleep while I settled down too. Baby Jack was placed on my breast as soon as he'd been cleaned up. 'Skin to skin' the midwife kept repeating, good for bonding, but he was asleep now beside my bed in a little plastic crib. I turned to lie on my side where I could see him, to wonder at the miracle of birth and rest peacefully knowing that my family was at last complete.

I managed only a couple of hours of sleep before the constant activity of the hospital woke me up. I was now in a ward with seven other beds, most of them occupied. A young nurse helped me get up to visit the bathroom, and then it was time to feed Jack again.

I hoped Simon managed to get more sleep than me. I was keen to see him again. It was only a few hours since we'd been together, but being positively bursting with happiness I wanted to share it with him and our wider family. It was only seven a.m., but the nurse said that I could be discharged as soon as the doctor had seen me.

At nine a.m. Simon arrived, claiming to have had some sleep, but the bags beneath his eyes told me otherwise. He was as excited as I was and couldn't wait to get Jack and me home. The doctor was on the ward by then too and stopped at my bed to check if we were set to go. Reading the notes at the bottom of the bed, he seemed satisfied that all was well, and after reminding me that I could ring the ward for advice any time if needed and that the midwife would be visiting tomorrow, gave me the all clear to leave.

Tiredness was trumped by excitement when we arrived home, and my first task was to ring my parents and then Grace. I would happily have had an open house for all to visit, but my mother's sense prevailed and she insisted that they would only come for ten minutes, maximum and then we had to rest. My sister (oh how I love those words) was so pleased when we spoke on the phone and agreed to visit the next day. I then rang Bea, who would also visit tomorrow. She was baking and no doubt would arrive with enough food to feed us and all our visitors for the next few days.

I was so keen to show off my son to everyone that Simon needed to rein me in. All our visitors, however, were sensitive to our needs, and no one stayed for long. My parents were the first to come, both with tears in their eyes as they gazed at little Jack, a name they both approved of.

'He's exactly like you were, well, apart from the obvious!' Mum laughed.

I hadn't seen my parents looking so happy for years. For us, finding Grace now put an end to the years of sadness and not knowing — we could at last move on and dare to be happy again. For Grace, however, the nightmare was just beginning. It was difficult to imagine how she must feel; the world she'd inhabited and loved suddenly disintegrated along with the couple she'd known as parents, who'd provided the only security she knew. True, she had us now, but up until a few days ago Grace didn't even know of our existence.

It would take time, but we had all the time in the world. As Grace's true family, I was confident that our love would support her and she would survive this difficult time and one day feel as if she truly belonged with us.

Chapter 28

Margaret Bryson

Last night I became a grandmother! My grandson is almost two weeks early, but a healthy weight at six pounds three ounces. Life has been so strange for Elise lately, and it's not surprising the baby's put in an early appearance. I certainly approve of their choice of name. Jack Priestly has been a true friend to our family throughout some of the most difficult of times, and even now we have him to thank for finding Grace.

Elise came home only hours after the delivery — things have certainly changed since my two girls were born. I can say 'my girls' now without the pain it used to bring. Grace is with us again, and although it will take time I'm sure we will be able to build a relationship.

When I first saw her, I understood why Elise was so certain of her identity. Grace shares some of my features and Elise's but also has Stephen's bone structure — a true Bryson, unmistakable. Finding her is most certainly a miracle.

Over the years, I've experienced both periods of hopefulness and of despair. I was advised by some to accept that my daughter was dead and to move on with life, but how could I when we never actually knew what had happened? As the years went by, I did try to accept that our daughter was never coming home, but deep inside there was always that tiny seed of hope, which at times I cherished and clung to, though the stark reality of the world we live in often snatched that hope from me.

At times I became almost obsessed with news items of other children who had disappeared and imagined a place where they were all together, waiting to be found. Yet I knew it was merely a fantasy, and when some of these children were found, dead or alive, I almost envied their families for the knowledge they had about their child's fate when we had none. Closure they call it, don't they? But now we have Grace back, I've held her in my arms and although the relationship is as fragile as a gossamer thread, we can build on it. She needs us and has no one else now, so we will be there for her and I'm certain it will all work out in time.

Our years of heartbreak are over, but for Grace, the most difficult period of her life is only just beginning. The Solomons stole our daughter from us, but they also stole Grace's identity. Bringing her up as their own child was a falsehood, which duped Grace into believing she was someone else. They lied to her each time they called her Jane.

Over the last few days, Stephen and I have talked much about the future, and we've decided to move back here to be near our family. Leeds no longer seems hostile to us, and we can hold our heads high, having been vindicated and proven to be innocent of a crime that we never committed but which many people believed we had.

Perhaps we can keep the house in Rouen as a family holiday home. Renting it out for part of the season will help to fund it and as our family has suddenly grown, we could all benefit from the property that Stephen and I have come to love. We'll find a new home here near to Elise, and then I can be a true doting grandmother and a mother to both Elise and Grace. I've missed my sister too; it will be good to see more of Bea and Peter — we always had a strong bond with them, which we can build on once again and share this new period in our lives with those we love.

Baby Jack is absolutely gorgeous, but then all new babies are. When I held him in my arms it was like holding Elise again, he is so like she was as a baby. Our lives are now complete with a grandson and our daughter back with us. I feel as if I might burst with emotion — we never expected to feel this happy again. Life has a strange way of twisting and turning along roads we least expect to travel, but now for us our journey can be travelled with joy.

Chapter 29

Jack Priestly

Sarah received a phone call from Margaret Bryson, sharing the family's good news and she rang me at work to tell me that Elise had had her baby. Initially I was confused, knowing that there was another two weeks or so to go. I wondered if there was a problem, but my wife reassured me that all was well, which came as a great relief. Elise and her family have been through so much, and it was unthinkable that more tragedy should befall them.

Sarah then told me the second reason for her call — Elise and Simon had decided to name their son Jack, after me. It was such an honour that I didn't feel I really deserved. True, we'd once again drawn close as we did in those dark times after Grace was taken, but I was only doing my job. It was quite humbling and spurred me on to find out exactly what had happened on the day of Grace's third birthday.

The visit to Elizabeth Solomon proved fruitless and the consultant, Mr Thompson, was unable to give any kind of prognosis. The fact that Elizabeth had experienced similar trauma previously seemed to suggest that any recovery may only be temporary, or at the very best, incomplete. The loss of her husband and the other events surrounding Dr Solomon's death were too much for his wife to cope with.

Retreating into this present, almost comatose state was a way of protecting herself from the pain. There was no incentive for Elizabeth to live anymore; she'd lost both husband and 'daughter'. Subconsciously, she would always have been aware of the fact that Grace Bryson was not their daughter and chose to live a life of pretending, not only to the outside world but to herself as well.

Mr Thompson explained that the symptoms Elizabeth presently displayed were a coping mechanism and her mind's way of dealing with such severe trauma. It was as good as we would get by way of an explanation but absolutely no help at all in finding out the extent of Mrs Solomon's involvement in the abduction, or anyone else who may have been complicit.

When it was made public that Grace had been found, there was an insatiable demand for details from the press. It may have been fourteen years down the line, but most people could remember the case clearly. Although the press learned that Grace had been living as Jane Solomon, fortunately they remained ignorant of where she was living presently. My family told no one, and the Brysons certainly wouldn't either.

The press did, however, have access to recent photographs of Grace through social media, and these covered the front pages of almost every newspaper in the country.

DI George Wheatley gave a press conference as soon as the DNA results confirmed what we already knew — reciting a prepared speech, one that naturally showed the Force up in a good light. 'We do not rest even when the world has given up hope,' that sort of thing. It was good PR but inaccurate in the omission of it actually being Elise McDonald who had never rested.

There were one or two interviews with so called 'friends' from college, which we read incredulously. Most of those named didn't actually know Grace, yet either they themselves, or the reporters, invented stories that held little or no truth at all. These things didn't make life any easier for Grace. Part of her wanted to go back to college to pick up her studies again, but the unprecedented interest in every detail of her life from the press and these so-called 'friends' made it impossible for the time being.

The media attention was, however, thankfully ebbing as other stories made their way into the headlines, and we lived in hope that the attention would wear off completely and life would return to normal. From our point of view, Grace was under our protection and could remain with us as long as she wished. The Bryson family also had her best interests at heart and were sensibly taking things slowly and not exerting any undue pressure on their youngest daughter.

It was impossible to say whether we would ever find out from Mrs Solomon what role she played in the abduction, but she certainly bore some degree of culpability.

Yet still I want to persist with the inquiries to find an accomplice — it makes sense that there was someone else. I cannot imagine a scenario where a medical doctor, someone in the caring profession who has sworn the Hippocratic Oath, would snatch a child at random without thought of the consequences for that child's family.

DI Wheatley is keen to wrap this up — it looks good for the statistics — but I know there is more to it than we have so far discovered.

Dave Bennet is with me on this and diligently continued searching through the doctor's personal papers in the hope of finding the missing link. He requested bank statements from the doctor's bank going back fifteen years and is hopeful that they will still be able to supply them. He is also meticulously going through other documentation and the laptop we found in the Bamburgh cottage.

For myself, I'm trying to be inventive in my thought processes, not easy when things have happened so quickly and my mind gets used to one idea, which is then suddenly shot down in flames. There is something else, however, something I would like to try but need the DI to sign off on. I would also need the family's consent, but maybe, just maybe it will work.

Chapter 30

Elise McDonald

My tiny son is nothing short of a miracle. It's been such a special experience, and I know how fortunate I am to have my family close by. Mum and Dad were the first to visit but sensibly put their own restrictions on how long they would stay. I was longing to see them and show Jack off, but Mum was right — I was very tired, and after they left I slept for an hour while my son was also asleep.

The second day brought more visitors — Bea and Peter, Grace, and Simon's parents, who travelled many miles to meet their first grandchild. The McDonalds booked into the same Travelodge where my parents were staying, and I imagined the four of them celebrating the birth of their grandson together.

Mum told me of their decision to move back to Leeds, and it was the icing on the cake! Leeds held no more fear for them now, and it seemed to be the right thing to do both for them and for Grace.

When my sister came to visit her new little nephew, I knew she was smitten when he grasped her finger with his warm little fist. Grace seemed to recover some of the vitality she'd had when I first saw her in the store in town. Unsurprisingly she appeared drawn and tired these days, but little Jack helped to change that. Perhaps it was that she wasn't the only newcomer to the family; they were kindred spirits and I hoped Grace would play a big part in our son's life.

With Jack sleeping in his crib, Grace told me of her visit to Elizabeth and described what had transpired.

'There was nothing, no recognition, no eye contact. I was convinced that she didn't even know I was there until we began to leave and she actually spoke, telling me she was sorry!'

'That must have been so hard on you, Grace, but such a brave thing for you to do.'

'I don't know about being brave or why I actually wanted to go. Yes, there was the obvious chance that she might open up when seeing me, but I felt I wanted to see her now that I know she's not my mother. Perhaps I expected to feel differently about her, I don't know.'

'And did you feel any different?' I asked.

'Yes, surprisingly I did. Elizabeth Solomon, the woman I've known as Mother, is now somehow relegated to the past. Even as we left it was like saying goodbye, to her and to that part of my life. Now all I have to do is work out who I really am.'

'You are Grace Bryson, my sister.' I was crying again, totally out of control of my emotions, and Grace moved closer to put her arms around me and softly wept with me.

Simon walked in on our little sobbing party and stood looking bemused as we turned from crying to laughing. We remained sitting close together on the sofa as we attempted to explain our actions. My husband shrugged with a face that said 'women' and went to put away the shopping he'd been out for.

Bea and Peter arrived as Grace was leaving, but she stayed a few more minutes to get to know our aunt and uncle a little better. The focus of course was still Jack, who began to grizzle — just the excuse Bea was looking for to lift him from the crib.

Peter soon disappeared into the kitchen to find Simon for a bit of sensible conversation that didn't include coo's and ah's and also to deposit the dishes of food he was precariously balancing — Bea's contribution to help us through these first few days.

After a few minutes, Bea passed Jack to Grace, who held him as if he might break, but it was such a wonderful sight and one that I'd never expected to see, my sister holding my son.

Chapter 31

Jack Priestly

Dave Bennet caught my eye as I passed by his desk. I could tell from the expression on his face that he was pleased about something.

'Okay, what is it?' I asked.

'The bank got back to me with Solomon's account history, and it goes back fifteen years — exactly what we needed. I've been checking off any activity around the dates of the abduction and Solomon made an unusually large withdrawal. Unfortunately, it was in cash: ten thousand pounds on 26th August, just over two weeks after the abduction.'

'I suppose it would have been too easy for us if he'd paid someone by cheque with the recipient's name written nice and clearly for us to see?'

'Yes, that would be too easy and highly unlikely.' Dave smiled. 'There are also a couple of other large withdrawals in cash, almost a year after the event and again two years after that, both for two thousand pounds. It seems as if our abductor tried to squeeze as much out of Solomon as he could, though fourteen thousand is a paltry amount for the life of a child and the distress it caused.'

'It is if we're on the right track with looking for a paid accomplice. I'm just off to see the DI, and this gives me a little more leverage for what I have in mind next. Is he in a good mood this morning?'

'Seems to be — he's still basking in the reflective glory of finding Grace, glory which should be yours by rights.'

'It doesn't bother me, Dave; solving the case and having Grace alive and well is all I ever wanted.'

Dave handed me a printout of the relevant bank statements, and I took it to show the DI. I needed as much ammunition as possible.

Dave was right; George Wheatley did seem in a good mood and offered me a seat when I knocked on his door.

'What can I do for you, Jack?' he asked.

'I'd like to do a reconstruction of the Bryson abduction. Obviously they're no longer at the same address, but if I could get permission from the new owners I would like to get everyone who was at the party that day together again.'

Wheatley leaned back in his chair and studied me carefully.

'Why the need to pursue this, Jack? The Bryson girl was taken by Dr Solomon; what more do we need to know?'

'There was an accomplice, I'm certain. Look at these bank statements; they show that the doctor made a large withdrawal just two weeks after Grace disappeared and then more after a year and the same again after two.'

'Bank withdrawals hardly count as evidence. They could have been having a kitchen fitted, or going on holiday. It's time to let go, Jack; the girl is back with her family, and it's not our brief to play social worker to them. And anyway, what good would a reconstruction do? Are you going to get the press and the public involved, look for new witnesses or what?'

'No, nothing like that; I think if we get all the main players together back at the house, it might trigger a memory from one of them or even from Grace herself. I know this is a good result, but I'm convinced there's more to it. If you would just sanction this one last try, then I'll let it go.'

'Okay, do whatever you think is right, but you might have a job in persuading everyone to go along with this.'

'That's great, thank you.'

I almost ran from his office before Wheatley could change his mind. Heading straight for Dave, I told him what we were going to do next. The look on his face told me he was on board.

'You talk to the Brysons — they trust you, Jack — and I'll take the new owners of Lilac House. What day are you looking at?' Dave's enthusiasm fed mine.

'See the new owners first and ask if it's possible in the next few days. If they agree, I'll ask Grace and the Brysons. When we get the okay from both sides, we can set a date and take it from there.'

Dave was already shrugging into his jacket. 'No time like the present.' He was out of the office in double quick time.

Settling down to study the case notes once again, I began compiling a list of who we would need to be present. Margaret and Stephen, Elise and Grace were obviously the key witnesses, followed by Bea and Peter, then the neighbours, Christine and Harry Robinson. I would have to ask Stephen if they were still in contact with them — I'd certainly like them both to be present.

I had a list of parents of the children who attended the party and wanted to have them there too, if at all possible. Admittedly, this was a long shot, but with Doctor Solomon dead and his wife unable to help it was the only way forward I could think of. My phone interrupted these thoughts; it was Dave.

'I've got the okay from the new residents at Lilac House. They're a lovely young family and know all about the history of the house and will do anything we ask if it helps to solve the case. They've suggested a few dates when they could be out of the house and are happy for us to have keys to go inside as well. Basically, we'd be looking at the next two weekends. I've promised to get back to them with a firm date. It's up to you now, Jack, to persuade the family.'

Rather than phone Elise, I decided to visit. It would be a good opportunity to meet my namesake — he was only a few days old, and we hadn't yet been introduced. As I'd hoped, Elise was at home, with the bonus of Stephen and Margaret being with her. Simon was upstairs catching up on some sleep.

Little Jack was fast asleep when I arrived, giving me a chance to study his face. I cannot pretend that the sight of a newborn baby doesn't affect me. Seeing some of the seedier side of life, it always did me good to remember that the world was populated with some truly good people as well. A policeman's view can easily become distorted through his work, and looking at this child who brought so much joy to his family gave me a more balanced outlook on life. But I was there for a purpose other than to admire Elise's son.

After drinking the coffee Margaret made, I began to outline my idea for a reconstruction.

'Won't it depend on the new people in Lilac House?' Stephen asked.

'Yes, but my colleague's been in touch earlier today and they're keen to help if they can and have offered to vacate the house on the day we choose, and to leave us the keys.'

'That's incredibly generous of them,' Margaret observed.

'It is, but I need to know how you all feel about participating in this.'

I waited for a reply but received only questions.

'Who will you want there?' Elise asked.

I listed the four Brysons, Bea and Peter, Christine and Harry and any of the parents of children who were at the party that day.

'I'm not sure how much I'll remember, and I think Grace will remember even less.' Elise spoke again. 'Will this really help, Jack? Are you sure there was someone else involved?'

'Yes, I'm sure. Even today there've been a few more indicators that Solomon didn't do this alone, and although it happened so long ago, recreating the afternoon might just jog a few memories.'

'It's fine by me.' Stephen was first to agree.

'And I trust you, Jack, so yes, I'm happy to go along with it.' Margaret spoke next.

'Me too. Have you asked Grace yet?' Elise was always thinking of her sister.

'Not yet. I'll be doing that when I get home this evening. Now, do you want me to approach Bea and Peter, or would you prefer to ask them?'

'I'll have a word and let you know,' Margaret offered.

'Thank you, and do you have an address to contact the Robinsons? I believe they no longer live on River View either.'

'That's right, but they separated years ago. I'm in touch with Christine; I can speak to her and ask if she has a number for Harry.'

It was going well. I suggested the days Dave had given me and we decided to opt for the following weekend. Before leaving, I asked them to let me know the outcome of asking the others. I would write to the parents of the other children asking for their attendance, as the more input we could get, the better the chance of a result.

Baby Jack was waking as I began to leave, and Elise lifted him from the crib and brought him over to me. I took the little man from her and smiled down at his furrowed brow and puzzled expression. I kissed the top of his head before handing him back to Elise and leaving. My connection with the Bryson family began during the most harrowing of times, but it had been an honour to help them and see those horrendous times being lifted from them, allowing peace and happiness to be theirs again.

Chapter 32

Grace

A letter arrived for me this morning with a date for an initial session with a counsellor. The GP arranged this, confident that it would help in dealing with my emotional problems, and at this point in time I'm ready to try anything that might help.

Sarah told me that she'd seen a counsellor at the time of her mother's death and found it a very positive experience. She advised me to try it, and if it didn't work out I could always stop going. Actually, Sarah seems to be the only person I can really talk to at the moment. Jake's a good listener, but I don't want to burden him too much with my problems. With Sarah, though, it feels quite natural to open up and I'll miss her when I eventually leave.

Each night I lie awake and think about my future — not years down the line but next week, next month, next year. I am nearly seventeen, and even I can see that that's too young to live alone.

I have an appointment with a solicitor tomorrow. Jack found his details in the paperwork he's been trawling through. I thought about asking Margaret or Stephen to go with me but decided that it wasn't the sort of thing they should have to worry about.

Sarah offered to come, which is perfect. In some ways I wish I could stay with them permanently, but that's not really a viable prospect. Margaret and Stephen have decided to move back to Leeds, and I know this is in the hope that I'll move in with them, which in a way would be okay, I suppose. The

Priestlys were strangers when I came to live with them, so it wouldn't be much different with the Brysons, and they are my parents.

I know of Mr Priestly's theory that there was a third party involved in my abduction, and it seems that he's not going to rest until he finds whoever it was. When he explained what he wanted to try, I almost wished he'd left it until morning to tell me. A reconstruction seems quite daunting, and I'm not sure exactly what part he wants me to play in it.

Truthfully, I'm curious to see the house we used to live in. From what I've picked up, mainly from Elise, we were all really happy there, but the family couldn't stay after the abduction, too many memories, I suppose. Mr Priestly talked about the key witnesses, who to me are mostly strangers, except perhaps Stephen, Margaret and Elise. I'm beginning to feel comfortable in their presence, and baby Jack is gorgeous!

Of course, I'll go along with the plan. I do so appreciate the work Mr Priestly has put in trying to piece everything together. He reassured me that his plan would not take the form of a full-blown reconstruction with press and appeals to the general public. I don't think that would help so long after the event. Only people who were directly involved with the party that afternoon will be there.

Mr Priestly also brought some mail for me, which had been delivered to the police station. There's been a huge pile of correspondence, most of which I've shredded. It amazes me how ordinary people follow cases like mine in such a ghoulish way. Letters asking questions about my life have arrived, most of which seem to be seeking sordid details, which for some reason they feel I should want to tell them.

I've received letters from journalists offering me huge sums of money to give them exclusive rights to my story. One was from a ghost writer offering to write my life story, a book he assures me will make a fortune! I am not, however, 'a story'; I am a human being who is trying to get my head around recent events and revelations.

I suppose I should be grateful that no one has yet found out where I'm living. I would hate to be hounded by the media or gawped at as if a freak. It seems as if I have become public property, but hopefully the media will soon forget about me and I'll be able to rebuild a new life.

Chapter 33

Jack Priestly

Grace is proving to be a very plucky young lady. When I asked how she felt about participating in the reconstruction, she asked a few pertinent questions and then agreed. So much is being thrown at her in such a short space of time, and Grace working with me is making my job so much easier. She was brilliant with Elizabeth Solomon, which was not easy for her and she's doing her best to get to know the Brysons, which must be so strange, having a whole new family who desperately want her back.

Sarah and Grace are becoming close, and it was my wife who she asked to visit the solicitors with her. Afterwards, they told me all about it. Apparently, the doctor had made a very detailed will in the event of him dying before Elizabeth or their daughter. Obviously, the big problem here is that Grace is not his daughter, but when he made the will it was her to whom he alluded.

Thank goodness I'm not a solicitor, as this poor man has a legal nightmare to work through, made even more complicated by Elizabeth's present unbalanced state of mind. It seems as if Grace could be the main beneficiary of Solomon's estate once provision for Elizabeth is determined.

Sarah told me later that Grace said very little, and when the solicitor began to talk about assets, showed very little interest, later telling Sarah that she didn't really want anything from the Solomons. I could understand the sentiment but, as Sarah wisely pointed out, she would need money to support herself in the future, through university or whatever life choices she would make. Personally, I would say she deserves everything after what they did.

It is now about six weeks since Elise first saw and recognised her sister, six chaotic weeks for each and everyone concerned. For myself, I knew that if the coming reconstruction bore no fruit, I would have to rest the case once again. That would be the least satisfactory result, but was I hoping for too much? It was fourteen years ago; Elise was only nine and Grace barely three.

Several of the parents of children who were at the party responded positively to the request to be at Lilac House on Saturday. Obviously the Brysons would be there and Bea and Peter. Margaret also contacted their neighbour, Christine, who was happy to come and to supply me with an address and phone number for her ex-husband, Harry. I'd rung several times and left messages, which were not returned, and a letter had been sent asking for his presence, but again with no reply. This was disappointing; Harry was, in my mind, one of the key players, and although he didn't arrive home to River View until after Grace disappeared, he was not completely out of the picture. I decided to pay him a visit one evening, hoping he would be at home and compliant to my request.

Dave Bennet continued his cyber search of the Solomons' affairs. The bank statements told us nothing else of interest but the unusual cash withdrawals that formed part of my basis for the reconstruction. Dave found evidence of the doctor's involvement in quite a few local charities, particularly the local hospice of which he was chairman. He appeared to play an active role in a couple of children's charities too, rather incongruous considering what we knew of the man. Perhaps he did this to salve his conscience or to show the world that he was a good man; we will never know, but surely every day when he looked at Grace he must have seen the product of the very worst side of his persona. He never was Grace's father and for a doctor, showed very little compassion towards her real parents.

So this is my last chance to prove my theory, and my confidence of achieving a result isn't particularly high. On Monday morning, if Saturday fails to get a result, Dave and I will be assigned to another case.

Chapter 34

Elise McDonald

Saturday morning began well, with a clear blue sky dotted only by the smallest of white fluffy clouds. I'd hoped for sunshine; it had been a glorious day when Grace was taken so it seemed appropriate that we should do this reconstruction under the same sunny sky. It was May now; the trees were in blossom and I wondered if the lilac trees would be in flower at Lilac House.

I nursed very mixed feelings about going there again. It was the scene of some of my happiest childhood days, which ended so abruptly on Grace's third birthday. Life was never the same from that day, and whatever Jack Priestly has in mind, those stolen years can never be replaced.

I'm not sure that even Jack knows what he's hoping for today. Simon will stay at home with baby Jack, his parents on hand to help although our son is no trouble at all. It will be good for Simon's mum and dad to have some time with their son and grandson, as my family are always around at the moment and I don't want them to feel pushed out.

The plan for the day is to meet at River View at three this afternoon. Mum and Dad are calling to pick me up, and Bea and Peter will make their own way there, as will Christine, and Grace will come with Jack Priestly and Dave Bennet. There are a few parents of children who attended the party that day coming as well, but as they only arrived after Grace disappeared I doubt they will be able to shed any new light on the situation.

After we moved away from the old house, I never thought I'd want to go back again. It will be equally difficult for Mum and Dad, but a whole lot better for us all now that Grace is with us. We've tried not to put pressure on her and haven't pushed for visits, but she's kept in regular contact. When Mum told her that they'd decided to return to Leeds to live, she was rather quiet, not passing comment at all. I've also offered a home here with us should she want to take it, but it will all take time.

The morning dragged, even though baby Jack kept me busy. Simon was almost avoiding me, trying not to get in my way.

'I'm fine, you know,' I eventually told him. 'This isn't half as traumatic as it would have been if we hadn't found Grace.'

'I know, love, and I'm sorry I didn't believe you at first. You've proved us all wrong, haven't you?'

'There's no need to apologise — it must have sounded impossible to you that I could recognise her after all these years, and I know you were only thinking of my welfare.'

Simon moved to hold me, an uninterrupted moment of tenderness that we both needed. I loved my husband so much, and my life now was far better than I ever dreamed it could be. I had Simon, baby Jack and Grace. Mum and Dad were coming back home, and the road ahead looked bright and sunny.

Chapter 35

Margaret Bryson

We arrived at Elise's house in plenty of time to have a light lunch before going to River View. Stephen and I were both anticipating this visit with mixed feelings. Lilac House was the backdrop to so many of our happiest times, but also the most horrendous experience of our life. Stephen was unnaturally chatty during the drive to our daughter's home, which was his way of coping with nervousness, while I withdrew quietly into my own thoughts.

The weather was smiling on us and it was perhaps the warmest day of the year so far, which would enable us to use the garden and more accurately recreate the events of Grace's birthday. We were all a little unsure of what Jack Priestly expected from this reconstruction, but probably he was too. It seemed to be a case of throwing everyone concerned into a melting pot and standing back to see what happened.

Thankfully it was to be a private affair without any media coverage, and we'd been told that it would be completely informal, just a gathering of people who'd been at Lilac House for Grace's birthday party in August 2000. It was incredibly generous of the new owners to entrust us with their keys and free access to their home, but with this lovely weather I didn't think we would need to go into the house except to access the garden.

I left the unusually stilted conversation in Elise's lounge to help my daughter in the kitchen. Six of us sat down to eat, all regretting the fact that baby Jack was fast asleep; he would have been a welcome distraction. Being asleep, however, didn't prevent him from being the focus of our conversation. Jack was the thread that drew us together, cementing us into a family. We lingered over coffee, needing something to do to take our minds off the afternoon ahead, but inevitably the time came to leave and so we did.

Pulling up in front of our former home was a strange feeling and going inside, even more so. Bea and Peter were already there, sitting in their car, solemnly waiting. As we arrived they got out and came over to us.

'Are you okay?' Bea asked, forever the big sister looking out for me.

I hugged her and said that I was fine. Truthfully, I didn't know how I felt: apprehensive perhaps, curious maybe. This afternoon could turn out to be a waste of time, or Jack's theory could be right.

Christine was next to arrive, walking down the road to join us and the little huddle of parents who were waiting to do their part. Jack pulled up with DS Bennet sitting in the passenger seat and Grace in the back with Jake, who I was a little surprised to see. We'd met Jake only once when Grace brought him on one of her visits, and I found him to be a very likeable young man. He had his father's height and good looks and was certainly attentive to Grace, clearly very fond of her, and they seemed to be well suited.

Jack jingled a bunch of keys and headed straight to the front door. Stephen followed on but turned to the right, expecting to go straight into the garden. There was a gate, however, preventing direct access, a new feature. I was following my husband, and when we were halted by this unexpected barrier I couldn't help but wonder if things might have been different if we'd erected that gate.

We turned to follow the others through the house and out of the French windows. For some reason, I kept my eyes lowered as we passed through the hall and into the conservatory from where we could get to the garden. The feel of the house was certainly different and had changed considerably since we lived there; new blinds hung at the long conservatory windows and rich honeyed oak flooring ran the full length of the hall, flowing beautifully into all the downstairs rooms.

I felt no desire to look around; even though Grace was safely back with us, there were still painful memories secreted in the back of my mind, which a tour of the house was likely to rekindle. I was, however, keen to watch Grace's reactions. Holding Jake's hand, my youngest daughter moved slowly through the hall and into the conservatory. Jack was already in the garden, and everyone gravitated towards him as if awaiting instructions.

'The gate wasn't there in our time.' Stephen nodded in the general direction of it.

'Yes, it was an open path between the house and garage, I remember,' Jack replied. 'What I'd like everyone to do is to walk around the garden, the areas you went to on that day and try to remember everything you saw or heard. Feel free to go into the conservatory and kitchen, and try to remember who was near you and if you had any conversations. Anything at all really, and then have a word with Dave or me and we'll take notes.'

We began to spread out from the patio. I looked around, undecided as to where to start. The lilac trees had almost doubled in height and stood majestically at the far corners of the lawn, bowed slightly to the south from years of resisting the wind.

Grace barely moved and I went over to her, suggesting we walk round together. Her smile showed relief, and letting go of Jake's hand she linked an arm through mine. Such an insignificant action, but to me it was a grand gesture, one of affection and hope for the future!

We walked to the south end of the garden, which appeared even more untamed than when we lived here. Quite understandable though; it was a garden that demanded much work and time. Letting nature take care of the bulk of it seemed to work well. I recognised a few of the shrubs, although they were all so much bigger now, with some of them showing new growth and blossom.

Managing to pick out the red brick path that meandered down to the far wall, we were both silent. Stephen was in the house — I don't know exactly where, but presumably he was doing what Jack asked and trying to recreate his movements as on the day of the party. I felt perhaps I should speak, to tell Grace about the garden.

'You always loved being outside, even in the rain and cold. When I wanted you in, you tried to hide down here and Elise had to find you.'

'Is the river behind the wall?'

'Yes. They trawled it after you disappeared...' I could say no more. Reliving that day brought all the pain back. Grace squeezed my arm.

'It must have been terrible for you all.' We turned to walk back toward the house. 'This is quite some garden, but I don't remember any of it.' My daughter sounded sad, as if she was somehow disappointing us.

Jack and Elise were talking on the patio, where we joined them. They both looked expectantly at Grace, who shook her head.

'I'm sorry, but none of it is familiar.' She looked around for Jake, who was waiting on a bench and came over to take her hand again.

'Perhaps if you take a look in the orchard?' I suggested.

This too was so much more mature than it was in our time. The trees looked well cared for with blossom suggesting a good crop for later in the year. Grace took Jake over to the orchard and I turned to Jack. 'She has no memories, Jack, so what next?'

'We'll stay a little while longer. Dave's been talking to some of the parents, but they don't remember anything more than they did fourteen years ago. Stephen and Peter have been inside trying to retrace their actions but again without much success as far as any fresh memories.'

Elise gave me a brief hug and Bea came to join us. She'd been in the conservatory and the kitchen with Christine; they'd both been in and out throughout the party, serving tea to the children.

'Sorry.' Christine looked sad. 'Nothing new has struck me, and the inside isn't much like it was back then.'

'Any word from your husband?' Jack asked.

'Ex-husband. No, but he wouldn't contact me. I thought he would get in touch with you directly.'

'He's a difficult man to pin down. I've left messages, written and even called round one evening, all to no avail.'

'That's Harry for you.' Christine shrugged.

I was beginning to feel uncomfortable at Lilac House and really wanted to leave. Most of those present gathered once again on the patio where Jack thanked us all, asking that we keep our little tour in mind over the next few days and if anything fresh did occur to us to ring him or Dave Bennet.

Our group dispersed, each of us wondering if we'd wasted our time. Even Jack looked downcast, having hoped for something to come out of the exercise, something that was maybe overlooked during the original investigation. I said goodbye to Grace and Jake, who got in the back of Jack's car, waiting for him to lock up the house. Bea and Peter were hovering in the front garden, apparently waiting to talk to Jack as we waved goodbye and pulled away.

'Did Grace not remember anything, Mum?' Elise asked from the back seat.

'No, nothing at all, I'm afraid. The house did look different, though, and even the garden has changed considerably.'

'That's sad. I suppose I'd hoped she would at least recall some of the good times, even if she didn't remember that awful day.'

Elise sat back and remained quiet for the rest of the journey. We'd all tried so hard, but perhaps Jack was mistaken about an accomplice. I honestly didn't know, but what I did know was that I really wanted to stop looking back and begin to look forward.

Chapter 36

Grace

As we pulled up at River View my senses were alert and expectant, but expecting what, I didn't quite know. This exercise was probably more difficult for Margaret and Stephen, having to relive such sad memories, and Elise too, who would certainly remember her first ten years spent here.

The garden was amazing and just beginning to show colour. Two huge lilac trees drew my eye; they couldn't be missed really, and their fragrance perfumed the air, carried on the light breeze of the day.

Looking around the garden with Margaret, it was easy to see why they had bought Lilac House; it was a fantastic place for a family, but seeing it had no effect on my memory whatsoever. Aware that the others assembled were watching my reactions, I somehow felt that I'd let them down, particularly Mr Priestly, who seemed to have pinned such importance on this venture.

We spent about an hour looking around and then, promising to visit Margaret soon, we said our goodbyes and she, Stephen and Elise left to go home.

Watching their car until it turned out of River View, I felt so sad for them — life had been so cruel, which they didn't deserve at all, and I felt determined to maintain the contact we'd already begun and try to make it up to them in some way. Although I'd been the one to be abducted, my grief was short-lived compared to theirs.

I climbed into the back of the car beside Jake and waited for his dad to lock up the house and finish talking to Bea. Peter was standing around too, waiting for Bea, who appeared to ask him to do something. Peter came to the car and I rolled down the window to hear what he wanted to say. He mumbled something about Bea wanting us to go for a meal, but I couldn't take it in. The words sounded hollow, as if they were coming at me from the end of a tunnel.

As Peter leaned his arms on the open window, head almost fully inside the car, I suddenly experienced what I can only describe as a vivid flashback. In my mind, I could see Peter in exactly the same pose, leaning through the window of another car with a man in the front seat. Being in such close proximity now, I could smell his aftershave, a woody pine scent that took me right back in time.

I was laughing then, playing a game before suddenly becoming confused as the man in the front seat pricked my arm with a small needle. That was it, a snapshot of a memory triggered by Peter's aftershave and the sight of him leaning into the car window!

I felt sick and turned towards Jake, backing away from Peter. At first, I couldn't clear my brain to make sense of this frightening experience and could only stare at the figure of my uncle.

Then his eyes narrowed, and he drew back from the window and almost ran to his car. What it all meant was not clear — it was like looking at something through muddied water — but I was left physically shaking, gasping for breath and almost clawing at Jake in an effort to draw closer to him, to be safe.

As Peter's car sped away, Bea and Jack stared after him, their conversation forgotten as they watched in disbelief. Everyone had now left River View, except for the four occupants of Jack's car and Bea. Dave Bennet climbed into the car, asking what had happened, but when he saw the state I was in he came round and opened the passenger door, kneeling beside me to speak.

'It's alright, Grace, just breathe slowly, you're fine now.'

I tried to control my breathing, closing my eyes in an effort to relax, but the trembling continued; my teeth were chattering and I felt chilled right through to my bones. Bea and Mr Priestly were at my side now too, Bea holding my hand and speaking softly, but the words didn't seem to be reaching me. I was aware of Mr Priestly asking what had just happened, but I felt ill and wanted to curl up in a ball and be alone.

Dave went back into the house and brought me a glass of water. I drank half of it and again felt my heart pounding and my face flushed and damp. The next thing I realised was that the car was moving, very fast. When it finally stopped, there seemed to be arms reaching out to me from all angles, voices coming at me with questions that I couldn't answer. I was afraid, terrified, but of what I didn't know.

It was a hospital. I realised that I was on a hospital bed but why, what had happened, was I ill? Jake was holding an oxygen mask over my face, and as I breathed into it my body relaxed and I became calm. A nurse was speaking to me, asking if I'd ever felt like this before. I shook my head, and she went through the curtain that was around the bed and Jake squeezed my hand, smiling.

'Dad and Bea are talking to the doctor. Are you feeling better?' His look of concern was touching.

'Yes, I feel fine, but what happened?'

'I don't know; Peter was asking if you would go to their house for a meal, and you just seemed to collapse. I thought it was a heart attack or something.'

'Sorry, but I'm feeling much better now. I need to talk to your dad, though. Can you get him for me?'

Jake went to find him. It was all coming back now. It was Peter who put me into a car all those years ago. The smell of his aftershave and the sight of him leaning in at the window brought it all back, a déjà vu moment, but a real memory.

I must tell Mr Priestly. It was my uncle, Peter.

Chapter 37

Jack Priestly

Thankfully, it was only a panic attack, for which I felt rather guilty, having pushed for the reconstruction when I barely knew what outcome I expected. It was a long shot that I hoped would pay dividends, not affect Grace's health.

When she was almost herself again, Grace asked to see me and began to tell me what happened in the car. Seeing Peter Cartwright in almost exactly the same way as on the day of the abduction precipitated a flashback so vivid that she actually felt she was being taken again, which resulted in the panic attack. I've come across this several times before in my line of work. Victims can blank negative incidents, but the subconscious still stores those memories and something quite mundane, a sound or a smell, can trigger a flashback. With Grace it was the combination of Cartwright looking through the car window and his choice of aftershave, which obviously had never changed.

When the hospital conducted their routine tests and was satisfied that this was nothing more than a panic attack, Grace was free to go home. After she told me everything I rang Dave Bennet, who was making his way home, with instructions to meet me at the Cartwrights' house as soon as possible.

'It's the uncle,' I told him, then I left Jake to call for a taxi and take Grace home, while I had the unenviable task of explaining to Bea what we now knew. Abandoned by her husband but more concerned about Grace, she'd travelled in our car to the hospital. I told her that Jake was seeing Grace home and that we needed to go to her house.

Alone in the car, I began to tell her what I knew would be a tremendous shock, beginning with the better news that Grace's little 'episode' was only a panic attack, but then I told her what had triggered it.

'No!' she shouted. 'Peter loves those girls as if they were our own and would never hurt either of them!'

I made no reply, concentrating instead on driving. The brutal truth would come out soon enough.

Arriving at the Cartwrights' house I was pleased to see Dave already there, waiting in his car. Peter's car was parked outside the gate.

'Thought I'd better wait,' he said.

I asked Bea to wait in the car, telling her I'd come and get her when we'd spoken to Peter. Her face was a stony mask; she was having trouble believing that her husband could have been an accomplice to such a hateful, evil crime. I asked for the door key, which she produced from her bag, and we went up the path, rang the bell and without waiting used the key to enter.

Peter Cartwright was at the kitchen table. In front of him was an assortment of medication, a few bottles of painkillers, a tranquiliser and several other medications. He was slumped over the table, and when I ran to check his vital signs I saw the blood.

Dave was already ringing for an ambulance. Then he helped me lift Peter, who was a big man, to place him on the floor in the recovery position. The blood was from his wrist, the left one where a trickle was running along his arm.

I grabbed a tea towel from the back of the chair and wrapped it around the wound, applying pressure to stem the flow of blood. The cut appeared to have missed the artery, otherwise the blood loss would be considerably more. Peter was breathing erratically and his pulse wasn't too strong, but he was alive.

'Peter!' Bea came into the house regardless of what I'd asked and knelt down beside his unconscious body. With tears in her eyes she began to beat him with her fists. Dave and I both reached to pull her away, but she fought like a tiger. 'Stupid, stupid man! How could you do this to us, to me?'

Bea was hysterical, and when we did manage to pull her away I took her into the lounge while Dave remained to monitor Peter. I could understand how she was feeling. It seemed incredible that a family member, someone who even helped in the original search and who visited the Brysons so regularly, could actually have assisted in abducting his own niece.

Bea eventually calmed down, and within fifteen minutes of Dave's call the ambulance arrived and the paramedics quickly began their assessment. Still unconscious, Peter Cartwright was carried to the ambulance and taken to hospital. I asked Bea if she wanted to go with him, and the answer was an emphatic 'no'. I sent Dave instead. As soon as Cartwright was able to understand where he was and why, Dave would caution him and arrest him for abduction.

'How am I going to tell Margaret?' Bea looked so pale and tired. My satisfaction at finding the accomplice was marred by the fact that it was a member of their family. I knew Elise was close to Bea and Peter, who cared for her during the most distressing time of her life. This revelation would shock them all, and I pitied Bea for having to impart such knowledge.

'Would you like me to tell them?'

'Thank you but no; you've done so much for us already, Jack.'

I couldn't leave her at home, alone. 'Shall I take you there — we could do this together?'

Bea looked into my eyes, her own reflecting the enormity of what she'd just been confronted with and the pain it brought.

'Thank you, Jack. I'd like that.'

Chapter 38

Elise McDonald

It was a disappointing afternoon. Simon was waiting anxiously for news, but there was none to impart. His parents tactfully left so we could be alone with Mum and Dad. Baby Jack was sleeping, which didn't bode well for a good night ahead for us. Still, we needed to talk, not about what happened but about our feelings and the future. Were we going to let the matter drop or not? Actually, that was probably more up to Jack and his DI than us.

'Was it okay, going in the house again?' My husband was concerned for us all. I answered first.

'Perhaps okay isn't the word. I remembered the events of the birthday party, yes, but then other memories came to mind, earlier ones. We had some wonderful times at Lilac House, and I was grateful to remember the good as well as the bad.'

Dad nodded. 'It was never going to be easy, but with Grace back it was bearable. Goodness knows what she thought of it all, but sadly she remembered nothing. What do you think, Margaret? You looked round the garden with her.'

'She was actually more concerned for us and almost apologetic for remembering nothing. But that's good, isn't it? I wouldn't want her to remember that awful day.'

Our conversation was interrupted by the baby waking, a most welcome diversion. Mum jumped up before me to lift our son from his crib. This was another positive. Jack was the symbol of the future, which now would be a complete one. I wished I'd asked Grace to come back with us, but Jake was there for her and I was sure my sister would come again soon.

Leaving Mum happily cooing at her grandson, trying to get a smile, I went into the kitchen to make coffee. Simon followed, weaving his hands around my waist while I filled the kettle at the sink. He kissed the back of my neck and I turned towards him.

'I'm good ... honestly, there's nothing to worry about. I rather think our life will be easier for getting this out of the way. Now be an angel and get the cups out for me.' I hoped my words were true, but why wouldn't they be?

As we drank coffee, Mum and Dad began to tell us of the estate agents they'd contacted and the folder already amassed of prospective houses to view. Their decision to come home was good news, and they could do so now without accusing fingers or whispered gossip. It wasn't only Grace who would benefit from their move, and I loved the idea of keeping the property in France as a holiday home, a bonus for us all.

The doorbell rang and Simon answered it, returning to the lounge with Jack Priestly and Bea. From the look on Bea's face and the red circles around her eyes, all was not well. Mum ran to hug her sister, guiding her to a seat and wondering what on earth could be wrong.

'What is it, Jack?' I asked, for clearly something was amiss. Bea nodded at Jack, giving him permission to speak.

'After you left, Grace suffered a panic attack, but don't worry, she's fine. We took her to the hospital, and she's back home now with Jake and Sarah.'

'Whatever caused that — the visit?' Dad asked.

'Yes and no. Peter went to the car with a message for Grace while Bea and I were talking and it triggered a memory, a flashback, to the day she was taken. I'm really sorry, but it was Peter who helped Dr Solomon to abduct Grace.'

Stunned would be an understatement for such unbelievable news. Bea hid her face in her hands, sobbing openly, with Mum now crying softly too.

'Are you sure? Could it be a mistake?' I knew the answer before I asked. Jack wouldn't be telling us if he wasn't certain.

'Where is he? Have you arrested him?' Dad was furious and struggling to hold back his anger.

Jack went on to explain the events of the last couple of hours, events our weary minds could barely absorb. Peter had always been there for us, in the background maybe, but very much part of our family! We couldn't believe he could do such a thing, yet he must have or why would he attempt suicide?

The room suddenly felt cold. Poor Aunt Bea could hardly look at us and kept saying sorry.

'It's not your fault, Bea. You're not responsible for his actions. I just didn't know that he hated us so much.' Dad looked dazed while Mum still clung to her sister. Peter must have harboured such bitterness and jealousy to make him party to such an evil act.

'What happens now, Jack?' I asked. 'Is Peter going to be all right?'

'I think so. It was difficult to know what medication he'd taken, but they will pump his stomach out as soon as they got him to hospital. The cuts were barely more than superficial, so I don't think there's any danger from them. Dave will stay with him until he wakes up, and as soon as he's able to understand, he'll be arrested.'

'And you're sure Grace is okay?'

'Yes, but if you'd like to ring and speak to her…?'

We wanted to, so Jack dialled his own home number and Sarah put Grace on the line to speak to us. She sounded tired but relieved that it was all over. Mum spoke with her for a couple of minutes, then Dad and lastly me. We didn't go into details or ask anything other than how she was. There would be time enough for that when we all felt better and the shock had worn off. I said goodnight to my sister, reassured that she was well cared for. There was so much to thank Jack and his family for.

Bea looked all done in. The revelations of the day had unsettled us all but mostly my aunt. She could not go home to be on her own — we wouldn't allow it — and so after a brief discussion it was decided that Mum and Dad would go with her and stay the night. They eventually left, shortly after Jack, and Simon and I were left alone with our son, exhausted by the extraordinary events of the day and hopeful that our lives could now be allowed to settle into some kind of normality.

Chapter 39

Peter Cartwright

For fourteen years I lived in fear of this moment. Solomon was a bloody fool, who should have kept to his part of the bargain and moved away, far, far away. When Elise came round that day to tell us she had seen Grace, it was a shock. She was adamant that it was her sister, and I had to put her off as kindly as possible. I couldn't have it all dragged up again. But Elise persisted, bringing that Priestly man in again.

A bloody reconstruction was all I needed! Initially, it seemed to be an unproductive exercise and I really thought I'd gotten away with it again, until Bea asked me to invite Grace for a meal. I spoke to her in the car and she somehow remembered — it was clear from her expression and the horror reflected in her eyes. She was afraid of me.

Solomon never did pay what the girl was worth, or enough to compensate me for the risks I took. When I asked him for payment he became rather coy, pretending we'd only snatched the girl to rescue her from an abusive home. We both knew that was rubbish. Solomon knew from the beginning it was a simple transaction, even though he pretended otherwise.

It was I who took all the risks, and then the doctor began playing games with me. Ten thousand was all he would part with, barely enough to cover my debts at the time. I tried at regular intervals to squeeze more out of him, but was rewarded pitifully for the service I'd done them.

As for Margaret and Stephen, they deserved the shock to wake them up, to stop their superior 'I've got it all' attitude! All I ever heard from Bea was how happy her sister was and what a wonderful life they had, with a perfect home and perfect children. It made me sick! For all their supposed closeness, Margaret never offered to help us out, to treat us to a much needed holiday to thank Bea for all she did. It was always Bea who made the running, helping Margaret with this or that, taking care of the children to give her sister a break. She couldn't see that she was being taken for granted by her perfect sister.

To be honest, I've regretted it all over the years, but I was desperate at the time. I hadn't thought it through, but it's too late now, just as it was too late that afternoon in August when I took Grace from her own birthday party. It was almost too easy: Solomon waiting in his car as we arranged and little Grace, still thinking we were playing hide and seek and that I was helping to find the best place to hide. The child was laughing, trusting — too young to be aware that trusting in this world is a waste of time. Even when I bundled her into the back of the car she smiled at the doctor, excited at the adventure. A small scratch on her arm from the tiny hypodermic needle was probably the last thing Grace remembered before her old life ended and a new one began.

I mistakenly expected that Margaret and Stephen would eventually recover from the loss of Grace. They were young enough to have more children and it seemed so unfair that Bea, who so desperately wanted a child, could not conceive. Admittedly, it was a cruel thing to do, but I knew the child would be well cared for — I wasn't harming her in any way and I derived a strange pleasure from watching my sister- and brother-in-law suffer.

I wanted to teach them a lesson, but now it seems to have come back to haunt me.

It's over for me now; life holds nothing good to look forward to. Solomon's better out of it and as for his loopy wife, she's in another galaxy completely, still convinced the girl really is their daughter, unless it's an act, in which case she's put up a remarkable performance for all these years.

Chapter 40

Elizabeth Solomon

Guilt is such a heavy burden to carry, and one that grows heavier with the passing of time. I always knew what we did was terrible, but my mind contorted the facts to justify the act in some very inventive ways. Do we ever grow out of the childlike passing on of blame? I directed my guilt towards Arthur at times, or to circumstances, or simply to fate. There are dozens of lies we tell ourselves to absolve us from guilt, and in time we accept those lies as truth because it suits our purpose.

When Jane first came to live with us I was in a terrible state, which is not an excuse, I know, but my reasoning at that time was warped. I'd just spent ten weeks as an inpatient on a psychiatric ward, ten of the worst weeks of my life! The drugs they gave me took away some of the pain, but they wear off in time.

Group therapy sessions didn't work. Perhaps I am selfish, but listening to other people's sad stories only served to make me feel worse. They said it would help me to realise that others also suffered similar traumatic experiences and I would not feel so alone; it did not. Each time Arthur visited, I begged him to take me home, but his confidence lay with those colleagues who were deciding what was best for me — people who did not know me.

If I cried or pleaded, Arthur saw it as a sign that I was still 'ill' and needed to spend more time at the hospital. Eventually I resorted to pretending, to lying in an effort to make them believe I had recovered. But how can you ever recover from the death of your only child?

I was discharged and returned to our home in Jesmond, our empty, childless home. Still on medication, I became lethargic, disinterested in my home, my husband and life itself. The house held too many memories, which I could hardly bear, so Arthur began looking for a position in another area and Leeds seemed as good a place as any. Since then, I've often wondered if it was too soon to make such a life-changing decision. Would those memories eventually have brought comfort, and would the familiar setting have eased the pain? We shall never know.

Arthur gave his notice in at work and found a temporary position as a locum in a practice in Leeds. We took a short term lease on a flat so that I could go with him, and began to look for a house to buy, although my heart wasn't in the search at all. Strangely, when we viewed the house in Carlton Wells I felt comfortable with it and with the location. It was a pretty village and a period house fairly similar to the one we had left in Jesmond, so we decided to put in an offer. It was accepted almost immediately, but I felt none of the excitement that a new home should bring. The medication kept me stable enough to go through the motions of preparing for the move, but then one day Arthur came home from work and sat me down to discuss something important, something that was to change our lives yet again.

'A patient came in today, a man. He saw the photo of Jane on my desk, the last one we had taken of her.'

I winced at the stab of pain that accompanied the memory. Arthur went on.

'This man couldn't get over the likeness of Jane to a child he knows, a little girl of about the same age. When he asked about the photo, I found myself telling him that we'd recently lost our daughter; I don't know why — I don't usually share personal details with patients. He seemed genuinely sorry for us, and again remarked on how Jane looked so much like the child he knows. I thought no more of it until I left for a short walk at lunchtime, and he was waiting outside for me. He said he needed to talk to me, so we went back inside, where he told me more about this little girl's life. It seems she is very badly treated; some of the things he described were terrible, and her parents need locking up! Honestly, Elizabeth, if you had heard what he said it would have broken your heart!'

I couldn't believe what Arthur was telling me. Some people shouldn't be allowed to have children, and this couple obviously didn't know how fortunate they were. But I had no idea where this story was going, or why my husband was telling it to me.

'The girl is beaten regularly, and the parents almost boast about knowing how to "discipline" her without showing the bruises!'

Tears welled up in my eyes; I couldn't bear to listen.

'Stop it, Arthur! Why are you telling me this? I can't listen to any more!'

Arthur took my hand and continued. 'Elizabeth, I'm sorry, but there's a reason for telling you. These parents are obviously sadists; they shouldn't have a child at all, and that's what this man thinks too! He said that he could bring the girl to us, take her out of that violent, hateful environment, and we could raise her as our own!' Arthur's eyes were wide as he searched my face for a reaction.

I was stunned and couldn't think straight. 'That's insane. If he wants to do something, he should go to the police or the social services — we couldn't just take another couple's child!'

'That's what I said, but apparently the father works in local government in some kind of senior role and if he was reported, no one would ever believe it. It's not only poor families on council estates who beat their children, Elizabeth; I've come across this before.' He looked at me, pleading, and it dawned on me then that Arthur was actually considering this ridiculous idea.

Arthur talked much about the child over the next few days, and I know he'd spoken again with the man who suggested this insane plan. It was so absurd and shocking that it occupied most of my thinking, and my heart went out to the poor little girl. I wondered how anyone could mistreat a child; such cruelty is beyond me, unthinkable. I seem to feel the pain of the world's injustices even more keenly since we lost our own daughter.

On a beautiful Saturday afternoon in early August, Arthur left the flat without saying where he was going, and after two hours I was beginning to worry. I hated the place we were living in — it was small and oppressive — but thankfully it was only temporary. We were both ready to move into our new home in Carlton Wells, something that would happen in less than two weeks if all went to plan.

I remember pacing around the flat, anxious for my husband to return and unable to settle or do anything constructive. I think I knew where he was and what he was doing but pushed such thoughts out of my mind. Arthur always made any important decisions and I generally agreed, but there had never before been anything as reckless as this. At that point in time, I was incapable of even deciding what to make for our next meal and anything more taxing than that was completely beyond me.

I took some clothes off the airer in the box of a kitchen, feeling suddenly sad that on such a beautiful day there was no outdoor space to dry clothes. It didn't take much to plunge me into depression, and although I constantly made attempts to pull myself together, it was impossible. Bracing myself for only two more weeks in this rabbit hutch of a flat, I wondered if moving to Carlton Wells would make things any better.

Arthur was starting his new post a week after the move, in a city centre practice with seven other GPs. He would enjoy the challenge of grassroots medicine; he always did and never held ambitions beyond being in general practice, dealing with the huge variety of problems that came his way. But then I would be left alone in that lovely old house all day with only my thoughts to keep me company. Or would I?

If Arthur was doing what I suspected, life might change for us both. It was an audacious plan, totally out of character for either of us, but there are times in life when risks must be taken. And this was certainly risky. I only hoped the end justified the means.

When my husband finally arrived home he was carrying a sleeping child, a girl, limp in his arms, a beautiful child who captured my heart as soon as my eyes rested on her. Arthur laid her gently on the sofa, and I couldn't stop staring; he had done it, he had actually done it!

As I watched the child, my heart skipped a beat and I heard myself say the word 'Jane', a name I'd not spoken since we lost our daughter. This girl could be Jane; the likeness was uncanny, and I decided there and then that she was meant to be with us and had been sent for us to care for and love. We'd rescued her!

She slept for another two hours, during which time I watched her peaceful slumber, sweet rosebud lips parted and breathing steadily. Long fair eyelashes rested on pink cheeks — she was perfect, and I could hardly wait for her to open those eyes so I could learn their colour. When she did wake up, there was fear in her eyes — blue eyes, as expected.

I can see now how my mind tried to justify our actions, and I was mentally telling myself that this child really was Jane, who had come back to us never to leave again. The girl's initial fear turned to panic and the child began to sob, great heaving sobs as she gasped for air and cried out for her mother. I held her in my arms, and at first she struggled but then relaxed into my embrace, allowing me to stroke her hair and whisper soothing words as I'd done so many times in the past.

When the tears dried up, she asked again for her mother and then her father, and I was struck by the sad thought that the child should want them, even though they had abused her so badly.

'You're going to stay with us now; you'll be happy here. Would you like something to drink and some cake?'

Jane shook her head, the soft honey blonde hair clinging to her damp cheeks. I brought a drink anyway and a slice of cake.

'I want Mummy!' she sobbed again, but this time allowing me to comfort her. Her warm, slim little body felt so good in my arms; she was trembling, and I could feel her heartbeat next to my own. I loved this child already, and we would make a life for her that was so much better than the one she was living. When the bout of crying ceased, Jane picked up the juice and drank it. Her eyes strayed to the cake.

'You can have it if you like.' I smiled and watched her pick it up, have a bite and then put it back on the plate. She asked for her mother again but this time without the tears.

'I can be your mummy now; would you like that?'

The child stared at me and stepped back.

'It's okay, you'll be happy with me.'

Arthur had been out again and returned with several carrier bags of new clothes and a large sack bearing the name of a high street toy shop chain. He could have been Santa Claus bearing gifts. Smiling at Jane, he said hello and after looking warily at him from beneath those beautiful lashes she moved closer to me.

This was heaven. For a while, I allowed myself to believe that Jane was actually back, yet I knew deep inside that this girl was not our daughter. I steered my thoughts, however, twisting and turning them, telling myself that it was a good thing that we were doing, we being totally altruistic, saving this girl and offering her the best possible life she could have.

Those first few hours were difficult. Jane tried to be brave, but the sobbing continued at regular intervals during which she allowed me to comfort her. She ate very little and became tired soon after six that evening. I'd shown her where she would sleep and eventually, after more tears, I sat by the bedside and stroked her hair until sleep finally came. Arthur said it was the medication he'd administered that made her so tired, but she was peaceful and we left the room with a light on and the door ajar in case she woke.

Arthur began to tell me what had happened that afternoon, but I stopped him.

'I don't want to know the details. It's done now and she's here.'

My husband nodded, but we did need to talk about how to proceed during the next few days.

'No one here knows us, and in a couple of weeks we'll be at Carlton Wells in our new home where the neighbours will accept us as a family — why should they think otherwise? If we cut her hair it should change her appearance, and I'll continue the sedatives over the next few days to help her settle down.'

Arthur could always be trusted to think of everything. Before we retired to bed I switched on the late news, knowing there would be something on the child's disappearance and also that I'd be better off not watching, but some strange masochistic desire prompted me. The incident got a brief mention on the national news, followed by a more detailed report on the local news. A photograph was shown of the smiling child, not what I expected, but then children are resilient and if she'd been born into an abusive family, she would know no better. The news cameras tracked frogmen trawling the river. We knew they would find nothing.

'Switch it off, love,' Arthur asked and I did. We went to bed, but neither of us could sleep and talked in whispers about the days ahead. I did not want to know any details of how Arthur had taken this child. I compartmentalised the sordid aspect of the situation and we discussed only the future, a future in which we were reunited with Jane.

If I wavered at all, it was when I watched the late news broadcast on Sunday. Naturally, Jane was asleep and Arthur was out on call, otherwise I might never have put the television on. Stephen Bryson was seated behind a bank of microphones, flanked by police officers and pleading for the return of his daughter.

At first I felt as if my heart was beating so quickly it would burst; he had tears on his face and sounded genuinely distraught. I switched the broadcast off and went to make tea, needing to do something to erase that sorrowful image from my mind. I sat sipping the hot tea, telling myself that he was only acting, putting on a show for the world. I worked hard at convincing myself that he was not how he appeared to be and really didn't care what happened to his daughter. And his wife, I thought, why, she didn't even bother to turn up for the appeal!

Arthur eased himself slowly into Jane's favour. Naturally, she leaned towards me as I was with her every minute of the day, and when he came home she acted shyly. Initially, my husband had difficulty in calling her Jane and would talk about her as if she wasn't our daughter. I remember on one occasion getting terribly upset about this and insisting that she was Jane. That was my coping mechanism, how I perceived her; she really was Jane and had come back to us. After that little incident, Arthur never contradicted me and only ever talked about her as Jane.

The day of our move came, and it was such a relief. The first thing I did that morning was cut Jane's hair. She hadn't been out of the flat for over a week, but now we were to begin our new life and I needed to change her appearance. I tried to make it fun and said we were playing a game and I was going to cut her hair to make her look beautiful, but she sat solemnly, watching with wide eyes as the soft locks of hair fell to the floor around us.

She now displayed a quiet resignation towards being with Arthur and me. The new toys helped to some degree, and we explored them together. Our games even elicited an occasional smile, but in reality the spark of life that should be evident in such a young child was missing.

I told myself that her behaviour was due to the cruelty suffered at the hands of her previous family and that in time she would learn to laugh and play and be truly happy again. When I called her Jane, she looked perplexed and sometimes replied that she was Grace. I persevered with her new name, and she began to respond and eventually stopped saying that she was called Grace.

Arthur cut down on the sedatives, but on the day we moved he gave her more than usual; it would be another change, another trauma to go through, and we wanted to make it an easy one. The removal men did their job and by midday Arthur, Jane and I were following the van containing all of our possessions for the fifteen mile trip to Carlton Wells.

The first things we wanted in place were Jane's bed and furniture, so the men packed them last in order to unload them first. The room was at the back of the house, overlooking the garden. I sat with her in the car until things were in place, then Arthur carried a sleepy Jane upstairs to bed. Fortunately, she remained asleep for about three hours, during which time the van was unloaded and we had all our furniture in place.

When Jane woke, we shared a simple meal of scrambled eggs around the kitchen table. The French window at the rear of the house was open, and after she'd eaten, Jane stood in the open doorway looking out onto the garden. Our poor child hadn't been outside for well over a week, and it was obvious that she wanted to go into the garden. I nodded and went with her to explore, holding her warm little hand in mine. There was a swing left by the previous occupants, and she ran towards it, actually looking reasonably happy for the first time since she came to us.

I pushed her as high as she wanted and sang songs to fit in with the rhythm of the swing. When we were both tired, we lay on the grass gazing at the sky and Jane actually chuckled, watching a bird bathing in the old bird bath. Another first, and to me a sign that things were beginning to settle down. How could she have been happy in that small flat when even Arthur and I were not? It was this house that would establish us as a family, its spacious rooms and large garden. Jane would have everything she wanted; I would move heaven and earth to make her happy.

Early in the evening of our first day at Garden House, the doorbell rang. It jolted me from my thoughts, and a moment of panic swept over me. Arthur went to answer it and I heard him talking to a woman, whom he then brought into the lounge. My instinct was to hide Jane away but there was not time; the lady was coming towards me with a smile on her face and a huge chocolate cake in her hand. With her free hand, she shook mine and introduced herself as Helen, our next door neighbour. Arthur told her my name and then Jane's.

A shudder gripped me, and I was paralysed with fear — would Jane contradict him? This was the first real test. Helen bent down to speak to my daughter as I put a protective arm around her shoulders.

'Jane's rather shy.' Arthur sounded confident, much more so than I was.

'Good way to be these days,' Helen nodded, and I hoped she missed the fact that those words made me blush.

'Well, I won't keep you — you'll obviously have much to do, but if I can help at all just give me a knock.'

Our new neighbour must have been approaching seventy, very sprightly and certainly friendly enough. Arthur showed her out, thanked her for the cake then returned to the lounge.

'We have to start as we mean to go on, Elizabeth. We're a family now, the three of us, and people need to see us as that.'

'I know, but I worried in case Jane said anything out of place.'

'She's three years old; almost anything she says will be taken with a huge pinch of salt. I'm sure Helen accepted the situation for what it is: a new family moving into the village.'

He was right, I knew, and I hoped Jane hadn't picked up on my nervousness. But the evening passed quietly after that, and Jane seemed naturally tired by bedtime. The fresh air was considerably better than sedatives to help the child sleep.

During our first few weeks, we began to get the feel of village life. I learned that there was a playgroup but made excuses when I was invited to enrol Jane. It would take a good while longer for me to feel confident enough to let her become involved in any activity without being on hand to monitor what she said. We did, however, put her name down at the village school. It seemed to be a friendly place, and I liked the idea of small classes. We checked the Ofsted reports on their website, and the academic standard seemed to be good too. I knew it would come quickly but didn't want to think too far ahead. We needed more time to bond; it was small steps and perseverance that would win the day.

Jane never again referred to herself as Grace or contradicted me when I said Jane. It was almost as if she recognised that this new house was a new beginning for us all. In time, she began to smile and laugh too, a huge relief as secretly I had been afraid that I wasn't able to make her happy.

She only ever asked for her mummy two or three times after the move. My reply was always the same: 'I'm your mummy now, Jane.' And then I would distract her with a little treat or a game. However, it was not until October that she actually called me 'Mummy', and it was one of the happiest days of my life. Before our first Christmas together, she also began to call Arthur 'Daddy'.

As to the investigation into Grace Bryson's disappearance, it was no longer worthy of media attention, and I was relieved not to have to listen to broadcasts any longer. The New Year came with a flurry of snow, and Jane and Arthur made snowmen in the garden. I watched from the window as they ran around, laughing and throwing snowballs.

Life was good again, not only for Arthur and me but for Jane too. Each smile or laugh was an affirmation that we had done the right thing.

After fourteen years, I was reasonably confident that our secret would never come to light. Jane was such a wonderful daughter, and we loved her from the first day she came to us. Thinking back, we were extraordinarily fortunate that she was never recognised, but the timing of our move to Carlton Wells worked in our favour.

No one suspected a thing. By that time the initial press activity had died down somewhat, with other current sensational stories bandied around the media, and Grace Bryson became yesterday's news. They say that the best place to hide something is right under people's noses, which was exactly what we did and it appeared to work.

When the police officer arrived at our door, it was a shock; we'd assumed that after so many years they would no longer be looking for Grace Bryson. I knew that whoever it was must be a family member or someone very close for them still to be searching. The detective seemed satisfied that Jane was our daughter and apologised for troubling us, but the visit had troubled us, more than he knew.

For the first time in years we needed to make contingency plans, but disappearing with a sixteen-year-old girl was not as easy as it would have been with a three-year-old. Firstly we put our house on the market, with considerable regret. Garden House had been our true family home, where we learned to live in comparative happiness. But rather than panicking and moving away immediately, we waited, hoping the detective was convinced by our story, and after a week without hearing from the police again we almost dared to hope we were safe.

But it was not to be the case. Goodness knows what brought that same detective back to our home, but he arrived with a colleague in what seemed to be a more official capacity. DI Priestly told us that the Grace Bryson case had been reopened, words that sent a chill through my body. The visit lasted only about ten minutes, but when they left we knew something had to be done — staying in Carlton Wells was no longer an option.

We should have known we couldn't run forever.

Epilogue

Elise McDonald, August 8th 2014

Today is my sister's birthday. Grace is seventeen, and this will be the first birthday we have celebrated together, as a family, for fourteen years. It is only four months since we found her, alive and well and living barely more than ten miles away from her old home. These few short months have changed us all, shaping and moulding us back into a closely-knit family. But four months cannot erase fourteen years of pain and suffering.

Of course, we know now that Grace has been living an ordinary life, but our imaginations took us to some extremely dark places, robbing us of peace, of happiness, of hope.

We are having a party, well, more of a family get together really — I'm not a big fan of parties. A barbeque in the garden of Mum and Dad's new home, where they now live with Grace. There will be laughter and joy, hugs and kisses and all the ordinary, enjoyable things we've been denied over the years because our family was fractured, incomplete.

Grace is wearing a bright yellow dress, which matches her sunny mood; she is beautiful! The garden is colourful too, with raised borders stocked with geraniums, petunias, fuchsia and lavender. Mum is nursing baby Jack, relishing his chuckles, a light throaty sound that makes us all smile. Bea, who spends most of her time here rather than the home she shared with Peter, is in and out of the kitchen, replenishing food as it is eaten and topping up drinks, generally needing to be useful.

The exception to a 'family-only' gathering is Jack Priestly, his wife and two sons. Events over the years have brought us close together; they have shared our pain and sorrow, and now we want them to share our happiness. And of course, Grace is still sweet on Jake, their affection evident to anyone who cares to look. In a couple of months, Jake will leave for university when anything might happen, but they are sensible young people and time will tell.

I managed to catch Jack on his own to ask how the case against Peter was going.

'The plea hearing was straightforward as he pleaded guilty, which makes life less complicated and avoids an unpleasant trial. Sentencing will be a while yet and he'll remain in custody until then, as he's considered a flight risk. The sentence will certainly be custodial, and as he's co-operating that might be taken into consideration.

He's filled in a few blanks for us regarding the actual events of that day. Apparently it was pure chance that he met Solomon shortly after their daughter died. Peter, noticing the resemblance of Grace to Jane, spun the doctor a fanciful story about Grace being abused and neglected, made it seem as if they were the good guys, rescuing a poor child.

Whether Solomon and his wife actually believed the lies at the time is immaterial. They must have been aware of the enormity of the crime when the media splashed it all over. As to how much involvement Elizabeth Solomon had in it all, we'll probably never find out. She's made virtually no improvement and looks set to remain in some kind of secure care for a long time.'

I nodded and thanked Jack again for being in our corner. If he'd refused to do anything after I saw Grace, we probably would not have her back among us now.

Simon came to find me; it was time to cut the cake. The last birthday cake we had in the family had only three candles. Today there were seventeen, and as Grace blew them out there was no need for any of us to make a wish.

All our wishes had come true with the return of my sister, Grace.

A NOTE TO THE READER

Dear Reader,

Thank you for reading *Abduction*. I do hope you enjoyed it. The novel didn't begin life as a 'page turner', but the subject matter and the urgency of the chase quickly took over, and I was as keen to reach a satisfactory conclusion as the characters in the story. I initially wanted to write a compelling story (and what is more compelling than the abduction of a child?), which could be seen from several different perspectives. Those of us who are parents can imagine the horror of a missing child, and I was able to draw on my experience of a time when my own two-year-old daughter went missing from our garden. She was only out of my sight for a few moments and fortunately was found within forty minutes, but the gamut of emotions my husband and I experienced was terrifying. The fear, guilt and despair almost crippled us.

Jack Priestly is the lynchpin of the story. I chose to create a sympathetic detective, rather than the usual hard-boiled, divorced, alcoholic figure with a chip on his shoulder. He is an empathic character, determined to do his best for the family and the kind of detective I would want on my side.

If you enjoyed reading *Abduction*, I would be grateful for a review on **Amazon** and **Goodreads**. If you would like to offer your personal comments, please contact me on my **Facebook Author Page** or send a message through **Twitter**. You can also keep up to date with my writing projects on **my website**.

Gillian Jackson

gillianjackson.co.uk

Sapere Books is an exciting new publisher of brilliant fiction and popular history.

To find out more about our latest releases and our monthly bargain books visit our website: **saperebooks.com**

Printed in Great Britain
by Amazon